# TRUST

First published in 2001 by Infected Books

This edition published in 2012 by Infected Books

A CIP catalogue record for this book
is available from the British Library

ISBN 978-0-9550051-8-3

www.infectedbooks.co.uk

Cover design by Craig Paton
www.craigpaton.com

www.davidmoody.net
www.trustdavidmoody.com

To Charlene

# TRUST

## DAVID MOODY

July 2-12

To Charles

July 2013

# FRIDAY. 4:17PM

Once I get outside I'm fine. All the nervousness and trepidation disappears in seconds. You just keep putting one foot in front of the other. Focus on the run.

People often ask me why I do it, but I never give them a straight answer. They look at the state I get myself into and shake their heads. But they see only the physical effects. Truth is; I run because it's the only time I ever feel completely alone. It's the only time I'm fully separated from the distractions of the phone, the TV, the Internet, and other people. I usually fob them off with all the expected bullshit about keeping in shape and being out in the open, but that's only half the story. When you're out running like this, you're everything and you're nothing. You can pass a hundred people, and none of them know how far you've come or how much you're hurting. None of them know where you're from or where you're going. I tell people I like that isolation. I sometimes tell them I like to clear my mind and think, but I never tell them what I think about.

When I left home about forty minutes ago, there was a bank of grey cloud building up on the horizon. I thought I'd beat the bad weather back but the wind picked up almost as soon as I left the house and now the sky is almost completely black. A moment ago the clouds finally swallowed up the last of the sun, and the sudden drop in temperature was sobering. I'm glad I'm nearly back now. There's a hell of a storm blowing in, and I can feel the air pressure changing by the minute. My head's pounding, and it feels almost as if gravity itself is increasing, making it harder to keep lifting my feet. I look up, and above me the clouds have stopped following each other. They're criss-crossing the sky at random heights and different speeds, uncomfortably erratic.

I can see the war monument at the top of the last climb

before home now and I know I'm almost there.

Christ, here comes the rain. A few spots become a deluge in just a couple of seconds, almost like running headlong into a wall of water. Bloody typical – I've run miles along footpaths covered by overhanging trees and streets lined with buildings but it's only now, when I'm out here with absolutely no protection whatsoever, that this torrential downpour begins. The rain is hissing, filling the air with noise, and it's so hard it hurts. Moments ago this cliff-top tourist track was dry and hard, now it's dangerously unpredictable. Potholes and ruts are rapidly filling with water, making it almost impossible to see what I'm running through, and yet, somehow, the risk adds to the adrenalin rush. There's a hundred metre drop just five metres to my left. I'm literally on the edge, but none of that matters because *this* is the real reason I run. Me, the cliffs, the sea and *nothing* else.

I dig in and push myself up the last section of steep climb to the monument, my legs having to work twice as hard now to get any traction. It's downhill all the way home from here. Keep pushing. Don't stop. Just a few more seconds.

The ground steepens again – the sting in the tail of this bitch of a climb – and the slope turns to steps, worn into the ground by countless ramblers and dog walkers who've come this way over the years. I slip, my foot sinking into a rain-filled pit I didn't see, but I manage to keep my balance and keep myself moving. Can't afford to lose momentum now.

Almost there. Last few steps.

And then I've done it. I pass the needle-shaped stone monument and the ground ahead of me levels out then drops away. My lungs are on fire but I know the pain will ease with the descent. I've followed this dirt footpath countless times since I've lived in Thatcham, but the view up here still takes my breath away no matter what. Even in the gloom I can see for miles in every direction, and the vastness of the sea and the land stretching away from here is humbling, reminding me in no uncertain terms just how small I am in the scheme of things. The rain is ice-cold, digging into me like needles, but suddenly it doesn't seem to matter. I don't feel it. Now I can see the gentle crescent curve of the bay up ahead. From here I can see virtually the whole of the village; a narrow strip of buildings dotted with occasional lights, sandwiched between the crashing waves on one side and endless fields and hills on the other. It looks as prone as I feel. And then I'm distracted as, out on the horizon, miles out to sea, a jagged flash of electric-blue light spits down from the belly of the clouds to the surface of the water. It's gone in a heartbeat, but I can still see it in negative.

Seconds later, the thunder arrives. A low and ominous warning growl, so deep I can feel it through my pounding legs, followed by an almighty crack so loud it seems to shake the whole world. I slip again and almost fall, and now I'm starting to wonder if I might be in trouble. There's still another half-mile to home, and I have no protection whatsoever out here, not even a tree. And I think to myself, if I get hit, I'm fucked. My brother knows I'm out, but I didn't tell him my route. I'm exposed and vulnerable, but I love it.

Another flash of light. This time I'm looking down at my feet when it hits, but the lightning illuminates everything like someone's taking photographs of the lone idiot out running. I splash through a puddle that's too big to run around and I'm taken by surprise when it's deeper than I expect. The ice-cold water soaks my feet, adding to the misery, but I keep going. I fix my eyes dead ahead, trying to pick out the outline of my bungalow on the hillside, aiming for home.

*Wait. What was that?*

*Something's not right.*

There's another sound now, lighter in pitch than the thunder but just as loud. It builds and builds, refusing to fade. I've stopped running before I've realised and I stand there, hands on hips, breathing hard and scanning the horizon. The noise is swirling with the wind, constantly changing direction, impossible to place.

There's a jet. It comes from behind me and flies overhead before I see it. Wait... there's more than one of them. I regularly see jets around here; there are usually a few each day, flying training missions up and down the valley and occasionally out over the sea, but surely not in atrocious conditions like this? They normally fly much faster and at a considerably higher altitude, reaching such speeds that you have to look way ahead of the noise to stand any chance of seeing them. This is very different. There are four more now, flying in an arrowhead formation behind the first, heading out over the water. They're getting lower. One by one they drop down through the low cloud cover.

The rain is relentless and I have to shield my eyes to keep watching. The noise is becoming unbearable. There's another flash of lightning, but the cumulative screaming of jet engines is such that the thunder which follows goes almost unheard.

Is there something else behind them?

Something's following them out over the ocean.

*Jesus Christ.*

Whatever this thing is, it's fucking huge. It's black, blacker than any of the clouds, and it's fucking enormous, dwarfing the jets. This thing is immense and yet it's hardly making a bloody sound. It's right above me now and seems to be going on forever – hundreds and hundreds of metres of Christ alone knows what, stretching down through the clouds, slicing through the storm with apparent ease. Parts of its surface are smooth and featureless, other areas covered with what look like probes and towers and clusters of pinpricks of light. About a third of the way along its length, its appearance changes drastically. There are a collection of unimaginably long, hexagonal-shaped containers, each of which looks to be miles in length but I can't even begin to accurately estimate the scale of this thing from here.

There are jets surrounding the entire machine. They look small up against it, like the shadows of scavenging birds. I can finally see the back end of it now as it powers through the sky. There's a huge ball of brilliant, blue-white light behind the ship. That must be what's powering it, but how can it be so quiet? I *can* hear it, but the noise of the jets and even the gusting wind are louder. How can something so huge move so effortlessly and make hardly any sound?

The light's so powerful that I can't keep looking at it and I have to turn away. I can feel my skin beginning to prickle and tighten with the heat, and for a moment the rain turns to steam. When the brightness reduces slightly I look up again. The sheer scale of whatever it is overhead is deceptive and the entire convoy is moving with remarkable speed. It feels like just a few seconds have passed since the first jet appeared, now the last one is disappearing from view. And all I can see is the vast ball of light moving out over the water, reflected on the choppy waves like a second sun.

A moment of silence, then the chaos of the storm seems to return with ten times the ferocity it had before. All I can hear is the crashing of the waves on the rocks far below, and I look down and realise I've walked away from the footpath closer to the edge of the cliff.

My legs are leaden, heavy with nerves more than effort now. It's a struggle to start running again, but I dig deep and make myself move.

I've got to get home

# Part i
# ARRIVAL

# 1

Tom Winter sprinted down from the exposed hillside, gravity dictating his speed more than any conscious control. His heart pounded, his body racked with exhaustion and fear. Up ahead, Thatcham remained visible through the inclement late-afternoon gloom, more lights being switched on in houses and shops by the second. Despite the atrocious weather, the streets were teeming with frantic movement. Cars raced down the main road, aquaplaning through the rainwater, brake lights burning through the haze as they caught up with those in front and bunched together. Faces were pressed against almost every sea-facing window, all looking upward for the return of that *thing* – whatever the hell it was – they'd all seen moments earlier. Some foolhardy souls braved the squall and gathered at the sea wall, looking out over the waves. A few more even dared venture onto the windswept shingle beach. Others ran through the streets in small huddles. Holidaymaking families looked for shelter, their temporary tent and caravan homes suddenly feeling hopelessly insecure in light of what they'd witnessed.

Everything looked the same as when Tom had left the village to start his run, but suddenly *everything* had changed.

He pounded down off the dirt footpath and was glad to finally be running on pavements again. He glanced back over his shoulder at the cliffs and the ocean, all of it appearing reassuringly normal. If it hadn't been for the chaos unfolding in the village all around him, he might have convinced himself he'd imagined what he'd seen; a sweat-soaked, storm-addled hallucination of epic proportions.

He sprinted across the road to run up the final hill to the house, hardly paying attention, when his sudden burst of speed was matched by a swerving car coming the other way around a corner, all bright headlamps, clattering wipers and barely controlled acceleration. The driver blasted the horn at him and shouted abuse.

The bungalow loomed ahead of him now at the top of the climb. Even from here he could see his brother Rob in silhouette, standing at the living room window and staring out to sea, transfixed like everyone else. Tom dug deep, half-running, half-walking up the steep footpath rather than following the meandering slope of the road. Tom reached the front door and crashed inside, barely able to breathe. He leant against the hallway wall and kicked off his sodden trainers.

'That you Tom?' Rob shouted.

'It's me,' he just about managed to reply.

'Did you see it? Fuck me, did you see it?'

Tom limped into the living room, his legs unresponsive, shivering with cold. Or was it nerves? He wasn't sure anymore. 'I saw it,' he said, still fighting for breath.

Rob swallowed hard. He looked as bad as Tom felt.

'What the hell was it?'

'You tell me.'

'I mean, I know what I *think* it was, but where did it come from? Why here?'

'How am I supposed to know?'

'Do you think we're safe? Fuck, is it still out there? Tom, mate, are you all right?'

Tom slid down the wall, legs finally giving up. 'Drink,' he said. He felt faint, bright lights dancing in front of his eyes despite the room being dark. He tried to control his breathing and steady himself, but he could still hear the screaming of the jets, could still feel that intense white light burning his skin... and now, suddenly, all he could think about was how exposed and vulnerable he'd been up there, close to the edge. The storm had been so powerful, and whatever it was that had flown overhead had been so huge... It reminded him of the time he and Rob had been messing around on scaffolding on a drunken night out a few years back. They'd laughed about it at the time, but when he'd returned to the scene next morning and had seen the height they'd climbed – the stupid, unnecessary risks they'd taken – it had shocked him rigid.

Rob returned with a mug of coffee and an energy drink which Tom drained dry in a series of quick gulps. Rob returned to the window. The worst of the storm had passed now and the light was slowly beginning to improve. The sky was dirty yellow, the colour of a fading bruise. There was nothing to see out there, and he shifted his attention to the television instead, picking up the remote control and searching through the channels for one of the news stations, all the time talking nervously.

'I was in the kitchen when I heard the jets. Bloody hell, there were so many of them I thought we'd gone to war or something.'

'Maybe we have,' Tom suggested. Rob gave his comment a few seconds consideration before continuing.

'I came in here to see what was going on, and that was when it flew over. It must have been a couple of miles long at least. Christ, Tom, did you see the size of it?'

'I saw it,' he answered, beginning to feel marginally more himself again. He stood up, coughed hard, steadied himself, then took his brother's place at the window and looked down into the village. It was still mayhem down there. The petrol station forecourt had flooded, and several members of staff were doing what they could to block the kiosk door. The main street was still awash, drains struggling to cope with the sudden deluge. Abandoned cars had reduced the road to a single lane for much of its length, and the sudden volume of traffic still trying to get in and out of the village had caused a jam. Some pedestrians wandered aimlessly, others just stood there, watching. It looked like everyone wanted to try and get somewhere else, but no one was going anywhere.

'So what do you think it was?' Rob asked, still cycling through channels for the news.

Tom kept watching the people down below. It was easier to focus on them rather than answer his brother. He knew it was going to sound ridiculous.

'I think it was a spaceship,' he said finally. Regardless of what the immense vehicle proved to actually be, 'spaceship' seemed a trite and tacky way to describe the single most incredible thing he'd ever seen. 'But it can't have been, can it?' he added quickly, doubting himself. 'A spaceship. Bloody hell, that's just stupid.'

'Why?'

'Why what?'

'Why is that stupid? What else could it have been?'

'Come on... a spaceship? Aliens? Are you serious?'

Rob stood to one side so that Tom could see the TV screen. There it was: the incredible craft hovering out over the ocean. *Is that real or CGI?* he asked himself.

'Give me another explanation then,' Rob said. He pointed at the screen. 'What else could that be? A mass hallucination? *Dr fucking Who?* Are there Daleks in that thing? Cybermen?'

'But *aliens?*' Tom said again. 'Close encounters of the third bloody kind and all of that? I don't know, maybe it's something military? A prototype or an airship or something that—'

'Bollocks,' Rob snapped at him. 'Look at it. It's fucking enormous. Does that look like an airship to you?'

Tom walked towards the bathroom, still shivering, still nauseous. He hoped getting cleaned up and warm might help him make sense of everything. Countless questions and random thoughts continued to flood into his head. If it was aliens, it wasn't so much the sudden proof of their existence he was struggling with, he just wanted to know why they were here. Thatcham was nowhere. The arse-end of everything. Nothing much ever seemed to happen in this place, and that was how he liked it. That was why he'd moved here, for Christ's sake.

Rob remained in front of the TV, unaware his brother had left the room. 'Hundreds of thousands of people will have seen this, millions even,' he said. 'There's no way the authorities will be able to keep it quiet. I mean, it's only ever been balls of light or flying hubcaps before, never anything like this...'

He turned around and shrugged when he realised he was talking to himself. He turned up the volume and flicked through a few more channels. Same picture now, almost every station: that machine – the spaceship, uncovered military secret or whatever it was – hovering motionless over the churning waters. A number of clearly well-armed boats bobbed and rolled in the shadow of the behemoth, and countless helicopters and jets buzzed around like relentless flies, their trivial size serving only to emphasise the unimaginable scale of the craft. Rob thought it surprising there was so much military activity in the water already. Assuming the footage he was watching was coming from somewhere not that far from here, then this was happening in waters where there was rarely any call for war ships and frigates. Thatcham was hardly a warzone.

'They must have been waiting for it,' he shouted, not knowing whether Tom could hear him. 'They knew it was coming. That's got to be a good thing, right?'

When no one answered, he turned the TV up again, loud enough to be heard throughout the small house.

'...we'll be staying with this story for the time being,' a clearly flustered newsreader's voice explained. She sounded as dumbfounded as everyone else, tripping over her words with uncharacteristic regularity. 'Once again, these are live pictures you're seeing here. We repeat, this is not a hoax. The UN statement we brought to you a short while ago confirmed that there is no cause for alarm...'

In the bathroom, Tom turned on the shower. The pipes groaned and, after a brief pause, air cleared from the system and water began spitting out of the shower head, stopping and starting, then running steady, silencing the TV noise. Tom stepped under the flow and felt the water beginning to massage him back to life. And it was then, when the effort of his run and the initial shock of what had happened began to fade, that he finally began to comprehend the enormity of what he'd seen out there today. It was one of those life-defining moments, he realised, like all those years ago, when he'd sat between Mum and Dad and watched the twin towers collapse in stunned silence. One event with incalculable repercussions. Whoever was in that ship and whatever they wanted, the importance of what had happened today was already unquestionable. The only thing he knew with complete certainly was that *nothing* was ever going to be the same.

He switched off the shower and could immediately hear the TV newsreader again: '...there is no cause for alarm...' *Yeah, right*, he thought as he towelled himself down then went to the bedroom to get dressed. *If we're all still here this time tomorrow, I might believe you.*

He found Rob sitting cross-legged on the living room floor, a look of child-like disbelief on his face. A ticker-tape stream of information ran across the bottom of the screen:

**CONFIRMED CONTACT WITH ALIEN VESSEL – FIRST OFFICIAL WORD FROM DOWNING STREET DUE SHORTLY – GOVERNMENT SPOKESMAN URGES CALM – UN SECRETARY GENERAL TO MAKE STATEMENT – NO EVIDENCE OF HOSTILE INTENT**

'You okay, mate?' Tom asked. Rob glanced up, then immediately turned back to face the screen, as if he was too afraid to look anywhere else.

'What d'you think Dad would have made of all this?' he said.

'I know exactly what he'd have been doing,' Tom replied, 'he'd have been digging a bloody shelter. Either that or he'd have been at the supermarket, stocking up on supplies while everyone else was glued to the TV like you.'

'You reckon?'

'Probably. He'd have been in his element. Mum said he used to love a good crisis.'

'And is that what this is? A crisis?'

'I don't know yet. Ask me again in a couple of hours.'

'In a couple of hours I want to be down the pub, getting pissed.'

'That's if there are any pubs left by then.'

'Don't say that,' Rob protested, glancing back again and sounding genuinely concerned. 'Anyway, there's a government briefing on in a few minutes.'

'Oh, that'll help,' Tom said, not even bothering to try hiding his cynicism.

'What do you think they'll say?'

'They'll say a lot, I expect. Well, they'll use a lot of words, but probably won't actually *say* anything, nothing of any worth. You know politicians – it'll be ninety per cent bullshit, ten per cent facts, that's if there are any facts in there at all.'

'But this is big, Tom, too big. They can't cover up something like this, can they? Too many people have already seen too much. They'll have to come clean and tell us everything they know.'

'You think? Since when has any government ever done that? You wait, they'll probably arrange for us all to disappear. That-cham will become the new Area 51. Area 52.'

'Fucking idiot,' Rob cursed. 'This is different. Can't you feel it?'

'I'm knackered, Rob. I can't feel anything right now.'

'You're such a bloody pessimist.'

'I've got good right to be. We both have.'

'When are you going to give it a rest? What happened to Mum and Dad was out of our control.'

'And so is this.'

'Granted, but—'

15

'But nothing.'

'It was an accident, Tom. A freak accident.'

Tom wasn't listening. They'd had this argument too many times before. He got up to fetch himself another drink, groaning with pain as his legs began to stiffen. When he returned to the living room, he saw that the picture on the TV had changed. The ship over the sea had been replaced with the image of an uncomfortable looking stuffed suit – some government minister for something or other. The normality of the scene was reassuring. The faceless politician was bathed in a non-stop barrage of camera flashes. Tom didn't recognise him and he wondered who he was and why he was the fall-guy today? Where were the bigwigs? Holed-up in some secure bunker somewhere no doubt. So who was this guy? Minister for Alien Invasions? Secretary of State for Unexplained Phenomena? What did they call the odd-job men of Westminster? Wasn't it Minister Without Portfolio or something like that? The man's over-educated voice sounded understandably unsteady. He shuffled his weight uncomfortably from foot to foot.

'Earlier this week,' he began before immediately pausing again to clear his throat, 'various observatories and scientific outposts, both around the globe and in space, became aware of an unidentified object approaching the outskirts of our solar system at a remarkable speed. As the progress of the object was tracked, it slowed and changed course several times before heading towards Earth. The vessel was broadcasting a continual distress signal.'

'Bollocks,' Tom said, unable to help himself. 'That's how these things always start. How did they know it was a distress signal? Do they speak English or have we learned Alien?'

'Shh...' Rob hissed at him. 'This is important.'

The politician paused again, just long enough for the mass of assembled photographers to fire off another volley of camera flashes and for a hundred reporters to ask countless variations on the same question at the exact same time. The defenceless spokesman lifted his hands in protest, attempting to restore some order.

'Although there has been no direct communication with the occupants,' he continued, 'the vessel has so far obeyed our every instruction and is currently holding its position some fifty miles off the coast of the UK. An international air force is currently patrolling the skies around the region, and a number of warships from several states are also *en route*. At this stage we have no reason to believe the ship and its occupants are hostile, but no unnecessary risks are being taken.'

Rob looked around for reassurance from his brother again. 'If they were going to blow the shit out of us, they'd have done it already, wouldn't they?'

Tom shrugged his shoulders. 'Who knows? Thing is, if they are here to take over the planet or wipe us all out, I don't suppose there's a fat lot we can do about it. We should find out where we go to sign up for the resistance.'

'You're kidding me?'

'Of course I am, you dick.'

'Anyway, they won't try anything like that,' Rob said.

'Why not?'

'Were you not listening? They were broadcasting a distress signal. Why would they have done that if they were going to attack? You're right, if they'd wanted to they'd probably have already levelled the planet by now.'

'You're so bloody naïve,' Tom said, getting up and crossing to the window again. 'Did you not see *Alien*? That started with them answering a distress call.'

'Yes, but that's a movie, you prick. This is real life.'

Tom looked down into the village, no longer interested in anything either his brother or the government spokesman had to say. Neither of them were doing anything to calm his unease.

The sun peeked out through a gap in the thinning clouds, as if checking whether it was safe to come out yet. Down in the streets of Thatcham, more people had emerged from where they'd been sheltering from the torrential rain or the aliens or both. It seemed a little calmer out there now. A train pulled away from the village's small station, the traffic was beginning to move freely again, and there were several small groups of cagoule-wearing people gathering in bunches by the sea wall. The reality of an alien invasion – if that was what this was – had so far proved very different to all those movies Tom had seen. He kept thinking about stories like *War of the Worlds* and god-awful films like *Independence Day*. Any minute now, he thought, and the war machines will appear on the horizon. Huge metal-legged striders will march across the land, crushing everything in their path and killing thousands with their deadly weapons. By this time tomorrow, he decided, there'll probably be nothing left of any of us. He felt genuinely afraid. Helpless. He felt like he had the day he'd taken the phone call about Mum and Dad's accident.

'I think you're wrong about Dad,' Rob said suddenly. 'He'd have loved this. He'd have been right in his element. I don't think we've got anything to worry about, Tom.'

'I'll remind you of that when we're both in one of their slave labour camps, okay?'

'Fair enough. But here's the deal, if we don't end up in a slave labour camp – which we won't – then you have to start lightening up, okay? You're in a good place now. You've got Siobhan, you've got your house, and thanks to Mum and Dad you've got more than enough cash to keep you going for a good while yet. Apart from the fact we might have just been invaded by aliens, your life is good!'

# 2

The routine of living in the village frequently felt as predictable as Tom's pre-Thatcham life had been. He'd just replaced strategy meetings, targets, brainstorming and the like with more convivial alternatives: long walks, runs, and regular Friday evening drinking sessions.

Siobhan arrived just before half-past seven. Tom watched her from the window. He thought her extraordinarily beautiful. She was just short of his height, with shoulder-length blonde hair, steely blue-grey eyes, and the kind of body he'd only dared fantasise about previously. He didn't know what she saw in him.

She let herself in. 'Hello, you,' she said as she entered the living room. She walked towards him and kissed him gently on the lips, then hugged him. He kissed her neck, nudging away the strap of her top and nibbling her shoulder. 'Easy tiger,' she whispered. 'You know what that does to me.'

'That's why I do it.'

He pulled her down onto the sofa with him, wrapping his legs around her so she couldn't escape.

'Bloody hell,' Rob moaned as he walked past. 'Get a room.'

'This is my room,' Tom reminded him. 'Come to think of it, they're all my rooms.'

Rob shook his head and switched the TV back on. It hadn't long been off. Siobhan immediately disentangled herself from Tom and turned around to watch.

'Anything happened?' she asked.

'What, apart from the alien invasion?' Rob answered sarcastically.

'You know what I mean. Anything happened since then?'

'Not a lot as far I can see. I still can't get my head around any of it. Did you see that thing...?'

'I was at work. There was only me and Mona in the office. It was dark because of the storm, then it went even darker and I didn't think much of it. Then Mo saw that everyone outside was looking up. We went out front and watched it fly over. Scary as hell. Amazing, though.'

'I watched it from here. It was incredible. Your dickhead of a boyfriend was out running, weren't you, Tom?'

Siobhan looked around when he didn't reply. She thought he was watching TV, but he was staring at her, transfixed by the shape of her long legs, their shadows visible through her light summer dress.

'Put your tongue away,' she said. 'Perv.'

The doorbell rang and Rob went to answer it. When Siobhan remained standing in front of the TV, Tom got up and walked over. He wrapped his arms around her from behind and felt her leaning back into him.

'Love you, you know,' he whispered.

'I know.'

'You okay?'

She scowled and looked at him over her shoulder. 'Why shouldn't I be?'

'All this going on,' he said, gesturing at the TV.

'Not a lot any of us can do about it, is there?'

'No, but that's not the point. Things have changed today, Siobhan. Can't you feel it?'

'Yes, but that's not necessarily a bad thing, is it?'

'Bloody hell, how many science-fiction movies have you sat here and watched with me? How many of them turned out well for mankind once the aliens arrived?'

'You're always looking on the downside,' she said, turning around and looking at him with concern.

'I'm not, I'm just—'

'You are. How many of those films ended up with people winning against the odds?'

She had a point. 'But aren't you worried?' he asked.

'Of course I am. We all are. But what can we do? We can all spend the rest of our lives hiding under the kitchen table, or we can get on with things as normal and hope everything works out for the best.'

'I know, but—'

'But nothing. Lighten up, sweetheart. You're always worrying about something. Stop!'

She toyed with a strand of his hair, then gently ran her fingers down the side of his face. She looked up when Rob returned.

'Are you two coming? James is here.'

'There in a second,' Tom replied. He went to move but Siobhan kept hold of him a moment longer. She stared into his eyes, and he felt uncomfortable, foolish even.

'Everything's going to be all right. Believe me?'

'I believe you.'

'Good. Early night, tonight, okay? Just you and me.'

'Sounds perfect.'

The Badger's Sett was often busy on Friday evenings, particularly in summer, but never like this. The place was heaving with unfamiliar faces, and Tom had to fight just to get in through the door. It seemed that every tent-dwelling holidaymaker staying anywhere near the village had chosen the security of bricks and mortar and alcohol over their flimsy canvas walls tonight. The large-screen TVs dotted around the bar were clearly another factor. Groups of people were gathered around each of them, mouths hanging open, watching events unfold with continued disbelief.

John Tipper, running up and down behind the bar, looked exhausted – red faced and flustered but still grinning like a fool. He loved his pub, loved being the centre of attention, and more than anything, he loved the positive cash flow of a bumper night like this. His wife Betty had just shut the kitchen early, having run out of most of the dishes on her simple bar food menu.

John looked up as Tom and the others approached the bar, and nodded to let them know he'd clocked them. As Tom and the others were such reliable regulars, he often had their drinks waiting for them. Not tonight.

'Bloody hell,' James complained, 'I've come out for some peace and quiet. This is a joke.'

'Want to go somewhere else?' Tom asked.

'Like where? There is nowhere else.'

Siobhan noticed a family in the corner who'd just started collecting up their things. They were obviously holidaymakers – she could tell in an instant that they weren't local. Living in Thatcham helped you develop a sixth sense when it came down to differentiating *us* from *them*. That thought stuck in her head as she made a beeline for the table to claim it before anyone else. Tonight the *non-locals* were no longer the only invaders. In fact, tonight they didn't feel like outsiders at all.

James and Rob followed Siobhan, abandoning Tom at the bar. As he waited for John to serve him, Tom watched Siobhan collect the vacating family's dirty glasses, plates and cutlery and take them through to the kitchen. She'd even been known to help out behind the bar before now, though she much preferred drinking to serving. There were aspects of village life Tom still struggled to get his head around. The concept of helping out and doing something for nothing for the benefit of someone else just wouldn't have worked where he'd come from. He recalled a particularly offensive ex-colleague who used to regularly tell him: *Don't ever feed a beggar, they'll eat your fucking arm.* Things were different here in Thatcham. Stepping away from his old life had allowed Tom to appreciate just how intense and, ultimately, unimportant it had all been.

'How the devil are you?' John asked – his standard greeting

– when he finally got around to serving Tom. He neatly rolled up the sleeves of his sweat-soaked check shirt, adjusted his glasses and smoothed back his thinning white hair.

'Excellent, thanks,' Tom said – his standard reply.

'Glad to hear it. The usual?'

'Of course. Bit busy tonight, John.'

'Just a little. I'll tell you something, Thomas, these aliens are more than welcome to drop in every Friday afternoon if they're going to do this for my profits.'

'Just as long as it's not last orders for all of us, eh?'

John forced a grin at Tom's pathetic comment. Then his face dropped. 'You don't think it will be, do you?'

'Don't know. Not sure yet,' Tom replied, suddenly more serious. The moment reminded him of a scene from the beginning of *The Hitchhikers Guide to the Galaxy*: Ford Prefect ordering six pints of bitter *'and quickly please, the world's about to end.'*

'You worried?' John asked.

'Yep. You?'

'Likewise,' he said, passing Tom the last of his drinks. 'Glad to hear someone else keeping things in perspective.'

'What do you mean?'

'Some folks seem to be getting carried away. You know Barry Yates from Kemberton Boats, him and his mates were talking about sailing out there.'

'Bloody idiots.'

'That's what I said. I told him this is serious. Some people just don't get it. They'll get themselves killed.'

'More fool them,' Tom said as he handed John his cash. 'I'll reserve judgement until I'm sure we're not being invaded or anything like that.'

John's expression changed. Momentarily deep in thought, he'd allowed his permanently grinning landlord persona to drop. A shout for service from further up the bar brought him back to reality.

'Got to get on,' he said, handing Tom his change. 'Punters to serve, profit to make.'

'Something strong please, John,' he heard Phil Yates, another local, say. Tom glanced back at the others and managed to catch James' eye through the mass of people filling the pub. James came over to help with the drinks, weaving through the crowds.

'Cheers mate,' Tom said, handing him two pints. 'Listen, I hope you don't mind me saying, you look bloody terrible.'

'I feel bloody terrible,' he replied as they worked their way back to the table.

'Baby keeping you awake?'

'She's keeping me awake, the rest of the kids awake, the missus awake...'

'That bad, eh?'

'That bad.' James sighed as he sat down. 'And now we've got bloody aliens to deal with as well. I tell you, mate, I've had enough.'

The pub was loud, too loud. The noise levels, coupled with a reluctance to give James opportunity to moan about the miseries of family life, meant there was little conversation. The afternoon's events cast a dark cloud, but just being here helped. The familiar chaos of the place was strangely reassuring.

Tom looked up from his beer, noticing that both Rob and Siobhan were glued to the TV screen on the wall opposite. The same syndicated shot of the alien ship still dominated the news as it had all evening, only the lighting and the number of boats floating in its vast shadow seemed to have changed. As the sun had set, the sky on the horizon had turned a searing yellow-orange, making the ship look impossibly dark in contrast. It remained fixed in position: a featureless shadow which seemed almost to be sucking in the light from around it. Only occasional searchlights from the flotilla below disturbed the inky black, rippling across the hull and down the endless length of the titanic machine. The intense blue-white light at the back of the ship, Tom realised, had been extinguished. *I guess that means they're stopping,* he thought.

'Unbelievable, isn't it,' Rob said. No one answered, but he continued regardless. 'Don't know about you lot, but I'm still having trouble getting my head around all of this. We'll be talking about this day for years to come. Everyone will remember where they were and what they were doing when the aliens came. I know I will.'

'Me too,' James agreed. 'Christ, our little one will grow up never having known any different. Imagine that.'

Tom couldn't. It still felt like too bizarre a concept. Were the occupants of that ship explorers or an invading force? His mind wandered back to history lessons he'd struggled through many years earlier at school. Sir Frances Drake, Christopher Columbus, Vasco De Gama... there were many more. History had never been his strongest subject; he remembered little more than the explorer's names and the fact that the history books always seemed more sympathetic to the discoverer than the discovered. When he started to think about colonization, and the impact of these invading forces on the indigenous populations of hitherto unknown countries, he began to feel uneasy. *You can dress it up however you like*, he thought, *but is there really any difference between an explorer and an invader?*

Tom made himself focus on what everyone else was talking about, but that was inevitably the aliens too. He was beginning to wonder if they'd ever be able to talk about anything else.

The strange night evaporated with unexpected speed, faster even than their normal Friday sessions. It seemed that Siobhan had forgotten her offer of an early night. She was happy to stay where they were and to keep drinking until John called last orders and kicked them all out. Tom knew there was little chance of that happening. On nights like this – and whilst this was the first time aliens had been involved, there had been plenty of nights like this before – John tended to stay open as long as he was able. As long as there was no trouble or complaints, the local police were generally happy to turn a blind eye. In fact, Sergeant Phipps and several of his officers would no doubt be in here themselves before long, drinking with the rest.

After being wedged into the corner and trapped for much of the evening, Tom took advantage of Rob finally going to the bar to duck out for a quick toilet break. He wasn't the only person in the small restroom. Ken Trentham was standing at the urinal furthest from the door, holding himself with one hand and leaning up the wall with the other, wearing the same dirty grey overcoat he wore every day from the hottest day of summer to the depths of winter. Tom slipped into the nearest cubicle and cringed as the door creaked shut, hoping he hadn't been noticed. People generally avoided old Ken if they could help it.

Ken was still leaning against the wall and, judging by the noise, still pissing, when Tom emerged. Tom caught Ken's eye in the mirror, nodded and then looked down again quickly as he washed his hands, hoping that would be the end of it. It wasn't.

'What's all this about then?' the older man asked. On the few occasions Tom had come across him before, Ken was usually shouting, spitting, or starting fights. He seemed unexpectedly lucid tonight, no sign of his usual volatility.

'What?' Tom replied

Ken shook his hands then ran his fingers through his greasy grey hair. He was blocking Tom's way out. 'These alien things, what they doing here?'

'I don't know. You're better off asking someone else. I don't know anything about them.'

'That's the thing though,' Ken said, becoming animated and pointing his finger wildly, beginning to wind himself up. 'No one knows anything. We're all in the shit together, ain't we.'

Tom tentatively moved forward, keen to get past but not wanting to piss Ken off and risk his notorious booze-addled wrath. Tonight, however, the old drunk simply moved to one side.

'You okay?' Tom asked, momentarily surprised, almost concerned.

'Makes you think.'

'What does?'

'All this business.'

'Suppose.'

'Never known anything like it.'

'None of us have.'

'Frightening, innit.'

'It is. Look, Ken, I need to get back to my—'

'You think this is a good thing?'

Tom thought before answering. 'I don't know. I'm not sure yet. You?'

'Me neither. Never trust nobody until I've looked into their eyes, I don't.'

'Good advice,' Tom said, sliding past and holding his breath to avoid getting a nose-full of the stench of liquor, stale sweat and piss stains.

'Remember the eyes,' Ken warned.

When another unsuspecting punter crashed into the bathroom, Tom seized the opportunity to get out.

'You took your time,' Siobhan said when he finally returned to the table. 'What were you doing in there?'

'I've heard about blokes like you,' Rob sniggered.

'I got caught.'

'Caught by what?' Siobhan said. 'Or shouldn't I ask.'

'Caught by Ken Trentham.'

'Ken Trentham! That pickled old bastard. He wasn't causing trouble again, was he?'

Tom shook his head. 'No, he was fine. He was talking about the aliens, that's all. Same as everyone else.'

'He's been talking about aliens for years,' James said. 'Remember that, Siobhan? That night he came in here ranting about being abducted.'

'And John threatened to give him an anal probe with a pool cue!'

'Maybe this is how it starts,' Tom suggested. 'Maybe he's their first victim.'

'What are you on about?' asked Siobhan.

'These aliens. You always have to watch out when people have sudden personality changes like Ken. It's mind control, you know, just like in the films. They always start with the easiest people to manipulate, and since Ken's only got half a mind—'

'If that,' James interrupted.

'—then they wouldn't have any problems controlling him.'

'You think?' Siobhan said, suddenly deadly serious.

Tom laughed. 'Of course I don't, you silly sod. He's just scared like everyone else.'

'I'm not scared.'

'Uneasy, then. You know what I'm saying.'

There was a momentary pause in the conversation as each of them considered how they were feeling. Was it fear? James cleared his throat, the way he always did when he thought he had something important to say. 'That Stephen Hawking, he said we'd all be fucked if any aliens turned up here.'

'His language is appalling,' Rob sighed.

James continued, unimpressed, 'He says if they've managed to get here, then they're obviously more intelligent than us, so they'll inevitably end up wiping us out.'

'Who rattled your cage?' Tom asked.

'Fuck me, Jim,' Rob added, 'most people get more stupid when they're pissed. You're the first person I've met who smartens up.'

'Piss off,' James said, hiding his embarrassment by drinking more beer, the bottom of his pint glass covering his face.

'No disrespect, Jim,' Tom continued, 'but since when did you start following Stephen Hawking's work?'

'I don't,' he admitted. 'Steph was watching this programme on TV when I got home, and they were talking about it. They were saying how we should all just keep calm and carry on.'

'So let me get this straight,' Tom said, 'they're asking people to keep calm and carry on, but at the same time just happening to mention that Stephen Hawking thinks we're all screwed?'

'I guess.'

'I saw some of that programme,' Siobhan said.

'I thought you were at work?' Tom sounded surprised.

'I was, but do you think we took many phone calls after what happened this afternoon? The place was dead. Me and Mo were watching TV online to try and find the news. As usual Jim, you've got hold of the wrong end of the stick. They were disputing what Stephen Hawking said, trying to put people at ease and *not* wind them up.'

'Interesting though, isn't it,' Rob said, watching the ship on TV again. The sky was even darker now, and there seemed to be no let up in the levels of activity around the massive craft. Its vast underbelly was illuminated from below in places, but very little of the machine was visible now.

'What's interesting?' Tom asked.

'How it's already changing everything. You know something's up when you've got Jim quoting eminent scientists and an anti-social wino like Ken Trentham suddenly feeling the need to talk.'

'So what are you saying?' Siobhan wondered.

'That the rules changed today, that's all,' Rob replied. 'All the boundaries and demarcation lines we used to know were rubbed out and redrawn.'

'I must be pissed,' James sighed, 'because I don't have a bloody clue what you're talking about now.'

'There's a new player in the game,' Rob explained, 'and that makes everyone else consider their own position differently.'

One of the most notable differences Tom had found since moving to Thatcham was the lack of ethnic diversity here. Like most of the country, Birmingham was a richly diverse place. Thatcham, in comparison, was not. Eddie Williams was the only black man in the village, and he was in the pub with a couple of friends, leaning up the wall next to Tom's table.

'Takes the pressure off you, don't it, Ed?' Tom heard one of Eddie's frighteningly bigoted friends joke.

'So what is it you're studying?' James asked Rob.

'Social sciences and the adaptation of social policy in deprived urban areas, why?'

'Because it sounds like a load of old bollocks to me, that's why.'

'It's not,' Rob replied, indignant. 'Remember when Tom first bought the bungalow? Remember the grief he was getting from the neighbours? Remember all the crap Ray Mercer gave him when he cut down that tree?'

'What about it?'

'Well, he was the alien back then, wasn't he? Just for a while, until someone else turned up to take the flack. As soon as the summer season started and hundreds of bloody tourists started filling the streets, all that was forgotten. He stopped being one of *them* and became one of *us*. Isn't that right, Siobhan?'

'It does sound like a load of old bollocks, Jim, I'll give you that,' she said, 'but Rob is right.'

'So are you saying these aliens are neighbours or tourists? And is this what you'd call a deprived area?'

Rob looked at James with despair. 'I'm not saying Thatcham's deprived, but if I'd just come halfway across the universe in a bloody huge spaceship like that, I think I'd be well within my rights to turn my nose up.'

'Do you think they've got noses?' Jim asked, confirming beyond doubt to the others that his earlier demonstration of intelligence had indeed been a fluke. No one bothered to answer.

'They can't be that intelligent,' a shrill voice said from an adjacent table. Tom looked around. It was Wendy Grayson. She worked in Thatcham's small supermarket, and she was a bloody gossip. When she realised how many people had heard her she continued talking, always happy to have an audience. 'I mean, all that space... the whole of the bloody universe to choose from and those soft buggers end up here at the back-end of nowhere!'

'Imagine the odds,' Tom said to no one in particular. 'Can you imagine what the chances of them ending up here were?'

None of them could, though each of them did find themselves thinking about the impossible scales and measures of the day now ending. Siobhan moved closer to Tom, and took hold of his hand under the table.

'Hard to believe, isn't it? The whole world's watching this. Millions of people – billions, even – all watching what's happening just a few miles from here.'

'Most things that get this much news coverage only affect part of the world,' Rob said, pausing to knock back the dregs of another pint. 'This is different. This has implications for *everybody*.'

Tom gripped Siobhan's hand even tighter. 'I just want to know what they're here for,' he said. 'I mean, I just want to know whether it's *ET* or *Independence Day*, you know? Are they here because they want to be friends, or are they going to blow the shit out of us then...'

He let his words trail away, suddenly aware that the rest of the pub had fallen silent. He looked around and saw that every face was fixed on one of the various screens around the bar. Then he looked up himself, and felt his pulse start to quicken.

Something was happening.

The pictures now being broadcast were coming from the same general location as the footage they'd already seen. As they watched, however, the camera panned right then zoomed into close-up on one particular section of the vessel's endless underbelly, near the front of the ship. It was difficult to see at first, but Tom was eventually able to make out a long rectangular opening appearing, some kind of hatch. Siobhan nudged him as he continued to tighten his grip on her hand, hurting her. He let go and reached for his pint.

'This is it,' Rob whispered ominously. 'Make or break. Handshake or heat-ray.'

Nothing happened for what felt like forever. No one moved. No one spoke. It was as if someone had pressed the pause button but rather than the pictures on the screen, everything else had frozen instead. And then, just when the first whispered conversations were on the verge of striking up again, an intense beam of searing white light spilled down through the opening in the ship's belly.

There was something in the light. Tom squinted, unsure what he was seeing. Hard to distinguish at first, its movements were slow, graceful and precise. It drifted down until it was midway between the ship and the ocean, then it stopped and held its position with the same unnatural ease as the craft from which it had just emerged. No juddering. Not being blown by the wind. Completely motionless.

'What the hell is that thing?' James asked.

Tom could taste fear in the air now, a definite change. People had begun to relax throughout the course of the evening and now, almost instantly, their earlier anxiety had returned, amplified ten-fold. Still no one moved. No one reacted. The entire pub remained silent. The TV volume was up, but no one was saying anything.

The thing which had descended from the alien ship dropped

down again, swooping towards the water. As its distance from the source of the light above increased, it became possible to make out more detail. It was a small, dart-shaped object, as black as its parent and similarly featureless. Without warning, the light from the first ship was shut off as the hatch closed.

The camera tracked the smaller machine as it came to rest in a space above the waves, surrounded by frigates and gunships of different nationalities, hovering a metre above the water.

# 3

For a long time nothing happened. The uneasy silence in the pub continued, punctuated only by occasional noise from the fruit machines. Barely anyone moved. John Tipper stood with his wife and watched the nearest screen, arms folded defiantly. Even Darren Braithwaite, the long-haired lad who worked in the petrol station, and his gang of mates were quiet. This time last week John had threatened to bar them because of the way they'd been taunting a group of blokes from out of town. Today they were subdued, clearly as nervous as everyone else.

'I need to go,' James whispered to the others. 'Have you seen the time? I said I wasn't going to be out late.'

'It's been a strange day,' Rob whispered back. 'Steph will understand.'

'I should be back home with her and the kids. She'll have my balls.'

'She's already had them, mate.'

'She'll be okay,' Siobhan reassured him.

'You think?'

'She'd have phoned if she needed you home. Tell her you just lost track of time. She'll be fine about it. Anyway, she'll only be sat watching this.'

'No, I should be there,' he said, pulling on his fleece. 'I probably shouldn't have come out. What happens if...?'

James didn't finish asking his question. An audible collective gasp from around the pub silenced him. He turned back to the TV and saw that the smaller alien machine on the screen was moving again. It climbed to a slightly higher altitude, almost as if it wanted to be seen. Or was it being aimed?

'Shit,' Rob said quietly, 'is that some kind of missile?'

The camera angle and the lack of visible references made it difficult to gauge the machine's precise size and height. Tom was trying to estimate its proportions and guess its intent when, without warning, a series of lights appeared on the surface of the ship, all around its perimeter, all pointing upwards.

'What's happening?' James asked pointlessly. He knew no one could answer, but it helped him just to ask. The relative silence in the pub was replaced with a low buzz of nervous voices when a hatch slid open on the top of the machine. And then, slowly – cautiously – a lone figure appeared, lifted gracefully into view on some kind of platform. There was a heart-stopping moment of confusion as the picture shifted and blurred, but it was only the camera operator struggling to keep up with events. As the picture came back into focus, they watched the figure step off the platform and take a few steps out onto the hull of its vessel.

Tom stared at an alien.

It was an undeniably unsettling and yet strangely inspiring sight. Standing somewhere between six and seven feet tall, Tom thought, it looked to him to be distinctly male, not that he had any reason to assume these creatures had human-like sexes. It had smooth, dark pink skin and he thought it looked burned, as if it had spent too long unprotected under the strong summer sun. Its head was unexpectedly disproportionate, and looked too large and heavy to be supported by such a gaunt frame. It had a light covering of grey, almost silver hair which was swept back at the temples, giving it a distinguished appearance. The alien wore a simple yet formal-looking uniform made of dark material with little in the way of decoration.

The creature stood still for the longest thirty seconds in history, its large eyes fixed straight ahead, apparently unfazed both by its exposed position and the fact it must have known it was now the sole focus of attention of the entire planet. Tom wondered what thoughts were running through its head. Whatever it felt, the creature (and that suddenly felt like too derogatory a term given its dignified appearance), remained regimentally stood to alert as it was scanned, scrutinised and inspected by the population of the planet.

'Is that thing really an alien?' Tom asked the question without thinking.

'What else could it be?' Rob replied.

In the hours since he'd witnessed the ship's descent through the storm clouds, Tom had almost begun to get used to the fact that it was here. But this new development – this first confirmed and indisputable visible contact with an alien life-form – had made all the nervousness he'd felt out on his cliff-top run immediately return. Back to square one again in a heartbeat.

The alien on the screen continued to stand its ground, unperturbed by the chaos of movement and light which was now beginning to unfold all around it. What was it waiting for, Tom wondered? Was it going to surrender, or give the signal to attack? Neither option seemed more likely than the other. As he watched, it seemed to take in a long, deep breath, then tilted its oversized head back on its relatively slight shoulders and looked up at the mother-ship above. The TV coverage abruptly switched to a close-up of the alien's head from another angle, and the similarities with a human face caught Tom off-guard. Other than an unusually pronounced forehead (which gave the alien an unfortunate Neanderthal-like profile from this angle), its basic facial features were instantly familiar. It had a wide, thin-lipped mouth, a small nose (too small, Tom thought), two ears which were quite flat and smooth and which were tilted back at a more obtuse angle than a human's, and a pair of sharp, crystal-blue eyes. As still as the rest of its body remained, its eyes moved constantly, alert and intense, absorbing every detail.

When the camera angle switched again, the picture revealed that a boat had come alongside the shuttle craft. Filled with at least twenty heavily-armed soldiers, it bobbed and rolled with the waves, looking increasingly precarious in comparison to the unnaturally steady alien vehicle. The alien finally looked down from the mother-ship, took another deep breath of salty sea air (was it nervous, Tom wondered?), then raised its hands and struck an unmistakably passive pose. For a few seconds Tom was preoccupied with the unnatural length of the alien's limbs – its elbows were lower down than expected, and it's wrists higher – and he cursed himself for allowing himself to be distracted by trivialities at such a monumental, historic moment. The alien then began to move. It walked to the end of its ship, then stepped down onto the military boat. The soldiers all edged back slightly, leaving the new arrival standing alone in a small bubble of space on the deck. It continued to hold its hands up, keen to demonstrate that it was unarmed and had nothing to hide. The soldiers retook their original positions. For a few seconds longer the alien's bulbous head remained visible in the midst of the crowd, then it disappeared as it was taken below deck. The small boat immediately began to move away from the scene at speed, banking hard to port. The camera operator scrambled to keep it focused and in shot as it raced towards the shore, desperate for a final few frames of alien footage.

On the TV, the news channel cut back to the studio. The anchor man whose face filled the screen looked lost for words. He was about to speak but was rudely truncated when all the TVs were switched off. John Tipper's distinctive voice rose above the sudden noise of everyone else. 'Thank you very much, ladies and gentlemen, let's have your glasses please. I think that's quite enough excitement for one day. I'm sure you've all got homes to go to.'

Without complaint, the pub began to empty.

# 4

Tom woke several times during the night, to the point where he felt he'd been lying awake longer than he'd been asleep. He had a few very definite recollections of what had happened in the hours since they'd returned home, but they were muddied by confused, alcohol-induced dreams of running through storms and alien ships.

He clearly remembered falling into bed with Siobhan, wanting to make love to her, but not knowing if he physically could with all the beer still sloshing around in his gut. He remembered how those doubts had immediately disappeared when she'd slipped beneath the sheets and had started stroking, nibbling and licking. He remembered her sitting on top of him, the covers having long since fallen away, looking up at the ceiling and biting her lip as she held onto his shoulders and pulled herself down onto him. He remembered her face, barely illuminated but completely beautiful, and the shape of her arched back and perfect breasts. The warmth of her body...

He'd fallen asleep after sex but had woken a short time later, dizzy with booze, bladder about to burst, unsteady on his feet. He remembered leaving the light off in the bathroom because it was too bright, then missing the toilet and pissing up the wall because he couldn't see properly, then tripping over his discarded jeans on the way back to bed. He remembered Siobhan getting up for work and leaving just before eight, but what had happened since then was largely a blur. He didn't know what time it was now. He opened one eye and tried to focus on the clock next to the bed, but the bedroom was filled with light and he could barely make out any of the numbers. Instead he grabbed his phone and checked the screen. Eleven thirty-eight. Bloody hell, it was late. He had a message from Siobhan. Short and sweet:

is it me or the beer u can't handle?
get up u lazy fucker x

In contrast to the ferocious weather yesterday afternoon, today was a gloriously hot summer day. The air in the bedroom was stifling. With considerable effort, Tom forced himself up. He swung his legs off the bed and sat up too fast, then screwed his eyes shut and waited for a wave of self-induced nausea to pass. His head was pounding, and for a moment he wasn't sure if he was going to black out, vomit, or both. It was a relief when the sickness faded enough for him to get up and stumble over to the window.

And then he remembered: The run... The alien ship... Last night in the Badger's Sett, watching mankind's first confirmed contact with intelligent life from another world...

His hangover immediately forgotten, he picked up his phone again and checked the news headlines, genuinely concerned that something terrible might have happened while he'd been asleep. *Surely I'd have heard,* he thought as he waited for the page to load. *Wouldn't Rob or Siobhan have woken me up if it was the end of the world?*

It was hard to focus on such a small screen with his head so fuzzy. Satisfied that it wasn't the end of everything just yet, he pulled back the curtains and looked out over Thatcham.

The village looked very different; as busy as carnival day, but without the flags and floats and bouncy castles. The streets were teeming with activity – more people around than he'd seen all summer, and there were no free parking spaces either. The car parks were full and there were vehicles parked up on the grass verges with still more arriving. From his window he could see the road coming into Thatcham from the north, and it was unexpectedly busy, clogged with a queue of slow-moving traffic. There was no doubt about it, Thatcham was *the* place to be this morning. It was no surprise, really. He guessed this entire stretch of coastline would probably be the same.

Tom took a clean T-shirt and a pair of shorts from the wardrobe and kicked his dirty clothes into the corner. He stumbled through into the bathroom where, after doing everything he needed to do and cleaning his teeth twice to get rid of the taste of last night, he got dressed and gradually began to feel human again. *Human*, he thought as he looked into the mirror. *Doesn't seem to have the same impact as it used to.*

He headed for the kitchen to get coffee and toast to settle his still volatile stomach, but Rob had beaten him to it. Tom found him leaning against the back door, looking as bad as he himself felt. The kettle was boiling. With much moaning and groaning, he made drinks and passed one to Tom.

'All right?' Tom asked. Rob grunted something he couldn't make out. He tried again. 'Feeling rough?'

'Fucking terrible. You?'

'Same.'

Rob went through to the living room, dragging his feet along the carpet as if they were too heavy to pick up. He crashed onto the sofa and groaned again as he reached for the TV remote.

'You seen how busy it is out there today?' Tom asked.

'It's been like that all morning.'

'Have you been up long?'

'Don't remember going to bed.'

'Idiot.'

'Thanks.'

'So has anything happened?'

'What, apart from a ship full of aliens turning up in the skies over Thatcham.'

'Yes, apart from that.'

'Well they're not here to kill us, if that's what you're worried about.'

'How do you know?'

Rob turned up the TV sound on one of the news channels.

40

At first glance it looked the same as usual: the forced smile of an overly made-up, plastic-faced presenter, the ticker-tape running across the bottom of the screen, distracting graphics and icons constantly appearing then disappearing... but the headlines were anything but usual. It was still bizarre to hear the newsreader talking about alien contact and *'entering a new era for mankind.'* Was there anyone left alive on the surface of the planet who *hadn't* heard what had happened here? In these days of the Internet, mobile phones, digital TV, and everything else, when information was harder to avoid than to come by, could there be anyone who still wasn't aware of the arrival of the aliens? *More to the point*, he thought as he waited for the headlines, *there's no way anyone could keep something like this quiet, even if they wanted to.* The picture cut to a montage of shaky phone footage of the arrival of the ship, taken from various locations. *How many thousands of people have video like that on their phones?*

Back to the studio. The woman on the screen was annoying him now. Was that a smile or a grimace? Her skin was too perfect, her lips too red, not a hair out of place. *Can I trust you? Are you an alien?*

Midday. Headlines. The monumental events of the last twenty-four hours were condensed into two minutes of sound-bites and recycled footage, much of which he'd already seen, but that was sufficient. A little more information followed: an observation station in Southern Australia had, apparently, been the first place to pick up the distress signal (and Tom still wasn't sure how they knew the aliens were in distress), and from there the progress of the ship had been continually tracked until a coordinated military task force under the command of the United Nations had guided the vessel out over safer waters.

Old news. What had happened since then?

The newsreader explained that direct contact had been made with the occupants of the ship shortly before they'd reached the Earth's atmosphere. Just after midnight UK time, agreement had been made for a representative of the aliens to be taken into custody to explain their sudden and unexpected arrival here.

Tom couldn't quite gauge the level of bullshit at play. This was mainstream TV news, so he knew there'd undoubtedly be some spin being put on the story somewhere along the line, but where, and from which direction? It was impossible to tell. But Christ, he thought, it all sounded so perfect. *Too* perfect, if anything. Maybe it was just him being a cynic?

Truth was, Tom was scared. He wanted answers no one was yet in any position to provide. He couldn't say anything to Rob or Siobhan – he didn't think either of them would understand – but he didn't feel particularly good about any of this. Maybe it was the lack of control that troubled him. Whatever these bloody aliens decided to do, there was bugger all he could do about it.

In comparison, Rob didn't seem to give a damn. He lifted his backside to fart, then groaned again.

'Dirty bastard,' Tom said.

'Hold up, this is new,' Rob said, ignoring him.

'What is?'

'This,' he said again, nodding at the TV. 'Haven't seen this guy before.'

The man on the screen wore a well-decorated military uniform and spoke in heavily-accented, clipped English. Like the bewildered politician they'd seen on TV yesterday, this man also struggled to make himself heard over the noise in the briefing room where he was standing. He stood at a UN plinth, waiting impatiently for quiet. Eventually the noise subsided enough for him to continue.

'Since the alien representative gave himself up to us in the early hours of this morning, we've been discussing the on-going situation constantly. They have complied with our every request, and have given us no reason to believe they will not continue to do so.

'We are aware that these developments have incredibly wide-reaching ramifications, not just for countries and governments, but for every individual person on the planet too. With that in mind, the Security Council has authorised the following statement in the belief that honesty and transparency is the only way forward given the circumstances.'

'Sounds ominous,' Tom said.

'Not necessarily.'

The UN representative continued. 'Since the days before mankind took its first tentative steps beyond the atmosphere of our planet, we have dreamed of the moment we make contact with intelligent life from another planet. That day was yesterday.

'Our science-fiction writers and film-makers have, unfortunately, always tended to put a rather dark and overdramatic slant on such events, portraying them as the beginning of the end, rather than anything more positive. Let me reassure you all today, we have no reason to be afraid of these visitors.'

'Visitors!' Tom laughed. 'Reminds me of that old programme we used to watch. Remember $V$? I've been thinking about that show a lot today.'

'Funny, that,' Rob said. 'Suppose visitors is as good a word as any.'

The man on the screen had paused for the assembled throng of reporters to absorb his words and calm down again. He continued, 'As you already know, the alien ship is currently surrounded by an international military force which will remain there as long as necessary. The visitors have made no attempt to respond to their presence with anything less than complete humility.'

'Odd choice of word,' Tom said. Rob grunted.

'This first contact between our two worlds was not planned,

it came about by chance. I can tell you that the aliens were on a mining expedition on the outskirts of our galaxy. Their ship was damaged in an accident, leaving them unable to return home. It seems that we are the only other intelligent life-forms in an almost incalculably vast region of space. The aliens have, therefore, come to us for help.

'This is not an invasion, this arrival is not a precursor of doom for our world, this is an *opportunity* for all of us. Despite being a considerably more advanced race than ourselves, the visitors are at our mercy. Their ship is incapable of making the return journey back to their world. Put simply, without our help, they will not survive.'

'Do you buy that?' Tom asked. 'All that intelligence and technology, but they can't fix their ship?'

'Why not?' Rob quickly replied. 'Remember when you had that blowout on the motorway the other month?'

'What about it? Hardly the same league.'

'Same principle, though. You didn't have a spare, so you were stuck standing on the hard shoulder for hours until the recovery truck could get to you.'

'So?'

'So, you know how to replace a tyre, but you didn't physically have one, so there wasn't anything you could do.'

He had a point, but Tom's head still wasn't clear enough to be able to see it. He tried to concentrate on the TV again, but the UN official had drifted into rhetoric about 'new beginnings' and 'the dawn of a new age', and he lost interest.

'So how come they're able to talk to us?' he asked.

'What?'

'That's one of the things I could never work out from *Star Trek*. Wherever they went and whoever or whatever they met, everyone spoke English.'

'Newsflash, mate,' Rob laughed, digging his brother in the ribs. '*Star Trek*'s made up. This is real.'

'I know that, you prick, but that just makes it even harder to swallow, doesn't it?'

'Why?'

'Because it does. Christ, we don't even bother learning new languages when we go abroad. We just shout louder and hope the locals understand us.'

'Well maybe we should make more of an effort. Anyway, if they can build and pilot a ship like that, something like Google Translate will be a piece of cake for them. They've probably got it implanted in their brains or something like that.'

'Now you're just taking the piss.'

'I'm not! I'm serious. You can get things for your phone that'll give you a translation if you take a photo of a sign written in a foreign language, and you can get software that understands speech. Put the two together and you're not a million miles away. It's a logical next-step.'

'There's nothing logical about what's going on around here.'

'Like I said, mate,' he sighed, 'they've got a great big, fuck off spaceship, remember? If they can manage that, I'm sure they can out-Google us too.'

'Suppose. You've changed your tune. You didn't sound so sure about all of this last night.'

'I've had time to think about it, that's all. Your problem, Tom, is that you're a bloody cynic. I reckon it's all those years spent shafting people in your job, all those takeovers and acquisitions. You need to start being a bit more altruistic. Not everyone's always out to get you, you know.'

'I know.'

'When we were little, you always said you wanted to go into space. Well now you might have a chance. Imagine that! They'll share their technology and there you go, the sky's no longer the limit.'

'I hope you're right. I already know how it'll pan out though. They'll show someone how to build a ship, then someone else will want to build a better one, then we'll be racing to build bases on the Moon and on Mars...'

'I know what you're saying, but let's hope this is different, eh?'

'Why should it be? In fact, why should they show us anything? Why not just take what they want then leave us broken and in pieces? When has a superior power ever truly given a damn about the people they've conquered?'

'You're still looking at this all the wrong way, Tom. It's not about battles and fighting, is it? These aliens aren't here because they want to pick a fight. They're not here because they want to be here either. Their ship is fucked, and we just happen to be their only hope, even if all we're doing is offering them bed and breakfast until they can get back. Thing is, when you step back and look at it, it looks like they need us far more than we need them.'

# 5

Whether it was because of his hangover, the constant barrage of news overload, or his brother's endless conjecture, Tom felt like he needed a change of scenery. The chance to visit Clare Austin, a good friend, presented him with an opportunity to return to the welcome normality of life for a while and shut off from all the talk of aliens and *new horizons* and the like. He didn't know anyone who was more grounded and down-to-earth than Clare, and that was probably why he liked her so much. A spade was a spade to Clare. It wouldn't have mattered if the aliens had touched down in her back garden instead of just flying over it, he knew she wouldn't have given a damn.

As was often the case, Clare needed Tom's help. She was perfectly capable, she just didn't have time to waste, and that was something Tom had in abundance. A recently-separated single mum with a young daughter, she felt like she had to work twice as hard as everyone else just to keep standing still. Her partner had walked out on her and their daughter, Penny, at the end of last year, leaving behind little more than bad memories and a heap of jointly-held debts. There was no disputing the fact that Aiden had been a selfish, inconsiderate shit (any of his many girlfriends would agree), and Clare knew it was for the best.

Tom had been helping Clare out with odd jobs for almost as long as he'd been living in Thatcham. They'd been introduced to each other by James, and they'd immediately got on. It was a purely platonic relationship. Tom sometimes got bored. There was only so much daytime TV and video games he could take. His lack of motivation was becoming a serious concern, and putting up a shelf or painting a wall for Clare often provided him with a welcome kick up the backside and gave him the impetus to do something constructive. Today he hoped that fixing her computer would bring some purpose to this incredibly strange day.

The traffic in and around the village remained heavy, the single carriageway which wound along the length of Thatcham far busier than Tom would have typically expected, even at the peak of the season at this time on a Saturday afternoon, when one lot of tourists left for home and the next moved in to take their place. He sat at a junction waiting to turn right to get out of the village, watching the chaos deeper in the heart of Thatcham. The place was, in reality, little more than a meandering line of shops, cafés, takeaways and houses, most of which looked out over the ocean or, more accurately now, over the recently bolstered sea defences. The council had spent a small fortune dropping tons of boulders at strategic points along the coast to reduce the risk of the village flooding, as had happened in previous years. Parking space along the main road was severely limited at the best of times, with residents claiming those spots where there were no markings or warning signs. Today, however, all such warnings were being ignored.

An unexpected gap in the traffic (Tom might have been wrong, but he thought he heard Ken Trentham screaming at a hapless motorist) allowed him to nudge forward, then finally make the turn and start heading out of the village. He accelerated as he broke free from the congestion, and with his windows down, his music playing and the smell of the sea hanging in the air, for a few seconds everything was reassuringly familiar again. No sooner had he got up speed, though, than he was forced to slow once more as he joined the back end of another queue of traffic waiting for a large truck to reverse into the car park of one of the many campsites dotted around the village. He thought it strange, and not a little surreal, when he saw the truck pull up alongside several more of a similar size. Some had satellite dishes and huge aerials bolted to their roofs, and they all belonged to various media companies: BBC, ITV, SKY, and a few more he hadn't heard of besides. The campsite itself resembled something from the outskirts of a music festival: a sea of wildly coloured canvas roofs with barely a scrap of space between them. Still, he thought, this sudden media influx was by no means the strangest thing which had happened in Thatcham recently, and his mind wandered back to this time yesterday when he'd been out on the hills...

The road ahead was clear again now, Tom put his foot down and continued out towards Clare's. He passed a lone house about a mile further down the lane, the people who lived there enjoying a barbeque in the sun. He caught the sound of their laughter on the breeze, their relaxed noise making him realise how uncertain he still felt. *Maybe Rob's right*, he thought. *Maybe I just need to lighten up and stop overanalysing everything.* He couldn't help himself, though. Everything looked the same today as it always had done, but somehow it all *felt* different.

Clare's house was near Welbeck, a small village on the way to Drayton, the largest town in the area. Even with today's traffic it didn't take Tom long to get there. He pulled up outside her terraced cottage, behind the heap of a car her ex-in-laws had given her to appease their guilt over their son's behaviour. The house door was open before he'd even rung the bell. Penny stood in the hallway, grinning at him.

'What did your mum say to you about opening the door to strangers?'

'She said don't do it. But you're not a stranger, are you.'

'No, but...'

'Let Tom in, Pen,' Clare shouted from inside the house. 'I'm in the kitchen.'

'Mummy's been swearing at the computer again,' Penny explained.

'I heard.'

Tom shut the door then side-stepped the little girl to get through. Clare was ironing, and dinner was cooking on the stove.

'You were quick,' she said.

'Not a lot else to do,' he replied without thinking.

'It's all right for some,' she grumbled, semi-seriously. 'Bloody hell, Tom, it's a sad state of affairs when you've got nothing better to do on a Saturday afternoon than come here.'

'There's nothing happening at home. Siobhan's at work and Rob's still half-drunk from last night. He was asleep when I left him, actually.'

'How the other half live, eh?' she said as she hung a pair of trousers on a hanger then picked a crumpled shirt out of the washing basket. Tom remained in the doorway, feeling redundant and slightly awkward. He was glad of the distraction when Penny reappeared.

'So how are you, mate?' he asked her.

'Okay.'

'Been up to much since I last saw you?'

'Not really.'

'Enjoying the holidays?'

'They're all right.'

'Only all right? You live near the seaside and you don't have to go back to school for another week, how can it only be all right?'

'I was in day club most days. Some days Mum and me had chips on the beach when she finished her work.'

'Sounds great. Were the chips good?'

'Chips are always good.'

With that she was gone again. End of conversation. She caught a glimpse of her ever-elusive cat out of the corner of her eye and went chasing after it with predatory speed. Clare shouted after her to slow down but her warning had little effect. Tom watched as Penny chased the cat down the length of their short back garden, then saw it slip through a hole in the wire-mesh fence and run out into the fields beyond.

50

Clare watched her daughter from behind the ironing board, standing on tiptoe to make sure she was okay before returning her attention to the laundry. Again Tom felt awkward, and a little sad too. Clare never seemed to relax, never switched off. He'd only come into her life at the tail-end of her relationship problems, but he knew the break-up had taken its toll. He hadn't had it easy himself since the death of his parents, but there was a major difference in their relative situations: he had no one to think about but himself. If Tom wanted to cry, he could cry. If he wanted to get drunk and smash something up, he'd do it. If he wanted to stay in bed all day and not say a damn thing to anyone, then that was what he did. Clare, on the other hand, had to keep everything bottled up and hidden away for her daughter's sake. He could see the strain etched on her face.

'So how are you doing?' he asked, slightly cautiously, treading a fine line between caring and patronising.

'Okay,' she said as she folded up the ironing board. 'Been better, been worse.'

'Work all right?'

'I'm a dental nurse, Tom. I spend my days sterilizing instruments, checking notes and looking into people's mouths. Work's as all right as can be expected.'

'Well that's something, I guess,' he said, and she managed a subdued grin as she passed him the ironing board to put away. She immediately turned her attention to the oven, and served up Penny's dinner then called her inside.

'Drink?'

'If you're having one,' Tom replied.

'I am. Hot or cold?'

'Whatever's easier.'

'Juice or beer?'

'Don't mind.'

Clare grinned again. 'Typical bloody man, couldn't make a

decision if your life depended on it.'

'Juice then,' he answered quickly. 'I'm driving.'

'That's better,' she said, deliberately patronizing.

'You're not going all feminist on me are you, Clare?'

'What if I am? What's wrong with that?' she asked as she led him through to her over-cluttered but comfortable living room.

'Nothing,' he replied, backpedalling furiously. 'It's just that—'

'I've had enough of men,' she said. 'You're more trouble than you're worth, you lot. That guy next door, Jim Franks, he's such a bloody chauvinist. Him and his wife are both in their eighties, and I can't believe how he talks to her. You can hear him out in the garden, shouting for her to get him something to eat. And she puts up with it too, silly cow. Has done for years'

'But they're ancient. It's probably just a generational thing.'

'That's no excuse. Honestly, she's scared to do anything without checking with him first. Spends her entire life cleaning up and fussing around him. You try talking to her and it's pitiful. She's got no conversation, absolutely nothing to say for herself. Christ, I think she has to check with Jim before she goes to the toilet.'

'Bloody hell, Clare, who rattled your cage?'

She sighed and shook her head. 'Sorry, bad week.'

Tom sensed he shouldn't pry. 'Want to show me what the problem with the computer is? Let this useless bloke try and fix it for you?'

'I could probably do it myself if I tried. I just don't have the time.'

'No worries. You said something about it not connecting?'

'Yes, bloody thing,' she said as she led him upstairs. The computer was in her cramped bedroom, set up on a dressing table littered with loose cables, CDs and data sticks, unused user guides, and a layer of dust. Tom sat down and turned it on. Clare cleared her throat. 'Sorry.'

'What for?'

'For going off on one just now. For ranting.'

'It's water off a duck's back. Honest, it doesn't bother me.'

'You're a good punch bag at times, Thomas Winter.'

'I aim to please.'

'No, seriously, you're a half-decent bloke. Best of a bad bunch. I didn't mean to lump you in with the rest of the shysters.'

Tom watched the computer beginning to boot up. Should he say anything else or just let it go? He didn't want to, but decided he probably should. 'So what's he done now?'

'He's messing me around, that's all.'

'More than usual?'

'Not really. I just get fed up of it, you know? Everything's a battle with Aiden. He's a spineless, selfish bastard.'

'Bloody hell, don't hold back.'

Clare had no intention of doing so. 'I mean, just look at the way he left here. No hint there was anything wrong until he told me he was going. No discussions. No negotiations. Right before Christmas too. Bastard. Now I look back I feel like such an idiot. I should have seen it coming. The warning signs were there. All those bloody business trips. And he never wanted to get married either. It's obvious why now. It would have been harder for him to walk out if we'd been married.'

Tom seized on a pause in her rant to try and divert the conversation elsewhere. 'You said you were having trouble getting online...'

'It gets this far,' she explained, 'then it freezes up. See?'

'Ahh... I think I can fix this. You installed anything new recently?'

'No idea. Aiden probably emailed me a virus or something stupid.'

'He wouldn't do that, would he?'

'I don't think he'd have the intelligence. He's such a shit, Tom. You know, I don't think he gives a damn about Penny. He keeps making excuses for not seeing her. She hasn't seen him for over a month. It's Pen I feel sorry for. She's the one who's suffering most in all of this, but she's too young to express how she's—'

'We got any more ketchup, Mum?' Penny asked from the doorway. Neither Tom or Clare had heard her creep upstairs. Clare smiled at her daughter, hoping she hadn't overheard.

'There's some in the cupboard. I'll come down and get it for you in a sec, okay?' Clare replied quickly, her voice overly bright. With that Penny disappeared back down to her dinner. Tom looked over his shoulder and saw Clare staring into the space where her daughter had just been.

'I've got this,' he said. 'Shouldn't take long.'

Clare nodded and went downstairs.


The computer problem turned out to be a relatively simple one to fix, which was a relief because Tom definitely wasn't an expert. He'd picked up a fair amount of knowledge from his time working in the city, but until he'd moved to Thatcham he'd always had the support of an IT helpdesk to fall back on whenever he hit trouble. But he had a logical mind, and he managed to work his way back through the problem by adjusting and readjusting various settings until something happened, removing a couple of redundant programs, and turning the whole thing off and on again several times.

'Done,' he announced triumphantly as he returned downstairs. Clare looked up from where she was sitting on the sofa, watching TV with Penny.

'Brilliant. Thanks, Tom.'

'You're welcome.'

'What was the problem?'

He tried to fob her off with some bullshit or other – a string of words he'd seen but didn't quite understand – but she could see straight through him. 'Not sure really,' he admitted. 'I just kept messing with it until it started working.'

'Thank you, anyway. You've got to let me give you something for your time.'

'Another drink will be enough.'

Clare got up and disappeared into the kitchen. Tom sat down next to Penny on the sofa. The programme she'd been watching finished, and she grabbed a handful of remote controls. With remarkable speed and dexterity, she switched off the DVD player and surfed through several of her favourite channels.

'You're faster than me with those things,' Tom said, genuinely impressed.

'I use them a lot,' she answered. 'There, I like that programme,' she said, pointing at the screen as the channel numbers and programme names flashed past.

'What, the news?' Tom asked, surprised. The TV had stopped on one of the many channels still broadcasting footage of the alien arrival.

'No, not that. After the news. It's on next.'

Clare called for Penny who got up and scrambled away, leaving Tom alone in the living room. He struggled to find the right button on the right remote control, but eventually managed to increase the volume slightly. A cursory glance at the headlines running across the screen revealed that nothing much seemed to have changed in the few hours since he'd last checked. He was relieved. He felt like he'd taken his eye off the ball coming here. Anything could have happened.

Clare passed him his drink and sat down next to him.

'So what do you think about all of this?' he asked.

'Not a lot.'

'You're not excited? Intrigued?'

'Not really.'

'Plenty of other folks seem to be. Thatcham's rammed.'

'I know. Drayton's the same. I tried to do a bit of shopping first thing this morning but I ended up turning back and coming home.'

'Still doesn't seem real, does it? I mean, actual confirmed contact with another form of intelligent life.'

'*Another* intelligent life-form? What, you think mankind's intelligent? Jesus...'

Tom sensed another anti-male, anti-Aiden rant coming, and he moved fast to head it off. 'Let's just hope some good comes of it, eh? You'd think with that kind of technology they might be able to help us make a few advances and—'

'The only kind of advances I'm interested in,' she quickly interrupted, 'are advances on my salary so I can afford to pay the bills and keep a roof over our head. Do you have any idea how much Penny's childcare fees have been this summer? I couldn't give a damn about bloody spaceships and the like.'

'Fair enough.'

'I don't want to piss on anyone's parade,' she continued, fired-up again, 'but I'll be honest with you, Tom, because I always am. I don't give a shit what's happening next door, never mind the next town, the next country, or the next bloody galaxy. All I'm concerned about is making sure my little girl is safe and happy and that she has everything she needs. I have to put her first, because no one else gives a flying fuck. And if everyone's now going to spend their time looking up at the stars, thinking about buggering off into space, then there's less chance than ever of me getting any help.'

Tom had touched a raw nerve, and he immediately regretted saying anything. But Christ, all he'd done was mention what was on TV. 'Look, I'm sorry,' he said, not entirely sure what he was apologising for. 'You know I'm here if you need anything.'

She smiled and gently squeezed his hand. 'I know. Look, I'm

sorry I'm such a bitch at the moment. Like I said, it's been a bad week. I know I can rely on you, but...'

A moment's silence.

'But what?'

'But it's not the same, is it? I don't want to offend you, Tom, so please don't take this the wrong way, but you've got Siobhan and your brother, and you don't owe me or Penny anything. By rights we should be at the very bottom of your list of priorities.'

'Thing is, I don't have much in the way of priorities right now.'

'I understand that. I'm being clumsy here... I guess what I'm trying to say is we're not your responsibility. Aiden's the one who should be providing right now, and no matter what he's done, for Penny's sake I can't shut him out of her life completely. All I want to do is punch the fucker in the face or worse when I see him, but I can't. I have to stay positive and keep trying, even if it kills me.'

'I'm not trying to take anyone's place, I'm just—'

'As much as I hate him right now,' Clare interrupted, not listening, 'and I *do* hate him, he's still Penny's dad.'

Tom resolved to keep his mouth shut and was relieved when a change on the TV brought a welcome distraction. *Breaking News,* a gaudy graphic announced.

'Mind if I...?' Tom asked, picking up the remote control again. He turned up the volume as yet another stuffed suit took up position behind another UN plinth. Tom's mouth was dry and he felt uncomfortable, half-expecting the diplomat to be about to announce the beginning of hostilities or something similar.

'I bet it's all gone belly-up,' Clare said, and it made Tom feel slightly better knowing he wasn't the only person left who was still looking at glasses which were half-empty rather than half-full.

'Further to the information we shared with you earlier to-day,' the spokesman began, 'we can now provide you with an important update.'

'They've brought space germs with them and we're all fucked,' Clare said. 'I saw a film like that once.'

'Either that or we're all being ordered to report to process-ing centres first thing Monday morning so they can turn us into mindless drones.'

'I think they've already started. Have you been into Drayton recently?'

'A thorough inspection of the alien vessel has been carried out by their technicians,' the man on the screen continued. 'They have reached the conclusion that the ship is damaged beyond repair. Contact has been made with their home-world, and we've been advised that a rescue mission is already being prepared for launch. Current estimates are that it should arrive by May next year.'

'Next year?' Tom exclaimed. 'Bloody hell.'

'They managed to get in touch quick enough, though.'

'Ten months,' he repeated. 'At the speed that thing moves? Why's it going to take so long?'

'Can't say I'm surprised. Ten months is plenty long enough for them to get themselves well and truly settled. We're never going to be able to get rid of them now, are we?'

'We don't know that.'

'Let's be honest, Tom, we don't really know anything yet.'

He didn't bother trying to argue with her logic. On the screen the UN spokesman was still in full flow.

'By unanimous agreement we have today passed a United Nations resolution which permits these travellers – our guests – asylum here until such a time as they are able to leave. It is hoped that both the visitors and ourselves will be able to take advantage of our time together in order to learn about each other's planets, cultures and technologies. This is a tremendously exciting time for *all* of us.'

'Bollocks,' Clare interrupted. 'Who are they kidding? Does anyone really believe they're going to learn *anything* from us? Bloody hell, look at the state of their spaceship. Do you honestly think we'll be able to tell them anything they don't already know?'

'You're right,' Tom agreed. 'They've got halfway across the universe. We can't even get a bloody unmanned probe to Mars without fucking it up.'

'This is all spin,' Clare said, 'no substance. It's all so bloody vague. I used to have the same problem with Aiden. He could talk the talk and he was full of big ideas, but when you looked deeper, there was nothing there.'

Tom glanced across at her. She picked up a magazine and started flicking through the pages, her limited interest in the aliens clearly exhausted. It was obvious from her tone that, to Clare, the sudden arrival of these visitors was just another unnecessary complication to her already unnecessarily complicated life.

The man on screen still had more to say.

'We have been informed that there is a slight danger of a leak from the ship's engines. Having fully considered the information provided to us by the visitors, the Security Council has agreed that the most sensible course of action available is for the aliens to destroy their ship. Arrangements are being made to launch the vessel away from Earth on a course which will guide it directly into the sun. We are assured by our solar experts that this will have no detrimental side-effects and that it is the safest and easiest way of avoiding potential dangers. Furthermore, when the—'

Tom didn't get to hear anything else. Clare snatched up the remote and switched the TV off.

'Sorry,' she said, 'I've heard enough for one day.'

Tom looked across at her again, concerned. She caught his

eye momentarily, then looked away.

'Listen, I'm only going to ask you this one more time. Are you sure you're okay?'

She paused, and she seemed about to say something before deciding at the last possible second that she shouldn't. 'I'm fine,' she said. 'I'm sorry I'm such a miserable bitch.'

'You're not,' he said instinctively.

'I am.'

'Okay, you are. But I understand. You don't have to apologise.'

'I'm probably just hormonal.'

'Too much detail.'

She smiled. 'It's just that sometimes I feel like I can't breathe, you know? It's not Penny's fault, and I feel like a bad mum just for saying this, but I'd just like a break. I'd like to go out and get pissed. I want to pick up my studying again and try and finish my degree. I want to be more than just a mum and an employee. Does that make any sense, or am I just being selfish?'

'It makes complete sense.'

'I just want to have a little control back, you know? It's like every minute of every day I'm doing stuff for other people, and there's never any time left for me. I think that's why I'm not interested in these bloody aliens. I've already got too much to think about.'

There was nothing Tom could do or say. He waited a few seconds longer before making his excuses. 'I should go...'

'I don't blame you. I would if I was you.' She smiled. 'Thanks for your help with the computer, Tom.'

'No worries. If you need anything else...'

'I'll call.'

'Promise?'

'Promise.'

# 6

It took Tom over an hour to get back home from Clare's. He could have run to Thatcham in half the time, and he would have if he'd known how bad the traffic was going to be. He even considered abandoning the car and coming back for it later, but there were no spaces in which he could leave it, and no sign that the congestion was going to ease.

He eventually parked up outside the bungalow and stretched his back, glad to be out of the car.

'You leaving that there?'

Tom looked around and saw his neighbour, Ray Mercer, storming towards him. They'd had their differences from the outset, after Tom had savagely pruned several of Mercer's Laburnums which had been overhanging his garden, blocking the light. Mercer had threatened to report him to the police. Tom had told him to stop complaining and find something better to do with what was left of his life, and things had gone downhill from there.

'Well seeing as I've parked on my drive,' he replied, 'yes. Is there a problem?'

Mercer grunted. 'Spoils my view of the sunset when you park there.'

'Oh well. I'll bear that in mind if I go out again later.'

'You do that,' Mercer said, turning his back on Tom and marching back to his house.

*Arsehole*, Tom thought, making a mental note to leave his car there more often. He found it strangely reassuring that, aliens or no aliens, Mercer was as objectionable a prick as ever.

From his high vantage point Tom looked down over Thatcham and the surrounding area. There seemed to be even more tents in the campsite just outside the village now, barely any spaces left between them. A flood of people disembarked from a usually half-empty train. Crowds of drinkers spilled out onto the street outside the Badger's Sett. Mrs Grayson was standing in front of the supermarket, leaning up the window and puffing on a cigarette as she did most times he saw her. *Life goes on*, he said to himself. This time yesterday, he hadn't been sure that would be the case.

The eyes of the world seemed still to be focused on Thatcham, and Tom felt that he was right at the centre of it all. He didn't like it. He'd come here to get out of the limelight, to find somewhere he could go unnoticed. Maybe the madness would die down as quickly as it had begun? Despite the intense media interest, he was surprised at how relatively normal things still felt. He'd half expected the scaremongers and prophets of doom to have been out in force by now, dispensing their fabricated stories about the visitors to anyone who'd listen. But they hadn't. It seemed the importance of this situation had been recognised by everyone. Every media outlet appeared to have access to every detail about the aliens. He guessed that there was plenty more being withheld at the highest levels but, even so, he hadn't yet heard much in the way of speculation. Enough information had been released to avoid the need for second-guessing.

*Maybe that's for the best,* Tom thought. *Sensationalism and scoops have been put to one side temporarily. Just for now it's all about disseminating the news as efficiently as possible. It'll all be about ratings, circulation figures and profit again in no time.*

He wondered whether things would ever get back to normal, before telling himself that this *was* normal now. A few days back, everything that had happened would have seemed completely unbelievable, laughable even. But the fantasy of science-fiction had become reality within just a few seconds yesterday afternoon. The aliens were here, and nothing was ever going to be the same again.

# 7

Sunday was another lazy day – Tom had had a lot of those recently – and most of it was spent at home with Siobhan. With the new term looming, Rob had caught a train into Drayton, then another on to Willsham and the university where he studied and worked. After an afternoon spent dozing in front of the TV after lunch, Siobhan too went home rather than stay the night with Tom. She had an early start at the office on Monday, with several clients to see and the realistic possibility of a flood of new work after the events of Friday afternoon. She'd been on the telephone to Mona already. Working in recruitment, they knew the suddenly swollen population of Drayton and the surrounding area would be ripe for exploiting.

After being surrounded by family and friends almost all of the time for the last few weeks, Tom's small bungalow felt huge once they'd all gone and he was alone. He sat in front of the television with a sandwich and a few bottles of beer. He put a film on just after ten, but was asleep before the opening titles had finished. He woke up several hours later, the only light in the house coming from the TV. His neck was stiff, his back ached, and he'd knocked over his drink.

His planned lie-in the following morning didn't happen either. He usually enjoyed Monday mornings and the smug satisfaction of staying in bed when pretty much everyone else was having to force themselves to get up and begin yet another week. This Monday, however, at some ridiculously early hour, the phone rang. It was James, scrounging a lift because his car had let him down (again). Much as he wanted to, Tom couldn't bring himself to say no. He had no excuse and absolutely nothing else to do.

James worked in Drayton. The volume of traffic was just slightly heavier than usual rush hour levels and it wasn't a particularly long journey, but before they'd covered more than a couple of miles, James had left Tom in absolutely no doubt as to why leaving his job in Birmingham had been the best move he'd made in a long time. Sure, his life might have been lacking a little purpose and direction since he'd moved out to the sticks, but it still seemed immeasurably preferable to the alternative.

'So let me see if I've got this right,' Tom said, feigning interest 'your boss has said he wants you out.'

'Not in so many words, but that's the gist of it.'

'There must be a reason, though. He can't just sack you because he doesn't like your face.'

'We had a run-in last week.'

'And?'

James paused before reluctantly answering. 'And I might have said a few things I shouldn't have. A few home truths. Nothing that wasn't justified, mind.'

'But that's not the point. Bloody hell, bad mouthing your boss is never going to be a good idea, no matter how much of a shit he is.'

'Well you don't know Sachs.'

'True, but I do know a fair bit about employment law and disciplinary procedures.'

'Anyway, it's all right for you.'

'What's that supposed to mean?'

'No offence, mate, but you don't know what it's like. You don't understand the pressure. I've got a wife and three kids to support. I can't afford to lose my job.'

Tom shot him a sideways glance. 'Then don't piss your boss off. Anyway, you forget, I *do* know what it's like. I did have a job, remember? A frigging high pressured one at that.'

It was clear that James wasn't listening. 'Okay, here's an example,' he continued, unabated. 'This is the kind of thing I'm talking about. Last Wednesday we had this meeting about sales, and we all got given our targets. He gives me this ridiculous figure that we both know I'm never going to hit.'

'And what about everybody else?'

'What about them?'

'Did they get similar figures?'

'All us full-timers got the same.'

'Then you don't have a leg to stand on. Or he doesn't. He can't sack all of you if none of you hit the target.'

'Whatever. Anyway, I told him it was impossible, especially at this time of the year. Holidaymakers come into our store for phone chargers and the like, not flat screen TVs. They buy those things when they're back home. Then I told him I couldn't do any extra hours this month because of the baby, and he starts going on about my lack of commitment. Bloody hell, *my* lack of commitment! I've been there longer than the rest of them combined, and he has the cheek to question *my* commitment.'

'I know what you're going through, actually. I had a similar situation myself. I always found the best thing to do was to overachieve. It really used to piss my boss off, and she couldn't touch me. She'd set me a target, and I'd do everything I could to blitz it without making a noise about it. In the end she was the one who got kicked out, and I ended up being promoted into her role.'

'Yeah, but it was probably easier where you worked, sur- rounded by all those fat cats and crooks.'

'Is that right? Well you could try working somewhere else.'

'Like where? There's nothing else around here.'

'You could move away.'

'You trying to get rid of me now?'

'Not at all...'

'Anyway, how can I move? We can barely afford the house we're in.'

*Well, you could try hitting your targets*, Tom thought but didn't bother to say. 'I know, mate. It's a tough one.'

'There was a supervisor job came up last week. Sachs went and gave it to Marie, and she's only been working there a couple of months.'

'Is she any good?'

'Suppose. She's got no commitments, though, that's what it boils down to. She can put the time in, I can't. And she's not up all night with a baby before coming to work. Bloody hell, four o'clock I was up with Fliss this morning. Four o-bloody-clock!'

Tom pulled up at a set of traffic lights, willing them to change to green so he could deliver James to work and be shot of him. He knew it was probably just the Monday morning blues, or maybe even nerves, but he had little sympathy. He resisted the temptation to tell his friend a few home truths and avoided getting into a tit-for-tat game of 'my job was harder than yours', even though it clearly was. Christ, he'd had responsibility for a team of twenty-plus staff and a department with a budget running into millions. But he was glad that was all in the past. He didn't miss it. He didn't miss any of it.

'Just here'll be fine thanks,' James said, and Tom pulled over into a bus lay-by. 'Ah well, here we go again. The beginning of another shitty week at the coal face.'

'Here's looking on the bright side, eh?'

James shook his head. 'You don't know how lucky you are, Tom.'

Tom didn't bite. He didn't feel particularly lucky.

'You sure you're okay for getting home tonight?'

'Fine, thanks. Steph should have the car back around lunchtime. She'll come and get me later.'

'Okay. Give me a shout if you have any problems,' Tom said, hoping that he wouldn't.

'Will do. Cheers, mate.'

And with that the door slammed and he was gone.

Tom immediately felt the pressure lift. He watched James

sloping dejectedly away towards the white goods store where he worked. He had a piss-easy job, and Tom was finding it increasingly difficult to stomach his perpetual whining. Again he remembered the pressures he'd had to deal with in his career, and the contrast was stark. As far as he could see, the only real responsibility James had was ensuring his brightly coloured uniform polo shirt was clean, and that he had his "My name's James, how can I help you today?" badge on straight. Bloody waster.

He drove back home, looking forward to another day of doing fuck-all.

# 8

In Tom's isolated little bubble, the week passed slowly but without further incident. The unusually inflated population of the village meant that, surprisingly, he saw fewer people than usual. The recruitment agency was as busy as she'd expected – both as a result of an influx of people looking for casual work and existing employers looking to take on additional temporary staff – and he saw hardly anything of Siobhan. Tom didn't care much for the crowded streets – his quiet local pub was no longer quiet, instead filled with so many out-of-towners that it didn't feel particularly local – and so he spent much of the week either lounging around the house or out walking. He walked for miles one day, following the coastal path he usually ran along. He walked for several hours in one direction, before turning around and coming back again, just because he could.

Tom grew to hate the twenty-four hour news channels. He thought it strange how, in the space of less than a week, footage of the alien ship had begun to appear remarkably mundane. It was beginning to bore him as much as the politics, war reports and other news stories it had temporarily usurped on the screen. It was all mind-numbingly dull when played on a loop.

Rob returned to Thatcham from university early on Friday morning, complaining that he'd had to wait hours to get on the train. It seemed that more people than ever had descended on the village today, but it came as no surprise to anyone. The reason was obvious: today was the day the aliens' crippled ship was to be launched towards the sun. No one knew exactly when it was scheduled to happen, nor if they'd be able to see anything from the shore, but that didn't deter any of the thousands of people who came. According to the world's media (almost all of whom continued to report live from the village and surrounding area), sometime this evening the massive machine's engines would be fired for the final time.

Space in and around Thatcham was already at a premium, and the situation had deteriorated markedly today. Tom had heard from John Tipper that people had been renting out their spare rooms, such was the demand for digs near to this historic event. By late afternoon Tom himself had accepted fifty quid from a man to pitch his tent and let his family of four spend the night camping on his small front lawn, much to Ray Mercer's disgust. Rob said Tom could have held out for double that price.

Certain aspects of the bungalow afforded them a reasonable view over the ocean, but the largest windows overlooked the village rather than the water, and like everyone else it seemed, Tom, Rob and Siobhan chose to head for the cliff-tops to try and get a better view. Tom had taken a little persuading, finding himself unable to match the enthusiasm of the others. They'd been on the verge of heading out without him when he'd spotted John Tipper coming up the road and had gone out to speak to him.

'What are you doing out here?' Tom asked, mindful of the fact that this was the first Friday night in an age that he himself hadn't been hunkered down in the lounge of the Badger's Sett. 'Who have you got looking after the pub?'

'No one,' John replied, sounding uncharacteristically downbeat. 'I've shut up shop. There's no one there, Tom. I was waiting for you, truth be told. I left it as long as I could in case it started to pick up, but the place was empty. Don't know what all the fuss is about myself. Betty's already somewhere up on the hills with the rest of her bloody WI clan. She phoned me and said I should come up myself. I said I couldn't leave the pub, but she reeled off the names of more than half the regulars she'd seen on her way up there.'

'I'll probably see you there then.'

'You going too?'

'Looks that way.'

'No idea if I'll be able to find Bet, mind,' John said. 'Have you seen the crowds? Reckon I'll hover around until it's all over, then get back down quick and see if I can't get a few people in before last orders.'

'Good luck,' Tom said, and then watched John disappear into the masses before setting out himself with Rob and Siobhan.

Regardless of whether or not they saw the alien ship tonight, what Tom witnessed out on the cliffs was an impressive sight in itself. An unimaginable number of people were gathered there for as far as he could see into the distance, an unending mass. The media had been building the launch up all week as an incredible, once in a lifetime event. Tom wondered how much of a spectacle it was really going to be.

Tom looked back as they climbed, and saw that more people were still heading in this direction from the village. Further back, even more cars were trying to get into Thatcham, so tightly packed together now that the headlamps of each car did little more than illuminate the back bumper of the one in front.

Was this safe? Was there any form of crowd control up here? He'd seen Sergeant Phipps and a couple of other officers, but that was all. Makeshift cordons had been erected all the way along the cliff-side of the footpath to keep folks back but they were little more than traffic cones with warning tape strung between them and the fact remained that thousands of excited people were gathering close to the edge of a hundred foot drop in the dark. Christ, he felt like such a killjoy, but he was already imagining the newspaper reports tomorrow morning. There was inevitably going to be some idiot – pissed-up, stoned or just plain stupid – who wandered too far forward. But no one else seemed to be bothered. It was like a bloody festival further up past the war memorial where the ground levelled out. People had set up barbeques and were selling food. Another enterprising guy was selling cans of drink he'd pushed up the hill in a wheelbarrow. Several others worked their way through the masses, hawking torches, glow-sticks and other assorted bits of worthless tat.

Despite the fact he found it difficult – impossible, almost – to match the level of enthusiasm of the hundreds of people all around him, Tom had to admit to feeling some genuine excitement now. The media's hyperbole had been accurate to an extent – whatever happened here tonight, history was going to be made, one way or another. He didn't want to miss it. The events of the next few hours would inevitably be written into the history books and be immortalised in photographs and film footage which would be pored over by every subsequent generation. It was remarkable, really. He felt privileged to be here, but at the same time, as just one of many thousands, he also felt uncomfortably insignificant. If he hadn't been here, barely anyone would have noticed.

Siobhan found a patch of grass deep amongst the masses, just large enough for the three of them.

'This do?' she asked, already sitting down.

'Suppose,' Tom replied, still looking around for a better spot. 'Will we be able to see it from here?'

'Well, going on the basis that it's a fucking huge spaceship we're looking for, I guess so,' Rob said sarcastically. 'As long as you can see the sky, you should be okay.'

It all looked completely different tonight, of course, but Tom realised they were sitting not far from where he'd been when he'd witnessed the arrival of the alien ship. 'I was just over there,' he tried to tell Siobhan, but either she wasn't interested or she couldn't hear him. It was a still night with only a light warm breeze, but the collective noise of the crowd was astonishing. He glanced across at his brother, and saw that Rob had a pair of binoculars.

'Where did they come from?' Tom asked. 'Were they Dad's?'

'You said you didn't want them, remember?' he replied as he scanned the horizon. He focussed on what he thought was the alien ship in the far distance, although he wasn't entirely sure what he was seeing. The immense bulkhead of the vast machine remained almost entirely black. It seemed to blend into the darkness, its shape revealed only by occasional bursts of movement and light around it.

'See anything?' Siobhan asked.

'I think I've got it.'

'Let me see.'

Rob was about to pass her the glasses when an audible gasp from the crowds way over to their left distracted him. He looked out towards the horizon again, just in time to see an intense flash of white light near to the surface of the water, followed by several more in quick succession.

'Bloody hell, that's cool,' he said. 'Won't be long now. I bet that's the engine firing tests they were talking about.'

'Either that or the shuttles,' Siobhan said, taking the glasses from him.

'What shuttles?' Tom asked.

'They've been stripping anything worth salvaging from the ship and transporting it all to the naval base down near Abertreach. It's been all over the TV.'

'Haven't you been watching the news?' Rob asked him.

'Must have missed that bit.'

'They're using the shuttles to shift the stuff that's too big or too heavy to be transported by water.'

'What sort of stuff?'

'Fuel cells and engine components,' a man's voice said from somewhere just behind Tom. He turned around but couldn't see who'd spoken.

'And how do you know?' he asked, still not able to locate the eavesdropper.

'Like your friends said,' the voice replied, 'it's been all over the news.'

'Shame about those shuttles,' Rob said, speaking to the unseen man behind. 'I'd love to have seen one of them close up.'

'Oh, absolutely,' the man said, shuffling further forward and making himself known.

'What's a shame?' Tom asked, but no one answered.

'Something to do with the propulsion systems, isn't it?' Siobhan said.

'That's what I heard,' the man said.

'Do you even know what a propulsion system is?' Tom asked Siobhan, bemused.

'Of course I do,' she replied, offended.

'I heard it was something to do with the shuttles' relationship with the mother-ship,' the unknown man continued. 'They're powered by the main ship, as I understand it. They'll probably last for a while longer, maybe as long as a couple of months, but after that they'll most likely be useless.'

Tom looked at Rob and Siobhan. 'Did you know that?'

'Yes,' Rob replied. 'It's no great secret, mate.'

'Bloody hell, I need to start paying more attention.'

He sat up straighter and took the opportunity to turn around and get a better look at the man who'd muscled-in on their conversation. He appeared to be in his late-fifties, maybe early-sixties, and he was wearing a baseball cap and a long-sleeved formal shirt, buttoned-up to the top, the sleeves neatly rolled to just above the elbow. He wore a pair of thick, heavy-rimmed glasses, and had a dark little moustache. In the low light, Tom thought he looked bizarre: part-school teacher, part-Nazi.

'You really *should* pay attention,' he said to Tom. 'This is important. None of us can afford to be left behind.'

'He's right,' Siobhan agreed. 'What's happened has changed everything, Tom. I don't want you to miss out.'

'I haven't missed out so far. Bloody hell, I was standing right

73

here when the damn thing first flew over.'

'You were that close?' their uninvited friend babbled excitedly. 'It must have been incredible.'

'It was, I suppose,' Tom said, belying any enthusiasm he felt, not wanting to prolong the man's involvement in their evening.

'Could you see much?' he asked.

'I saw everything. Like I said, it flew right over me.'

'What was it like?' he demanded impatiently. 'I've watched the footage over and over on the TV, but to have actually been here when it happened...'

'It was just like you saw,' he said with a nonchalant shrug. 'Big and black and—'

Tom's attempts to wind the man up were halted temporarily by a sudden rush of wind and noise and a sweeping white light. The crowd reacted immediately, convinced that this was it, all of them up on their feet and shielding their eyes from the brightness overhead. But it wasn't the aliens. The sound became more familiar – a steady *chop, chop, chop* – and a huge military helicopter flew out from over the village, skirting along the cliffs then heading out towards the intermittent lights flickering on the horizon. A subdued, disappointed silence took the place of all the sudden noise and bluster.

'So you're local?' the man asked.

'He lives just back there,' Rob replied, gesturing in the general direction of Tom's small house.

'You're not from around here?' Siobhan asked as she passed the binoculars to Tom.

The man (who had his own set of well-worn binoculars and was busy looking into the distance) eventually replied, 'No, I'm not. It's taken me hours to get here today. I was on the train before seven this morning. Wouldn't have missed it for the world, though.'

Tom couldn't understand why he'd gone to such lengths to sit in a field on a cliff-top along with thousands of other people just to watch a few seconds of alien activity. Perhaps he was just spoilt, living so close to the epicentre of all the interest. Maybe he'd feel differently if he was elsewhere and he hadn't been subjected to the alien overload of the last seven days. *Aliens*, he thought, *it's old hat now. Passé, almost.* It felt like it had been longer than a week, like they'd been here forever.

Tom peered through the binoculars and was just about able to make out the shape of the mother-ship, its endless bulk still hanging effortlessly over the sea. The longer he stared, the more he could make out. There were lights flitting to and fro from near the stern of the ship, the shuttles the others had been talking about, he presumed. He watched one of them make a quick, darting descent, perhaps to unload its cargo onto one of the many boats waiting below. Some of the ships were as large as tankers. He could see a line of them stretching back to the shore.

Rob nudged Tom to hand the binoculars back. He did as he was asked, then lay back on the grass and looked up into the sky. Siobhan playfully slipped her hand underneath his T-shirt and began to stroke his stomach.

'You okay?' she asked.

'I'm fine. You?'

'I'm good.'

'Just good?'

'Very good,' she laughed. 'Very, very good!'

'What are you doing tomorrow?'

'Work first thing, but I'll be done before noon. There was some talk of James having a barbeque, wasn't there?'

'Oh, that'll be great. Screaming kids and food that's either half-cooked or burned to a crisp.'

'It'll be okay. It'll be nice to see them. I'm sure it's at James'. Might be Clare's... tell you the truth, with all this going on I've hardly thought about it.'

'I think this might be it,' Rob said suddenly, rising to his knees and straightening up as if a few extra inches height was going to make a difference.

'What's happening?' the flat-cap wearing man asked anxiously, desperate not to miss anything. He glanced at Rob to see where he was looking, then angled his own binoculars accordingly and spoke again. 'I think you're right,' he said. 'The rest of the ships look like they're starting to move out. There's definite movement down there...'

'Just the aliens themselves to get off now then?' Tom said, propping himself up onto his elbows.

'Most of them will already be long gone, I guess,' Rob said.

'They going to quarantine them or something like that?' Tom asked.

'Something like that,' he replied. 'They'll have already been checked for diseases and bugs. There's probably more chance of them catching stuff from us than us getting sick from them.'

It was another ninety minutes before anything significant actually happened. The ever-expanding crowd on the hill had continued to grow and had reached such a size now that it was standing room only. Tom was uncomfortable. He needed a piss, but he didn't dare move. It – whatever *it* was – could begin without warning at any moment. Siobhan and Rob weren't going anywhere. He was sure he could find a bush to pee behind or even run to the house and be back out on the cliffs fairly quickly, but he didn't fancy his chances of finding Rob and Siobhan again when he returned. He wished he'd brought a radio with him. He had his phone, but the signal was poor up here and when he did manage to get online, updates were sparse.

'Here we go,' Rob said suddenly, the binoculars still pressed to his face.

'What can you see?' Siobhan asked. 'Come on, Rob, let me look.'

He passed the binoculars over, knowing that they wouldn't be needed much longer.

'The shuttles have almost stopped,' he explained. 'They've been slowing down for a while, but it looks like they're finally done now.'

Siobhan watched as the white lights from the rear of the last two shuttles sped across the water, quickly catching up then overtaking the slowest few human boats in the ragtag fleet now heading back to land. Around them, those people who had radios and better Internet connections started to react to events.

'Dad would have loved this,' Tom said to his brother, his voice tinged with sadness.

'I was just thinking the same thing,' Rob replied.

'Remember how he used to go on about little green men and stuff like that? Got it all wrong, didn't he? They're not little and they're not green.'

'I don't think he was being literal, you idiot. But you're right, he'd have been lapping this up. He'd have been in his element, right in the middle of it all. Knowing Dad he'd probably have been out there on one of those boats.'

'Never one for sitting at home watching TV, was he?'

'If he hadn't been able to get here, he'd have been online researching every aspect. He'd have known more than anyone.'

'You think?' Tom said. 'You lot seem to know a fair bit yourselves.'

'They've made it easy though, haven't they? Imagine what it would have been like if we hadn't had access to all that information? There'd have been panic on the streets. If there hadn't been so much on TV recently, people would have assumed the worst, wouldn't they? They'd have assumed we'd been invaded.'

Tom considered his brother's words. He was absolutely right, of course. To have withheld information about this most visible of close encounters would have been a huge mistake, doing infinitely more harm than good. He was actually looking forward to it easing up now, to seeing more typical news stories again. He longed to have a conversation with someone which didn't feature aliens in one way or another...

The noise of the crowd was increasing as news spread like wildfire from those following events on radios and computers and phones. The launch of the ship was imminent. People scrambled further up the hillside to get a better view. Excited kids were hoisted up onto their parent's shoulders. Others climbed trees or stood on walls.

The wave of excitement was just beginning to die down to a hesitant hum of expectation when, at precisely eleven-seventeen, it began.

Without warning, in a fraction of a second, the ocean for miles around the rear of the immense alien ship was illuminated by a flood of searing, incandescent brilliance as the engines were fired. Rob watched in wonder as it began to move, turning a slow and graceful three-quarter-circle towards the shore. Billions of people observed from every last corner of the globe as the beautiful black machine lifted its nose to the stars and began to climb at a ferocious speed and an impossibly steep angle. All telescopes and binoculars were discarded as it approached. For a few seconds it was so large that it filled the entire sky, appearing almost near enough to touch. And then it accelerated with incredible force, and the whole world seemed to shake. People steadied themselves as the air pressure changed and as a hot, downward wind buffeted them. Necks craned as it climbed higher and higher, unnaturally quiet and incomprehensibly fast. And then it was gone. In less than two minutes the incredible ship had disappeared completely from view.

Tom continued to stare into space, genuinely overcome by the scale of what he'd just witnessed. It had somehow surpassed the spectacle of the ship's arrival. He wondered if that was because this time he'd been surrounded by other people and not out here on his own, exposed.

As a huge wave of spontaneous cheering and applause filled the air, Siobhan grabbed his hand.

'What did you think?' she asked. He struggled to find the right words.

'Incredible...' was all he could manage.

'Fucking amazing, wasn't it?' Rob said. 'Did you see the size of that thing? And the noise – the lack of noise, I mean – Christ, how could anything that big be so quiet?'

'And the light,' Siobhan enthused, 'did you feel it? It was warm. It was beautiful. You could feel it on your skin. I've never known anything like it.'

They both looked at Tom expectantly.

'It was like that last week when I was out running,' he said finally. 'I thought I was done for when I saw it.'

'Come on, would they really have let all these people be out here like this if they thought it was dangerous?'

'No one knew anything about it last week, though. I could have been buggered, burned to a crisp.'

'Oh, but it was huge,' Siobhan continued, barely listening to him. 'I mean, I'd started to think there'd been so much build up it was going to be a let-down, but it wasn't. If anything, it was even more amazing than I imagined. Didn't you think, Tom?'

'I kind of knew what to expect.'

'And?'

'And that was what I got.'

'Bloody hell, you could try and show a little enthusiasm at least,' Rob sighed. 'What did you want, more lights and lasers? A few explosions? *Star Wars* music?'

Tom didn't bother to answer. All around them the crowds began to shift. Still gripping Siobhan's hand tightly, he began to lead her back towards home. She pulled back.

'What's the rush?'

'Need a piss,' he answered honestly. 'If we go now we'll beat the bulk of the crowds.'

'I want to stay for a while,' she said. 'It's great out here. You go on ahead. Come back out when you're done.'

Much as Tom didn't want to leave her, he couldn't wait any longer. Rob sensed his predicament. 'We'll stick together,' he said. 'Don't worry, she'll look after me!'

'Okay.'

Before he could leave, Siobhan hurled herself at him and wrapped her arms around him, squeezing tight.

'Tom Winter,' she whispered, 'you're a miserable bugger but I love you. Now go and have your piss then get yourself back here!'

'I'm not miserable,' he protested, 'I'm just—' She interrupted him with a kiss and a playful shove away.

Tom began walking back home, weaving through the sea of meandering figures. Many people were still rooted to the spot, standing motionless and looking up into the clear, star-filled sky, perhaps hoping to catch one final glimpse of the alien ship before it was gone forever. Some people were in tears, others grinning like idiots. He wished he could match their emotion, but the discomfort in his bladder was getting worse. In fact, he decided as he pushed his way through a bottleneck by the war memorial, he now felt positively anti-climactic.

'Well that's it,' he heard someone say, catching a snatch of excited conversation as he tried to push past a group of revellers, 'they're here to stay now.'

## 9

The barbeque the following evening was at Clare's house, but the location wasn't important – being in each other's company was all that mattered. Every member of this close-knit group of friends benefited from these regular informal get-togethers. They were a chance to relax in private with some of the people most important to them; a chance to forget about everything else for a while and unwind. Clare was more than happy to play host. It didn't involve any huge amount of effort or outlay on her part, and staying at home also had two very clear benefits: not only did it mean she didn't have to leave the party early to get Penny to bed, but it also meant she could drink. And Christ, after this week full of work pressures, stupid ex-partners and bloody alien invasions, she really needed to drink.

The day had been pleasantly warm and bright, down a few degrees on yesterday, feeling almost like summer's last fling. The atmosphere was peaceful, a stark contrast to last night's crowds. Although she lived mid-terrace, Clare's neighbours on either side were no trouble and the street was always relatively quiet. There were fields beyond the low fence at the end of her garden, which made the small square patio feel as if it was part of a much larger open space. There was a train line a couple of hundred metres out into the fields, running parallel with the row of houses, but the trains were infrequent and the noise low enough so as not to intrude.

The six adults – Tom, Siobhan, Rob, Clare, James and Stephanie – sat out on the patio by the light of a few scattered candles and the glowing embers of the long-abandoned barbeque. The children were indoors, ensconced in front of the TV.

'It's so good to be able to talk to someone over the age of eight for a change,' Stephanie said. She cradled her sleeping baby Felicity on her lap.

'I'm older than eight,' James protested, still picking at the remains of the food despite everyone else having finished almost an hour ago.

'Mental age or physical age?' Rob asked, deliberately winding him up.

'You don't count, Jim,' Steph said, 'and you know what I mean. I'm talking about *different* faces. I spend all day, everyday surrounded by the kids. Much as I love them, it's damn hard work. It's nice to have a break.'

'Tell me about it,' Clare said, finishing off her third large glass of wine. She watched Penny through the living room window. She was sitting wedged between Bethany and Mark, James and Stephanie's older kids. 'I know I've only got one child and I work, but I know exactly what you're saying. I love Pen more than anything, but there are times I could scream.'

'We haven't been out anywhere together for months now, have we, Jim?' Steph continued. 'I mean, he's been out and I've been out, but *we* haven't been anywhere without the kids in tow for ages.'

'We'll sit for you one night, won't we?' Siobhan said, surprising Tom. She was lying next to him on a plastic sun-lounger. He almost choked on his beer.

'Suppose...'

'We should sort something out,' she continued, ignoring her boyfriend's reticence.

'I'll drop Penny off as well, shall I?' Clare joked.

'Don't push it!'

'Think I'll give it a few more years before I think about settling down,' Rob said, stretching out on his deck chair. 'Listening to you lot is enough to put anyone off.'

'We're not that bad, are we?' Clare asked, concerned.

He shook his head. 'Not really. I like my freedom too much, that's all. It's like last night. I stayed out for hours. Didn't have to get back because anyone was waiting for me.'

'Where were you last night then?' James asked, scowling.

'Out on the cliffs. The alien ship. Remember?'

'Jim's sulking because he didn't get to go to the pub with you lot,' Stephanie laughed.

'No one went to the pub,' Tom said.

'So did you get to see it?' Siobhan asked.

'Oh, we saw it okay,' Steph explained. 'We watched the build-up on TV with the kids then took them out into the street and watched it fly over. Amazing, wasn't it?'

'I've never seen anything like it,' James agreed.

'Me neither,' said Rob. 'Kind of humbling, wasn't it?'

'I was just lost for words,' Siobhan said. 'Can't explain how it made me feel. It was the sheer size of it, you know? I just can't get my head around how something so huge could travel so far and so fast.'

'What about you, Clare?' Rob asked. 'Where were you last night?'

'In bed.'

'In bed! You're kidding me... You didn't see it?'

'I told you, I've had a bitch of a week. Standing outside for hours just to watch something I could see on TV didn't seem to make a lot of sense.'

'What about Penny?'

'Oh, she didn't miss out. She was full of it. Jim and Eileen next door had their grandkids over and they went out into the fields to watch it and took Penny with them. Sorry if you think I'm a miserable bitch, I don't mean to be. Fact is I lay down for a few minutes and fell asleep.'

'So you didn't see any of it?'

'All the noise they were making out back woke me up. I thought they were in trouble so I went running out. I got there just as it flew over.'

'Amazing, wasn't it?' said Steph.

'It was big, I'll give you that.'

'We went right up onto the hills,' Rob said, excitedly remembering the events of last night. 'Got stuck next to a right boring bastard, didn't we?'

'He wasn't that bad,' Siobhan said. 'Just don't think he got out much.'

'Anyway, don't worry, Clare,' Rob continued, 'you're not alone. Tom didn't think the ship was all that impressive either.'

'I never said that.'

'He wanted more lasers and lights and special effects. You know, the full *Close Encounters* thing.'

'That's not true. You're putting words into my mouth.'

'You couldn't wait to get away.'

'I couldn't wait to have a piss. We'd already been out there for hours. Anyway, I couldn't see any point in staying once the ship had gone. There was a lot of hanging around for something that was over in just a few seconds.'

'Well we stayed out a while longer,' Siobhan explained. 'There was a fantastic atmosphere out there. There were camera crews and everything. People started playing music and mucking about.'

'See, Jim?' Stephanie sighed. 'Now that's what I miss. A little freedom.' Her back stiff, she sat upright and gestured for James to have the baby. Clare intercepted. She took the child and cradled her gently. Tom watched her. She was leaning forward, instinctively protecting the little girl, shielding her. She didn't even know she was doing it.

'Ever thought about having another?' Stephanie asked.

Clare shook her head but didn't look up from the baby's face. 'The time's gone. I always said I wanted another, but Aiden didn't. And as you know, shit happens.'

'I think it's the most amazing thing,' James said, starting to sound like he'd had more than enough to drink.

'She certainly is,' Clare said quietly, still staring at Felicity.

Perfect skin, all creases and folds as she frowned in her sleep, mouth moving constantly as she dreamed and chewed on nothing.

'Sorry, Clare, I was talking about the aliens,' he said. 'But it is like when you have a kid. Them being here has changed everything.'

'We were talking about this last night,' Steph explained, hoping to make more sense than her half-drunk husband. 'You'll know this, Clare, it's like when you have a baby. It's the strangest thing. As soon as your child's born and you get them home, you can't remember what it was like without them. It catches me out every time, even when I'm expecting it.' She looked into Fliss' sleeping face. 'It just feels so right when you've got them with you. So natural.'

Rob agreed. 'I was saying something similar to you, wasn't I, Siobhan? We've spent too long looking inwards, and now it feels like we're ready to start broadening our horizons. We get so wrapped up in our own routines and problems that we miss the fact we're part of a much bigger picture.'

Clare glanced up and saw that he was looking at her. Was he trying to make a point? 'Life goes on though, doesn't it, Rob. I can't just drop everything because there are aliens on my doorstep.'

'And I'm not suggesting you should. It's going to be a gradual change, but I think things are going to be different from here on in. We've never been in a situation like this before. It's like they've come from nowhere and handed us a hundred years of progress on a plate.'

'Is that necessarily a good thing?' Tom asked. 'I'm not saying it isn't, but isn't the process of finding stuff out for yourself as important as getting the right answer?'

'Fuck me,' James slurred. 'Who invited Einstein?'

'Einstein?' Rob protested. 'What are you on about?'

'He was a philosopher, wasn't he?'

'No, he was a scientist. Bloody hell, Jim.'

'Same difference.'

'Just look at little Fliss,' Tom continued, ignoring them both and gesturing at the baby still being cradled by Clare. 'Imagine these aliens produce a pill which gives you fifteen years of schooling in a single dose. Would you want her to have it?'

'Not sure...' Steph admitted.

James was too drunk to answer.

Tom continued, regardless, 'If it was my daughter, I wouldn't want her to.'

'Why not?' asked Stephanie.

'Because it just wouldn't be right, would it? Going to school isn't just about getting qualifications. Obviously a lot of it is, but what about the friendships? What about the other things you learn? Relationships... wearing a uniform... dealing with authority... taking knocks... all the practical stuff.'

'This is all a bit rich coming from someone who does fuck-all for a living,' James said, the booze making him sound more antagonistic than he actually meant. Tom didn't think he merited a response. Was he jealous? Angry?

'Anyway,' Clare said, finally handing Fliss back to her mother, 'it doesn't matter what we think. The decisions are all out of our hands as usual. The aliens are here whether we like it or not, and nothing we say or do will change that. And now their ship's gone, they're here to stay.'

'You make it sound like that's a bad thing,' Siobhan said.

'Do I? I don't mean to. To be honest, I genuinely don't know what to think. I'm just too cynical. I've been disappointed too many times recently and I'm not about to roll over and let anyone else take advantage of me.'

'You'll probably feel different when you've got used to them,' Rob said. 'I'll admit, when they first arrived I was scared shitless. I think we all were.'

'And that's half the problem,' she continued. 'I don't think I want to know them. I just don't care, that's all. I've got enough to think about already. There's no room for aliens in my life right now.'

'Clare's not saying "aliens go home",' Tom added. 'She's just—'

'I'm just saying they'll have to wait until *I'm* ready for *them*. Like you say, I'll probably warm to them once I get used to the idea.'

'Give it a few months and it'll be like they were always here,' Siobhan said.

'Anyway,' Rob said, 'we'll all have plenty of opportunity to get to know our new friends soon enough.'

'Why's that?' Clare asked.

'Haven't you heard? They're letting them out.'

# Part ii
# RELEASE

# 10

The aliens' release was agreed with a surprising lack of legal wrangling and political manoeuvring. In essence, apart from a few lone voices of concern, the decision was met with very little opposition. The visitors were, however, given a first-hand demonstration of the frustrations of civilized life on Earth, as many days were subsequently wasted with discussions about "human" rights, and whether or not the term could be extended to include the aliens. Whilst they were inarguably inhuman, they were also inarguably equal to humans, if not superior in many respects. Of course no lawyer or leader would deign to commit career suicide by suggesting anyone or anything could be superior to man...

The irony was that once the necessary medical and scientific tests had been carried out and it had been concluded both that the aliens presented no threat to man and that living on Earth presented no threat to the aliens themselves, the actual event took place with little fanfare. Most people saw it as a logical next-step.

Tom kept one eye on the headlines. The expected deluge of pro-alien, pro-working together propaganda continued, and yet it didn't feel like there was any hard sell. People's questions were answered, their concerns satisfied. A steady stream of footage was available on TV and online, all designed to smooth out the differences and stress the many similarities between the two species: the aliens at work, them meeting with diplomats, celebrities and scientists, them relaxing in their accommodation... Further footage was also released showing things from their perspective: images of their home-world, the insides of their now-jettisoned ship, and more. Perhaps in an attempt to illustrate how dependent on mankind the aliens now were, with their help a space telescope was recalibrated and realigned in order to show a live feed of their ship ploughing headfirst into the sun. Tom watched that particular broadcast with interest. The visible loss of their transport seemed somehow to redress the balance a little.

There may have only been around three hundred and fifty of them here, but the media oversaturation made it feel like there were many more. By the last Wednesday in September, just over a month since they'd first arrived, the aliens were officially handed their freedom.

On the day of the aliens' release, Tom and Siobhan lay in bed together, watching a documentary which celebrated the occasion and summarised the events of the preceding weeks. It was hard to believe so long had passed since their first unannounced arrival in the skies over Thatcham. The time seemed to have flashed past.

Tom thought it funny how, in these newly enlightened times, the human race still stuck to its guns and refused to deviate. No one seemed to have much of an issue with the aliens being here, but when it came to having to make subtle changes to accommodate them, that was a different matter entirely. No attempt was made to use the aliens' indigenous names or languages. It was English or nothing. That didn't present too much of a problem, because the physiology of the aliens was broadly similar to human; their airways, lungs, vocal chords and circulatory and auditory systems were surprisingly alike, and it followed that their speech patterns were too. Although occasionally more guttural, and yet with a surprisingly wide vocal range, their language was far more difficult for any 'non-alien' to fully enunciate than it was for them to speak 'human'. And also, as an alien had pointed out in an interview earlier in the film, *they* were the visitors. As such, they thought it right and proper that they restricted themselves to only communicating in ways their kind and gracious hosts would understand.

'We're at your mercy,' he'd heard the alien say. 'Without you, we'd be lost.'

The precise location of their home-world was revealed, but its coordinates meant little to Tom. Which galaxy it was in, how many planets were in the same solar system, how large the star it orbited was, how many trillions of miles away and how long it would take to get there... in Tom's opinion these were all unnecessary details, and most of the population seemed to agree. In typically blinkered English style, they were content to simply say the visitors were from 'somewhere else' or 'the other place'.

The documentary was dragging now, bogged down with trivialities such as the aliens' predisposition towards eating overly sweet foods – something to do with their metabolism, he understood. Like most TV, the programme was padded out unnecessarily with clips and sound-bites he'd seen countless times before. These final scenes were intercut with talking head interviews with some of the key aliens. They all looked the same to Tom. They sounded the same too. And yet, despite being so unintentionally dismissive, he had to admit that he found them fascinating. There were subtle expressions they pulled, unexpected noises they made, unnatural (to him) movements and ticks... watching them made him feel like he was witnessing a bizarre collision between something inescapably ordinary and something completely unknown. The differences were striking, the similarities even more so.

'Shame about that, isn't it?' Siobhan said.

'Shame about what?' Tom had only been half-listening.

'The acidity in our air's different,' she replied. 'They might have to take medication while they're here.'

'Oh, right,' he said.

'It's nothing too serious,' she continued. 'Just a precaution, I think. If they were staying any longer then they'd probably have to do something about it.'

'Aren't they staying long enough?'

She dug him in the ribs. Siobhan shuffled, her naked body pressed up against his, legs entwined. He struggled to concentrate on the programme and not lose himself in semi-erotic daydreams. He hoped the hand she had resting on his chest would soon slide further down his body, but he knew there was no chance of that happening before the documentary ended. She was transfixed.

'I like this one,' she said when a particular alien appeared on screen. 'He's my favourite.'

'Your favourite? Why?'

'There's just something about the way he talks... the things he says. If you listen to him, he talks nothing but sense. And the way he speaks is really sweet.'

'*Sweet?* Bloody hell, just listen to yourself. He's travelled millions of miles to get here, he's probably more intelligent than you and me put together, and you're calling him *sweet?*'

She ignored him and explained. 'He's got a family. I heard him talking about them earlier. The way he speaks about them is lovely. You can tell he really cares, you know. You can see that he's devastated he's so far away from them, but there's no malice in his voice, no anger.'

'I should think not. I expect they're more relieved than anything. Imagine if they hadn't found us. I bet they would have just ended up drifting forever.'

'That's exactly what would have happened, I heard another one talking about it earlier. She said we're the first intelligent life-forms they've come across. This is as big a deal for them as it is for us, I reckon. They're probably sat on their home-world right now, watching documentaries about us like we're watching them.'

'You really think so? Jesus.'

'Why not?'

Tom gestured at images of the alien home-world on the

screen. It looked like an idyllic place. 'We get to see this, they get footage of Thatcham in return. Grey sea, grey sky.'

'Beautiful though, isn't it?' Siobhan said as the camera swooped low over a pink-tinged ocean.

'It's not what I was expecting. When I heard they were on a mining mission, I just presumed they'd sucked the soul out of their planet and used up all their resources same as us. I thought they'd finished with their place and were moving on to trash somewhere new.'

'You've watched too many movies.'

'I know. Part of me still thinks they're just here for our water or because they're going to start harvesting humans as slaves.'

'That's just stupid,' she said. 'You've got to stop talking like that, Tom. It won't do anyone any good.'

The documentary was finally drawing to a close, bringing the aliens' story up to date. Tom had seen teaser clips of the footage now being shown, but this was the premier of the scene in its entirety. He watched with genuine interest as an alien speaker addressed the United Nations. Would they be afforded member status, he wondered? Nothing was beyond the realms of possibility anymore.

There was something undeniably monumental about seeing the alien, dignified and proud, wearing some kind of dress uniform, standing alongside the UN Secretary General, both of them all smiles and handshakes and positive body language. Negotiations between the aliens and world leaders had been on-going since their arrival. The Secretary General seemed to take genuine pleasure in detailing the agreements which had been reached.

'Isn't it great that this is all so open,' Siobhan said. 'Suppose they don't have any choice really. If you don't tell people the truth, they'll make things up. That's not going to do any of us any good.'

'Since when have these people told us the truth?'

Siobhan thumped his chest and told him to shut up so she could hear. The unique double-act on the screen had begun to detail the formal relationship which had been established between the two peoples. *Peoples*, Tom thought... yes, that sounds about right. He'd been struggling with labels. Species, breeds, races, sides... it was difficult to think of an appropriate term which didn't sound borderline offensive. Switching his attention back to the screen, he listened to how the key principles, strategies and objectives of an on-going relationship had been identified, agreed upon, and then formalised. There was even talk of humans eventually heading off-world. It sounded like an extreme version of the foreign-exchange trips he remembered from school. He'd spent a really dodgy couple of weeks living in La Rochelle with a nerdy French kid back in the day...

'See,' Siobhan said, 'that's what I'm talking about. This is a really positive thing, Tom. You need to stop with the anti-alien jokes and focus on the positives. Maybe having them here will help us sort ourselves out. Stop us blowing each other up, you know?'

Tom didn't say anything. Tired of waiting for her to make a move, he slid down under the bed-sheets, human-alien relationships the very last thing on his mind.

## 11

'We should go out,' Rob called from the living room. Tom groaned and looked up at the kitchen ceiling.

'I don't want to go anywhere.'

'Well you should.'

'Why? I'm happy staying home.'

'No you're not. You're not happy anywhere at the moment. You've been a miserable bastard recently and you're spending far too much time shut away in this house on your own. Christ, the universe is opening up out there, but your world's getting smaller.'

'Maybe that's the way I like it.'

'Well I'm going,' Rob said, and he turned up the TV volume. Tom wasn't even sure what it was he was watching. He walked through to the other room and saw that it was just the local news. He immediately recognised the place on screen as being Drayton, although it looked much busier than normal – more like a busy weekday than a Sunday afternoon. He also recognised the reporter. He didn't like her. Too false. She smiled too much for his liking. Sometimes it seemed that the worse the news, the broader her sneer. He imagined her rubbing her hands together with glee when particularly bad things happened, constantly looking for the scoop which might get her promoted from the locals to national reporting. Her usual reports covered all manner of subjects from potholes in the road to pensioners dying in poorly maintained care-homes, all delivered with the same deadpan seriousness and a wholly unconvincing intent.

'I don't like her,' he said.

'I know. You tell me that every time you see her.'

'What's she on about anyway? Looks busy.'

'It was kind of a given that something like this was going to happen sooner or later,' Rob said. 'Couldn't be avoided, really.'

'What couldn't?'

'It's the aliens. First public appearances and all that. Looks like there's a few of them out and about in Drayton, and everyone wants to be the first person to shake their hand.'

'I don't.'

'Okay,' he sighed, 'everyone but you.'

Tom's reaction was instinctive, said more for effect than for any other reason. He sat next to Rob and watched the TV, genuinely interested but trying not to let it show. The reporter he disliked was still talking to camera – some pretentious bollocks about the dawning of a new age which he paid little attention to – but what was happening behind her was far more interesting: Overmill Park, a large, popular and well-tended public space in the middle of Drayton, was filled with people. And there, right in the centre of it all, he could see several aliens. For a few seconds his mind was occupied with needless trivialities: what was the correct name for a group of aliens? A tribe? A herd? A gaggle, pride, pod or clutch? But then he regained his focus, and the importance of what he was seeing began to sink in. Beings from another world were mixing freely with the local population, and everything appeared to be relaxed and good-natured. The broadcast cut to footage taken earlier in the day – the same aliens surrounded by different people in a different part of town, mingling with the locals. Some even stood and posed for pictures. Then the image changed again and an alien's face filled the screen, the strangest regional news talking head Tom had ever seen.

'It's an honour and a privilege to be here in Drayton,' the alien said. 'The people have been so quick to accept us, so gracious.'

*Gracious*, thought Tom. In his experience the people of Drayton were lots of things, but gracious was most definitely not one of them.

'Amazing, eh?' Rob grinned.

'Everyone here has made us feel so welcome,' another alien continued, his otherworldly inflexion and strangely laboured breathing occasionally audible. 'Much as we'd all like to be home, we're looking forward to our time here. We couldn't have picked a better place to be stranded.'

'Was that sarcasm?' Tom asked.

They seemed confident, not at all fazed at having a camera shoved in their faces by a local TV news crew on a world millions of miles from home. The alien still talking sounded relaxed and spontaneous, making a genuine effort to engage. It was only when the reporter asked him what he was most looking forward to doing during his stay in Drayton that he paused. Tom was quick to seize on his hesitation: 'He can't answer 'cause there's fuck all to do there.'

Rob got up and left the room, reappearing moments later, pulling on a jacket.

'You coming?'

'Where? I told you I didn't want to go out.'

'And I said you need to get out more. Come on, mate, let's go find ourselves some aliens!'

There were three hundred and sixty-eight alien visitors in total. Many of them had been dispatched elsewhere – the diplomats, spokespeople, chief scientists and the like. Others elected to travel the globe, keen to see as much of the world as they could while they were stranded here. Some decided to stay put and, somewhat surprisingly, a relatively large contingent remained in the area around Thatcham. It seemed they'd developed a strange affinity for the place. Perhaps, bizarrely, it had begun to feel like a home away from home. They were under strict instructions to integrate, not separate. The last thing anyone wanted was an isolated alien community springing up. Barriers were to be broken down and overcome. Less *District 9*, more

*Alien Nation*, was how Rob had described the policy.

There were at least twenty of them in Drayton, Rob had heard. He was desperate to see just one. Watching them on TV was one thing, and witnessing the alien ship's unexpected arrival and premature departure had been something he knew would stay with him until his dying day, but since the visitors had first come to Earth he, like everyone else, had harboured a burning desire to see one of them with his own eyes. It felt like a kind of holy grail, a badge of honour, almost. He wanted to be the first so he could brag to his colleagues at the university next week.

The small town was packed, the traffic heaving. It was six o'clock on Sunday evening, but there seemed to be more motorists trying to get in and out of the place than there normally would have been first thing on a typical Monday morning. Tom couldn't stand being stuck in queues like this. He'd always had a short temper in traffic jams, but since divorcing himself from the rest of the world, he'd grown to hate delays with a vengeance. Strange how the less he had to be late for, the more it bothered him. 'Bloody stupid idea, this,' he grumbled. 'We'll never get parked.'

'Give it time. Just be patient.'

'I don't want to be patient, I want to go home. Don't know why I agreed to this.'

'Because you want to see an alien close-up, same as me.'

Tom had no argument. His brother was right. Tom was feeling increasingly out of kilter with everyone else and he hoped seeing one of them would help him make the same kind of connection with the visitors that everyone else seemed to have.

'Your problem,' Rob said, 'is you're too cynical.'

'And your problem,' Tom quickly replied, 'is that you never shut up. Anyway, what are you on about? I don't have a problem.'

'Yes you do. You need to lighten up. You need to stop stand-

100

ing still and go with the flow. You're going to get left behind if you don't. The world's changing, Tom, and you have to change with it. Embrace it!'

'I don't have to change. I don't *want* to change.'

'Well maybe you should. This isn't science-fiction, you know. These aliens, they're just people like you and me.'

'Well, sort of.'

'They've been dealt a bad hand, that's all.'

'We can both identify with that, can't we.'

Rob shook his head sadly. 'It's not a competition, mate. You don't get a medal because you've been hardest done by. I know we lost Mum and Dad, but look at all the stuff we still have. You've got Siobhan and you've got the kind of lifestyle half the population would kill for. Look at the aliens. They're millions of miles from home and it's going to take them years to get back, that's if they ever get back at all. Their losses might prove to be a thousand times worse than yours and mine.'

The sudden seriousness in Rob's voice took Tom by surprise. Tired of driving, he was relieved when he spotted a car reversing out of a gap in a small gravel car park a short distance ahead. Fortunately, no one else seemed to have noticed. Tom drove the wrong way up a one way street, then pulled into the space the moment it was vacant.

The two brothers walked aimlessly towards the centre of town. 'So where do we go?' Tom asked.

'I don't know. Just follow the crowds, I guess.'

'It's all crowds.'

'You're a real ray of sunshine, aren't you.'

'Sorry, I just think we might be wasting our time. It's getting dark. They might have gone back to wherever it is they're keeping them. Where is that, by the way?'

'I don't know. Jesus, Tom, have a little respect. These are intelligent beings we're talking about here. You make it sound like they're animals in the zoo.'

Tom ignored his brother and turned left into a long alleyway which ran between two buildings then emerged out onto the main pedestrianised shopping area, perhaps two-thirds of the way down the high street. Most of the shops had closed up for the night, but a huge number of people remained. That damn TV reporter was still here, Tom noticed. She was standing on a corner with her crew, scanning the scene vulture-like for her next potential story angle.

'I need something to eat,' Rob said. 'Did you bring any money with you?'

'I've got a few quid. Forget your wallet again, did you? Funny how that keeps happening.'

'Sorry. Honest, mate, I didn't mean to. I was so made up with the thought of coming out here and seeing the aliens, I didn't even think to pick it up.'

Tom tugged Rob's arm and pulled him across the road towards a burger bar. 'This is my limit,' he said.

It hadn't seemed particularly dark on their way into Drayton, but the bright lights of the fast-food joint made the rest of the world look unexpectedly dull in comparison. They joined the end of a snaking queue which led halfway back to the entrance door.

'Busy in here,' Rob said.

'Busy everywhere,' Tom grumbled.

It took far longer than it should have to reach the counter, and when they'd got there they wondered whether it had been worth the effort. The few remaining members of staff of duty were run ragged, and half the items on the menu were unavailable. They left with a little food – a couple of plain burgers, some fries, and Rob's third and Tom's second choice drinks – then found themselves a place to sit on a low wall outside, every seat inside the restaurant already taken.

'You enjoying yourself?' Tom asked, wiping his greasy hands on his trousers as they'd both forgotten to pick up napkins.

'Yep,' Rob quickly replied. 'You?'

'Marvellous.'

'Can't get over how busy it still is.'

'Well that's because every bloody idiot is here trying to do the same as us. I tell you, if the aliens stood on a podium in the middle of town and let us all walk past and pay our respects, we could get this over and done with in half the time.'

'Give it a rest. Seriously, quit moaning and try and enjoy it, you miserable shit. There's a really good atmosphere here.'

Tom reluctantly had to agree. Despite the crowds, he'd seen no indication of there being any trouble, no hostility. It was rapidly becoming an over-used cliché, but it felt like carnival day had come around again. He glanced back over his shoulder at the main road in the distance; four solid lines of traffic clogging up the main route into town. *Not much of a parade*, he thought.

'So, do you think we're going to see one?' Rob asked.

'We might.'

'We'd better. I'm not going home 'til I have.'

'Bloody hell, grow up. You sound like a little kid.'

'I'm excited, that's all,' Rob continued to enthuse. 'Hey, do you think they have anything even remotely like this place on their planet?'

'What, a shit-hole like Drayton? I doubt it. Their cities are all futuristic and clean, aren't they. I bet this place is their worst nightmare. Remember when we were little and Mum and Dad dragged us around that living museum place in Dudley?'

'I remember.'

'All those traditional shops and the trams and canals and all that. Bloody horrible day out, that was.'

'I liked it. You had a face like thunder all day. Dad kept taking pictures of you, remember? Really wound you up.'

'Anyway, I bet this is like that for them,' Tom said. 'Like stepping back into the history books.'

'You might be right. They're going to show more on TV soon, apparently.'

'Can't wait,' he mumbled sarcastically.

'Yeah, apparently they've got loads of new footage coming. You can't help wondering what it's going to be like.'

'I can.'

'No, seriously, I bet it'll all be white and sterile like in the movies. All *Star Trek*, you know. They'll have everything there at the flick of a switch. They probably don't even need to flick switches, just think about whatever it is they're after and it'll be there.'

'You reckon? Don't forget they turned up in that bloody big black ship. There was nothing sleek and sterile about that.'

'It was a *mining* ship, remember?'

'That's as maybe. And it broke down, don't forget. They might—'

'Seriously, though,' Rob interrupted, cutting across him, 'I've been wondering how close their technology is to our science-fiction. I mean, do you think we got anything right, or were all our books and movies completely off the mark? Serious question, Tom, do you think we...'

Rob's voice trailed away. He stood up and threw away the rest of his burger.

'You okay, mate?' Tom asked, concerned. Rob started walking away, then he broke into a run. Almost as an afterthought, he turned back and gestured for his brother to follow.

'Come on!'

'What is it?'

'What do you think it is?'

Tom stood up and saw that a great mass of people was coming down the street towards them. The TV reporter and her team suddenly burst into life. Still finishing his food, he ran after Rob.

'Slow down.'

'Fucking hell,' Rob gasped excitedly. 'This is it!'

He wound his way through the furthest advanced members of the crowd, but it was already obvious they were going to struggle to see anything.

'Climb up,' Tom suggested, and he signalled towards a couple of recycling bins left in a particularly dank-looking corner. He scrambled onto the top of one, using a grubby drainpipe to haul himself up, then reached back down for Rob, helping him onto the lid of the bin next-door. They stood holding onto each other for balance as the heaving mass of people swept along the footpath.

The sun had all but completely disappeared now, leaving only the limited illumination of shop windows and streetlamps. Tom searched through what he could see of the crowd, looking for something different amongst the mass of heads. And then he saw them. Right in the middle of the gathering were two aliens. They were protected (*yes*, Tom thought, *protected*) by a respectful bubble of space on all sides. The crowd was well-ordered, with little squabbling or jostling for position.

From up on the bins, Tom had a clear view. But he'd still have been able to see enough had he remained at ground level. The visitors had a clear height advantage. Tom had noticed it before, but their size was even more marked in person. They stood a full alien head height above everyone else, and were able to look down and around and across at each other without any obvious distraction. He wished his eyes were sharper so he could better make out the expressions on their faces, and he wondered what they were thinking. Was this as incredible an experience for them as it clearly was for the people surrounding them? Of course not, he decided, they'd already had weeks of this kind of adulation – if that was the right word.

Both of the aliens had a sheen of silver hair, one slightly darker than the other. Their bodies were willowy and gangly, their limbs slight and long, and yet they walked with definite poise and confidence, apparently unfazed. Tom didn't know how they were managing to put up with it and remain so calm. He'd have cracked long before now had their positions been reversed.

When the bulk of the crowd, and the aliens themselves, had just drawn level with the bins, a man appeared. Neither Tom nor Rob noticed him at first. He looked, to all intents and purposes, like just another gawping face, here to get his fix of one-to-one alien contact, but it was immediately clear that there was something different about him. As the rest of the horde continued to move, he stood his ground. Several people knocked into him, excusing themselves and side-stepping him, but he refused to shift. They channelled past on either side as if he was a rock wedged in the middle of a stream. And as the mass of people continued to surge forward, he eventually found himself standing inside the pocket of space which still surrounded the aliens. He was blocking their way forward, and they were forced to stop. Everyone else stopped too, and the crowd fell silent. The sudden lack of movement and noise was stark. For a moment the only sound came from the traffic in the near distance.

'I want to ask a question,' the man said. Tom saw the two aliens glance at each other anxiously.

'Ask,' one of them said in a medium-pitched, somewhat monotone voice.

'I want to know why you're really here.'

'You know why we're here.'

'I know what you're telling us, but I want to know the truth.'

'Come on, mate, give it a rest,' someone said from just behind the lone protester. They grabbed his arm and tried to pull him out of the way but he was having none of it. He shook them off and returned his full attention to the two aliens.

'What do you really want?'

The second alien moved forward slightly. Its movements

went unnoticed by most of the crowd, but Tom saw it push out its chest and lift its head, giving it additional few inches of height advantage. The first alien held out his arm in front of his companion, clearly trying to diffuse the palpable tension.

'You know what we want,' the first alien said, the lack of emotion in his voice making him sound remarkably calm, 'and you know why we're here. You should also know by now that none of us would be here if we had any choice at all. We're grateful for your hospitality, and we're overwhelmed by the reception you've given us, but we'd much rather have needed none of it. Personally, all I want is to go home. I'd give everything I own, the clothes on my back even, just to see my family again.'

'I don't believe you,' the man said.

'Leave them alone, you stupid fucker,' someone shouted at him. Someone else tried to shift him out of the way and he tripped. He almost fell, but the first alien caught him and helped him back to his feet.

'I promise you,' he said, his voice loud enough for all to hear, 'all I want is to leave here and go home.'

A middle-aged woman rushed out and grabbed hold of the alien, hugging him over-enthusiastically. He thanked her and gently pushed her back towards her family in the crowd. He then took the protesting man's hand in his own and shook it firmly.

'Take a look around you,' he said to him. The man did as he was told, looking from left to right at the tightly packed sea of faces which all glared back at him. 'Do you see anyone else objecting to us being here? I'm sorry if you're not happy, but there's nothing any of us can do about it right now. We'll agree to keep a respectful distance from each other, if that's what you wish. Now please go home and spend time with the people who matter most to you. Don't waste your energy here. We really don't want any trouble.'

He shook the man's hand again, then carried on. Tom watched as the crowd continued on through the town, but as the mass of people disappeared, his eyes remained focussed on the protester in the street. He was largely being ignored, save for a few choice words and insults which were hurled in his general direction by stragglers.

Tom had seen enough. 'Let's go,' he said as he jumped down from the recycling bin.

'Why? It's still early.'

'You've got what you wanted, haven't you? You've seen your aliens. I want to go home now.'

'You're kidding me. I'm not going anywhere. Come on, Tom.'

'Look, I'm tired and this place is too busy, that's all.'

Rob considered his options. 'I'm going to stay a bit longer.'

'How are you going to get back? I'm not coming to pick you up.'

'I'll get a taxi or something. I'll walk if it comes to it.'

'Haven't you got work in the morning?'

'I don't have to be there until eleven. Sure you won't stay a bit longer?'

'No,' Tom replied. 'I'm going home.'

Tom knew Rob would be okay. He'd walked the few miles back from Drayton before, frequently half-pissed. It was a straight road. He watched his brother run after the crowd following the aliens, before heading back to his car.

A couple with a young child walked just ahead of him and their conversation was carried on the light evening breeze. Tom couldn't help overhearing. They had their little girl between them, holding one hand each, playfully swinging her.

'Was it as good as you expected?' the woman asked her partner.

'Better,' he replied. 'It's just... oh, I don't know. It's hard to put into words how it makes you feel, you know? When you think how far they've travelled to get here, and how lucky we are to be around at the right time... Meg will never forget this, will you, Meg?'

Both parents looked down at their daughter. She looked up and grinned at them.

'Makes you think, though, doesn't it?' the man said.

'What does?'

'Seeing them up close like that. All that distance between us, yet they're so much like us. Their faces, their body shape, the way they talk...'

'I'll tell you something, it makes me feel more optimistic. Remember how we felt that first night they arrived? When we didn't know whether we should have been celebrating or panicking? That all seems like years ago now. I don't know... you see the mess they're in and how they're dealing with it, and it makes everything else look trivial, doesn't it? Having them here puts things into perspective.'

Tom stopped at his car and watched the family walk away, thinking how increasingly out-of-step with the rest of the world he felt.

# 12

With everyone else busy all the time, Tom didn't dare admit to anyone that he was bored. He needed something to do with himself each day, something to focus on, but at the same time he didn't feel like doing anything. One day last week, he was embarrassed to admit, he'd sat down in front of the TV first thing and had played Xbox for seven hours straight. What was he, a grown man or a geeky teenager? He tried to convince himself that it was okay because he could only play the games he liked when there was no one else around now. Siobhan and Rob didn't approve. Shooting seven shades of shit out of an army of pixelated alien invaders wasn't as socially acceptable as it used to be.

Siobhan continued to be overworked, the business benefitting from the "alien effect" and the unexpected extension to the summer season their arrival had caused. She spent most nights at her flat, close to Drayton. With their time together greatly reduced, and with her being exhausted most evenings, Siobhan and Tom took every opportunity to see each other they could. When a client cancelled an appointment at the last minute, she phoned Tom and arranged to meet him for lunch. He jumped at the chance to get out, and found himself heading back into Drayton again.

Lunch was pleasant, if a little rushed. Their pub meal was interrupted several times by Siobhan's phone ringing and bleeping to let her know she had messages which, to Tom's annoyance, she insisted on immediately replying to, even when he was in the middle of telling her something he thought was relatively important.

'Sorry, love,' she said, 'I can't even begin to tell you what it's like right now. I've never known it this busy.'

He distracted himself with the rest of his food, resisting the temptation to tell her that he knew *exactly* what it was like, and that whatever temporary pressure she was feeling, he'd probably put up with far worse during his years in the city. The last thing he wanted was to start an argument.

Tom walked Siobhan back to her office, then spent a listless hour walking from shop to shop, just killing time. He didn't want anything – he didn't *need* anything – but it was good to be out. Although still busy, Drayton was back to its old self today.

Before going back to the car, Tom took a detour to Overmill Park, the place he'd seen on the TV news. It looked reassuringly familiar today, a few bags of rubbish stacked by each of the bins the only indication that there had been hordes of people crammed into this space not so long ago. He walked a circuit of the park, following the footpath which ran around its perimeter. He saw barely anyone else: workers were back in their shops and offices after lunch, and school children were in class. The late summer sun was warm and pleasant, and he slowed his pace, enjoying the silence and doing his best to think about as little as possible.

'Excuse me,' a voice said from behind him. He froze, not just because the unexpected voice had taken him by surprise, but also because there was something unusual about its tone and accent. He knew before he turned around that it was an alien.

Tom found himself face-to-face with one of the visitors. Just him and her and no one else. Except that, rather than being face-to-face, the height difference meant he was face-to-chest, and the fact he was staring at her slight bosoms just added to his sudden awkwardness. He looked up, but when he made contact with those eyes – those huge, piercing, otherworldly blue eyes – he immediately looked down again, lost. His mouth was dry, his legs weak with sudden nervousness.

'I'm sorry if I disturbed you,' the alien said, sounding almost as uncomfortable as Tom clearly was. 'I'm lost.'

'You come halfway across the universe, but then get lost trying to find your way around Drayton?' Tom joked without thinking, regretting his words the moment he'd spoken them. He cringed, fearing for a second that the alien might not understand sarcasm, concerned he might have unwittingly sparked an intergalactic diplomatic incident. Fortunately the corners of her wide, thin-lipped mouth began to curl upwards. *Please let that be an alien smile*, he hoped, *not a declaration of war.*

'It would seem that way,' she said, and her smile widened.

Tom cleared his throat and asked the question he should have begun with: 'Where are you trying to get to?'

'Lime Street,' she replied. 'I'm supposed to be meeting a friend there.'

Again, Tom clammed up. His brain was struggling to comprehend the extremes of this conversation. There he was, being asked to give walking directions to an obviously intelligent being who had travelled billions of miles through space. Either picking up on his unease or feeling equally awkward herself, the alien explained further.

'I'm a geologist,' she said. 'I can tell you anything about the geology of most of the planets and stars between here and home, but I'm useless at finding my way around Drayton.'

Her humility was touching.

'Well I know absolutely nothing about the geology of this planet, never mind any others, but I can tell you how to get from one side of this place to the other. You're a long way off, by the way. Lime Street's right on the other side of town. It's at least a half-hour walk.'

'I'm more than a trillion miles off the mark, actually,' she said. 'A half-hour's walk is nothing.'

Further along the footpath, nearer to the main entrance of the park, was a street map. Tom gestured for the alien to follow him. Was it too presumptuous of him to lead the visitor or walk alongside her? Should he hold back and let her go first?

His mind was rapidly filling with all kinds of nerve-induced rubbish. He needed to calm down and get a grip.

There were two kids on bikes cycling across the park, probably bunking off school, Tom thought. He noticed that they'd stopped and were both staring at the alien. The alien had noticed too.

'You must get sick of it,' Tom said.

'The novelty has worn off, yes.'

'Give it a few more weeks and they'll have forgotten about you,' he continued. 'In the nicest possible way, of course. We're funny creatures. We'll point and shout at something that looks a little different to us, then just accept it as normal when the next new thing comes along.'

'So you think people will stop staring as soon as *another* ship full of aliens arrives?'

Tom looked at her for a moment. Was she joking or being serious? It was impossible to tell.

'What I mean is,' he said, trying to dig himself out of a hole, 'it's just the shock of the new. Give it a little longer and everyone will get used to you. It'll get easier.'

'I hope so,' she admitted.

They'd stopped in front of the map. Tom showed her the park where they were standing, then slid his finger across towards Lime Street.

'You take a right here,' he explained, pointing along a pathway, then a road. 'Carry on until you reach the high street then turn right again. Follow the high street until you reach the junction with Fordham Street, then it's left, then left again. Okay?'

She scanned the map once more and then nodded. 'Right, high street, right, Fordham Street, then left and left again.'

'You got it.'

'Thank you.'

'Do you want me to take you. I could...'

'No, it's fine, thank you anyway.'

She smiled and started to walk away. Tom watched her go, feeling strangely deflated. Was that it? His first conversation with an alien, and all he'd found to talk about was how to get from Overmill Park to Lime Street?

'So how are you finding things here?' he shouted after her. She stopped and turned back to face him.

'I'm not,' she replied. 'That's why I had to ask you.'

'It was a figure of speech,' he explained.

Her mouth curled again. 'I know. What did you mean? How do I like the town or the planet?'

'Both. Either.'

She sighed (or at least that was what he thought it was) and thought for a few seconds before answering. 'I don't know how to give you an honest answer without offending you.'

'Then offend me.'

'Your planet is fine, and the people here have been very, very kind to us, but... but it's not home, is it?'

Her use of the word 'fine' to describe everything Planet Earth had to offer stung Tom somewhat. Perhaps she hadn't intended to sound so glib.

'Of course it's not your home. I just meant—'

'Don't get me wrong,' she said, 'I like very much what I've seen here. Parts of your world are beautiful, very different to where I come from.'

'Yes, but for every beauty spot, there are a hundred places like Drayton.'

'And it's exactly the same where I'm from, but that's not what I'm trying to say. It wouldn't matter if every square metre of this place was unspoilt and beautiful, it still wouldn't be enough. I'd rather be home. You'd feel the same way, I'm sure.'

'How long will it take you to get back?'

'A year and a half, probably longer.'

'And how does that make you feel?'

Her surprisingly expressive face changed. The definite smile

114

had disappeared. Her brow furrowed and her willowy shoulders dropped. 'Desperate,' she replied. Despite the unnatural twang to her voice, the inhuman lilt, he could clearly hear the sadness in her voice. They stood and studied each other for a few seconds longer, perhaps both trying to work out what the other was thinking, then the alien spoke again. 'I'm sorry,' she said, 'I have to go. My friend will be waiting. Thank you.'

Tom watched her leave.

'What did she want, mate?' one of the kids on bikes asked, finally plucking up courage to cycle over now the alien had gone.

'She was lost, that's all.'

# 13

Tom's plans for a quiet night in with Siobhan were thwarted by her decision to stay late at the office so she could try and get away at a decent time tomorrow. He ate half the meal he'd cooked, then threw the rest away. Too full of food to run, he decided to walk off his dinner along the cliff-top path he'd followed so many times before.

It was still pleasantly warm, and although he passed a couple of dog walkers close to the village, there was no one else about. Good. That was how he liked it.

He passed the war memorial, then stopped a short distance further along, close to where he'd been when the alien ship had arrived, and where he, Rob and Siobhan had stood and watched it disappear again. In contrast to both those times, it was peaceful and quiet out here tonight. It was still hard to believe what he'd seen, even harder to imagine the odds against him being in the right place at the right time to witness such historic events. He craned his head back and retraced the route the alien ship had taken when it left the planet's atmosphere. There was still a little light on the distant horizon, but overhead the sky was deep purple. The longer he stared, the more individual stars he was able to make out, peering down at him from millions of miles away.

*It's all about perspective*, he decided.

The contrast was obvious, but it still made him think: he could see hundreds of stars now, and if he stayed out here longer, he'd be able to see thousands more. And yet, from any one of those individual stars, he would be invisible. That was because of his comparative lack of size, of course, but the same was also true of the planet itself. In relative terms, the Earth was just a pinprick.

He walked on.

Along with the rest of the world, he'd had a month to get used to playing host to visitors from another planet. Like everyone else, he'd also managed to get used to the fact that the human race was nowhere near as all-powerful as it had long believed itself to be. He wondered how the people at the top were coming to terms with their newly adjusted position in the scheme of things. They'd been the leaders before – the teachers. Now they'd been demoted to being kids in the class, taking instructions from elsewhere. He thought about the Prime Ministers and Presidents, all of whom had gone from being the most powerful people on *the* planet, to the most powerful people on *a* planet. The difference was subtle, but important.

The technological advances the aliens had promised to share would no doubt have a profound impact on all aspects of life on Earth. Was that something everyone would welcome? What about the mega-rich, overly influential bastards who looked down on everyone else from a position of often undeserved privilege? Would they be content to play second fiddle to the aliens? Would they be willing to see their hold on power and influence lessened? He'd heard talk on the TV earlier of trying to harness the quieter, safer, and more efficient energy source which powered the alien ships. All well and good, he thought, but the oil barons, politicians, billionaires and dictators might not be so keen to give up the fuel and money-based stranglehold on power they'd maintained over everyone else for so many years.

Tom continued to climb the hills away from the village, although he stopped several times and considered turning back. He felt unnaturally tired. It was stupid – the less he did, the more effort everything seemed to take. Was he vegetating? He thought maybe he should be running. Maybe he'd start again tomorrow, if he could be bothered.

His increasing apathy was beginning to genuinely concern him. Everyone else seemed fine – happier than usual, if anything; buoyed up by the unexpected optimism of the events of the last month. He was beginning to feel more and more like an outsider, almost as if he'd been left outside in the rain, looking in at the party through the window. Too tired to go any further, though not yet ready to go home, he stopped walking and sat down.

The crashing of the waves on the rocks below was the only sound. Everything was dark save for the twinkling lights of the village he'd left behind and, further in the distance, the faint orange air-glow over Drayton. He felt separated from it all. Detached. He hated feeling this way.

*Is there something wrong with me?*

Depression, someone had once told him, always boils down to a person having a lack of control. *So how can I be depressed? I get up when I want to, go to bed when I'm ready, and do whatever I want in between. I've got more freedom than anyone else I know.*

But was freedom the same as control? He wasn't sure any more. It felt like something was missing. Tom had Siobhan and Rob and their small circle of friends, but beyond that he had very little. They all had their jobs to keep them busy and in regular contact with other people... what else did he have? Nothing. Not even any hobbies to speak of now he'd lost the impetus to run regularly. And yet the thought of getting a job or trying to find something else to do made him feel even worse. He wondered if the career he'd walked away from had given him a sense of purpose that he was now missing, or whether it had simply disguised the fact he'd never had one? Did he feel guilty because, as Rob had succinctly put it one drunken night, he was pissing on their parents' grave? One thing was for sure, whatever the reason, his life was in real danger of becoming a vacuum.

Recognising the problem was one thing. Doing something about it, another thing entirely.

He lay back, the dry grass tickling his neck, and looked deeper into the heavens. He found himself thinking about his conversation with the alien earlier. If anyone had a right to be depressed, it was them. Talk about a lack of control... Christ, they clearly had it far worse than he did. Separated from everything they held dear by an impassable gulf, no way of getting back to their loved ones for the foreseeable future, if at all... He pictured the visitor's face, the clear sadness in her eyes and the melancholy tone of her voice when she'd spoken about home. Bloody hell, in comparison to them, did he have *anything* to complain about?

And then it struck him that all of this might be the very reason why he found it impossible to connect with the aliens in the same way as everyone else. He didn't understand them. More to the point, he didn't understand how any of them could have allowed themselves to be willingly manipulated into leaving everything that mattered to them behind.

And then it struck him – *maybe* I'm *the one who's got it all wrong?*

# 14

Tom picked Siobhan up from work the following evening. After calling at her flat to sort out some washing and grab some clean clothes for the morning, they bought a takeaway and went back to the bungalow. Rob had gone back to university and was likely to be there all week. They had the place to themselves.

Tom was standing by the wide bay window in the living room, looking down over Thatcham. Although it was late in the season and late in the day, the streets were still teeming with activity, a stark contrast to how this place usually was in late-September, or so he'd been told. By this time of year, John Tipper had explained last Friday evening, the village should be half-empty. Not that John was complaining. As long as there was cash in his tills and people in his bar, he was happy.

Tom was looking at the nearest trees on the hillside, noticing how their branches were becoming more exposed as their leaves fell away, when Siobhan appeared behind him and wrapped her arms around his waist. She nestled her face against the back of his head and whispered in his ear.

'You okay? Feels like ages since we've had time together like this.'

'Too long,' he said, turning around and looking deep into her face. The only illumination came from a small table lamp and the TV at the other end of the room. The soft light and constantly changing shadows highlighted the intense beauty of her blue-grey eyes. He kissed her, a first delicate touch of lips, then waited for her response. It was immediate, beginning with light, fluttering kisses which rapidly became more passionate. She slipped her tongue into his mouth, then playfully chewed on his bottom lip. He felt her hands underneath his shirt, then felt her fingernails drag down his back, the perfect balance of pain and pleasure. 'I love you, you know,' he said, pressing his face up against hers.

'I know,' she answered, and she kissed him again as she pushed him back across the room then pulled him down onto the sofa. She took off his T-shirt then sat astride him. He looked up at her and wondered how the hell he'd managed to find someone as perfect as Siobhan. She was everything he wanted: beautiful, sexy, downright filthy when it suited her... he couldn't imagine being without her now. And yet, he'd been thinking earlier today that he would never have met her if he hadn't moved to Thatcham, and that he wouldn't have moved to Thatcham if he hadn't lost his parents. *Fate can be a strange fucker at times*, he thought. *Do we always have to suffer before we can experience pleasure? And if I experience pleasure now, will I have to pay for it later?*

To be honest, he'd have willingly taken any punishment as a consequence of what Siobhan was about to do to him. She undid his belt then popped open the button of his jeans and unzipped the fly, and he made a conscious decision to stop thinking and give his full and undivided attention to the perfect woman now sitting on top of him.

She leant forward and licked the length of his chest from just above his cock to just below his chin and then, almost lying flat on him now, she pressed her mouth close to his ear and whispered: 'Do you want me?'

Her breath tickled his skin, driving him wild. She hadn't needed to ask the question, she'd done it for effect and he'd already burst out of his open jeans with excitement. The hard-on she'd now wrapped her hand around was answer enough.

'I want you,' he said.

'Then I'm all yours.'

He pushed her upright and took off her T-shirt, lifting it over her head. She leant back to undo her bra, then looked up at the TV and froze suddenly.

'Shit. What time is it?'

'Who cares?'

'I do.'

'Why, have you got somewhere else to be?'

She slid off him and marched across the room.

'Christ, Tom, it's almost eight. It'll have started.'

'What are you on about?'

She hunted around in the low light for the TV remote, then changed the channel. Tom, rejected, stood up and held onto his erection, doing what he could to stop it disappearing.

'You've got to be kidding me,' he said. 'You'd rather watch a stupid bloody TV programme than—'

'It's not a stupid bloody programme,' she interrupted angrily, 'it's important. You should watch it too.'

'I don't want to watch it. I want to fuck you. This is a fucking joke.'

Eventually she stopped messing with the TV and turned around to look at him. Embarrassed, she reached out and took his hand. 'I'm really sorry. It's just that I've been waiting all day and—'

'We could record it.'

'I want to watch it. Please, Tom, watch it with me. When it's finished I promise you the fuck of lifetime. All night, if you want. Whatever you want to do. Whatever you want me to be.'

He knew there was no arguing. She gently kissed him, then sat down on the floor in front of the TV, still half-dressed. She beckoned for him to sit with her, but he didn't move. He remained standing where he was, limp cock dripping, feeling stupid like he'd been stood up on a date or completely misread her signals. As a series of trailers and announcements filled the screen, she looked up at him again.

'I'm sorry, Tom, I really want to watch this. I want us *both* to watch it. It's important, and if I don't watch it now I don't know when I'll get chance.'

She reached out and stroked his leg. Tom just nodded. He knew he couldn't compete.

'I'll make a drink,' he said as he traipsed miserably into the kitchen.

*Visitor Update.*

That was the name of the programme. Variations on a similar theme were broadcast on all the major free-to-air channels, in every conceivable language in every country imaginable. The BBC version, which Siobhan was now glued to, was widely considered the best.

The programme was intended to be an on-going education in all things alien, designed to lessen the gulf between the known and unknown, to break down any remaining barriers, and to eradicate any lingering doubts about the three hundred-or-so new arrivals on the planet. It had been showing twice-weekly for a while now, but this particular edition had been long looked forward to by many. Tonight the programme promised to show a wealth of previously unseen footage of the alien home-world.

The programme already had a fanatical following. The aliens' biology, psychology, history, physiology and more, broken down into easily digestible forty-five minute chunks. The presentation style was banal, Tom thought, bordering on being patronising. *They're aiming at the lowest common denominator*, he decided, *so everyone can understand this crap.*

His earlier disappointment aside, even Tom was forced to admit that tonight's episode was fascinating. Given the choice, he'd still have rather have been making love with Siobhan than sitting in front of the TV, but there was no point protesting. He could see her hanging on every last frame of footage.

'This is incredible, isn't it,' she whispered as she curled up against him.

'Suppose.'

'Don't be like that, Tom. This is important. This affects all of us.'

'Still don't know why you couldn't record it.'

'I'm sorry.'

She rested her hand on the inside of his thigh and began to stroke him, not even realising she was doing it. Her touch was a great pacifier.

Soon all Tom's disappointments were temporarily forgotten as the promised new footage was shown. It was all too brief and there had been far less of it than they'd been led to expect, but there was no disputing the sheer wonder of what had been shown. Vast, clean, quiet alien cities which seemed to cover entire continents of their unusually pink-hued world. Lush forests, home to an incalculable number and variety of alien species. Mountain ranges which stretched upwards and outwards forever. Floating cities resting on mill-pond still oceans. Intricate travel networks... Like the aliens themselves, Tom thought their world appeared to be completely different and yet bizarrely similar to his own.

The final credits had barely finished scrolling up the screen when Siobhan got up and switched off the TV. She turned around, dropped her trousers and kicked off her knickers. She stood in front of him, completely naked, arms open, offering herself up. Tom scrambled to get undressed, all the time looking up at her, her perfect body gently illuminated by the soft lamp light.

'You still want me then?' she asked. She didn't give him chance to answer. He lay naked on the floor and she sat astride him, knees either side of his crotch, and lowered herself down onto his immediately erect cock. The match was perfect, the movement precise and easy. Both of them were more than ready for each other.

'I love you,' he said, already breathless.

She grinned at him. 'And I love you too. Now shut up and

fuck me.'

The promised night of passion lasted less than an hour, but they both knew that would probably be the case, and neither of them cared. Lying in bed next to each other now, Tom felt himself falling asleep, still sweat-soaked and panting. He couldn't help it. He was exhausted. Siobhan, however, was having none of it. She had ten times his energy tonight, it seemed. She buried her face in his chest and gently nibbled his skin.

Tom wanted to resist, but it was inevitable. He wanted to stay awake and keep fucking, but the sleep was unstoppable.

'You have no stamina, Tom Winter,' she said, giggling, nudging him playfully to keep him awake.

'It's your fault,' he replied, still drifting. 'You wear me out.'

It might have been a minute later when she next spoke, it might have been hours. Tom couldn't tell, and he couldn't focus enough to see the clock. Siobhan was spread-eagled, one leg wedged between his, lying half on the bed and half on top of him.

'Question for you,' she said.

'Too tired,' he mumbled, fighting sleep again.

'If you had chance to travel to the aliens' planet, would you go?'

'It's never gonna happen.'

'It might.'

'Return trip or one way?'

'One way.'

'You coming too?'

'No.'

'Then I don't want to go.'

'Soft bugger. Okay then, what about a round trip?'

'Same question – you coming too?'

'Forget about me, this is hypothetical.'

'Doesn't matter. I can't forget about you.'

She thumped his chest. 'Just answer the question.'

'I'd like to go, of course I would, but not if it means spending years away from you. And I'm not being a soft bugger, I'm being honest. I miss you when I don't see you for more than a day. Hated it when you went on that course in July. I couldn't be away from you for years, I just couldn't...'

Siobhan looked up and watched his eyelids flicker.

'I think you'd answer differently if there was a real chance of going. I don't think you'd be able to say no. I don't think anyone would. Anyway, maybe they'd let us both go, imagine that. Sounds romantic, doesn't it... travelling across the universe together... being so far from home and the only person I know for millions of miles in every direction is you. Doesn't sound too bad, eh?'

She nudged him again but he didn't reply. He was asleep.

# 15

It became almost impossible *not* to keep learning about the aliens. The media's fascination with them and the public's appetite for news remained undiminished. If anything, the demand for new information continued to increase virtually by the day. Even the long-standing stalwarts of the TV schedules – the soap operas, the endless reality TV and talentless talent shows – were soon forced to give way to coverage of the visitors. Those people living in and around Drayton were fortunate to have an unusually large number of aliens on their doorstep. Most other places had to make do with the TV and with hastily arranged travelling road-shows and public appearances. It was almost as if some of the visitors had gone on tour, such was the demand to see them.

Sitting alone in his living room, watching yet another documentary as he waited for a film to start, Tom felt like he was learning about the aliens by osmosis. He had only a passing interest in them compared to most people, and yet he seemed to find out more and more each day without even trying. It was the contrast between their world and ours which intrigued him more than the aliens themselves.

Tom couldn't match the rabid curiosity some people showed, but being out of step with the majority was something he was becoming used to. He never could understand religion, for example. Billions of people around the world prayed regularly to whichever particular deity they chose to put their faith in, and yet to him it was all little more than unfounded superstition, as ridiculous as looking for fairies at the bottom of the garden or not walking under ladders.

He'd first become aware of this gulf between him and everyone else earlier in the year, and at the time it had threatened to bring his fledgling relationship with Siobhan to an abrupt end.

They'd driven to Cardiff to see a band. He'd paid a fortune for tickets, and the venue had been some soulless, warehouse-like place originally designed for trade exhibitions and sporting events, not the mass consumption of music. He'd hated every second of the concert, and yet everyone else – Siobhan included – had been in raptures. Tens of thousands of people were on their feet, cheering, singing and applauding, lifted by the atmosphere and the music. And then there was Tom. Sitting down. Bored shitless. Wishing he was anywhere else.

Siobhan had given him hell when they'd got back to Thatcham. But what would have been worse, he'd argued at the time, pretending to enjoy myself and not being honest? I can't lie, he'd said. I can't pretend to be something I'm not. You could have at least tried, she'd told him.

That particular argument, he remembered, had been over pretty quickly. Regardless of how he'd behaved, Siobhan had still enjoyed herself, and the fact they'd been able to deal with their disagreements actually left them both feeling surprisingly reassured about the strength of their relationship. He remembered another night, even earlier in their romance, when another mistake had had unexpectedly positive results. They'd only been out together a few times, and both were unsure as to how things were going to work out. Tom pulled out all the stops, arranging to pick Siobhan up and take her to The Black Swan, the most expensive restaurant within a hundred miles; a Michelin-starred gastropub with spectacular ocean views. He'd gone the whole hog – flowers, new suit, keeping his plans secret... he'd thought of every detail. Except one. In all his restaurant research, he'd only checked reviews, not news, and after booking the table several weeks in advance, he'd managed to completely miss the fact that the restaurant had been gutted in a fire the weekend before their date. He hadn't known anything until he'd pulled up outside the burned out shell of a place.

Tom had been devastated. Siobhan just laughed. 'When we're out together, what are you thinking about?' she asked him.

'You,' he said, side-stepping the most obvious answer, because they hadn't yet made love.

'I'm the same. I'm thinking about you. So it wouldn't matter if we were at the best restaurant in the country or some greasy spoon café where half the customers walk away with food poisoning, it's you I'm interested in, not the dinner.'

They'd made love in the car, there and then in the deserted car park of the restaurant, their first time together, and had followed it up with a quick drive to Drayton and a visit to McDonalds.

Happy accidents. A lack of planning. Chaos. Life was never completely prescriptive, and that was part of the issue Tom had with what he'd learned about the aliens' culture. Much of their lives, it seemed, were pre-planned to a frightening extent.

The programme on TV was recapping the basics, yet again.

'Alien families,' the narrator intoned over stock footage, 'are considerably larger than an average human's. Multiple generations live together under the same roof, siblings raising their own children alongside each other's, all under the collective auspices of parents, grandparents and, frequently, great-grandparents.'

The very idea of that made Tom feel stifled. He still missed his parents desperately, but even if they'd still been alive, there was no way he'd want to live with them. Siobhan felt much the same about her folks, not that she saw very much of them.

The aliens had two sexes (he hadn't needed a TV programme to tell him that – it was obvious). Promiscuity was unheard of. Aliens were free to choose a partner of either sex and from any background. Once the relationship had been given the blessing of the eldest member of both families, they were married. Perhaps the most bizarre fact Tom had discovered, was that whenever the aliens bred, there was a two-way exchange of genetic material. The upshot of this biological quirk was that, over time, both partners would gradually assume some of the physical characteristics of the other. There remained subtle differences (otherwise they'd long ago have become a race of clones), and yet it had resulted in there being a lack of any strong physical variation throughout the entire race. There were no 'black' or 'white' aliens, just 'aliens'.

Tom found another aspect of their lifestyles particularly disturbing, and yet it appeared eminently sensible too. The TV programme explained that once their preliminary schooling had been completed, the aliens were genetically assessed. Their anticipated potential strengths, weaknesses and intelligence levels were matched against the predicted future social, moral and educational needs to decide their ideal vocation. In essence, therefore, it was their biological and emotional profile which dictated the path their lives would take, not any personal choice on the part of the individual. Tom found that idea abhorrent. The TV presenter continued to enthuse. But it was the next thing he said which disturbed Tom the most.

'Having developed an incredible understanding of the minutia of how their minds and bodies develop,' he explained, 'the aliens are, incredibly, able to calculate their approximate date of death.'

*All the future-planning in the world wouldn't have helped Mum and Dad*, he thought as the presenter droned on. *Some things are beyond anyone's control.*

# 16

On an otherwise unremarkable Wednesday evening, Rob returned from university unannounced. He'd been due to stay away all week, but sudden changes of plan like this were not uncommon.

Siobhan was watching TV while Tom dozed on the sofa, having gorged himself on too much dinner. His swollen gut ached, he'd eaten so much. Rob let himself in and poked his head around the living room door.

'You two okay?' he said, and it was immediately obvious that something was different. He looked a little uncomfortable. Nervous, perhaps.

'You on your own?' Siobhan asked, thinking that at long last he might have managed to find himself a girlfriend. She'd tried to set him up with several of her friends recently, but he'd shown little interest. He favoured the occasional one night stand to long-term commitment, and steadfastly refused to talk about how he spent his evenings when he was back in his university digs.

'Actually no,' he replied. 'I've got someone here with me.'

She nudged Tom, who'd only been half-listening, and he groaned with effort as he sat up. Rob entered the room and then, several steps behind, an alien followed, ducking down to get through the doorway.

'Jesus,' Tom said under his breath.

'This is Jall. He's a friend of mine,' Rob explained. The tall, gangly figure next to him stood upright, the top of his head almost scraping the ceiling. 'I didn't think you'd mind if I brought him back for a drink.'

'No, not at all...' Tom said as he got up and walked towards them, trying to work out whether he *did* mind or not. He didn't know what he was supposed to say, how he was supposed to react.

'You okay?' Rob asked, immediately picking up on his older brother's understandable surprise.

'Fine,' he answered quickly. 'A bit spaced out, that's all. Sorry, I'm being rude... come in, please.'

The alien held out his hand. Tom hesitated for the briefest of moments and then shook it. The visitor's flesh felt almost too warm, unnaturally so. His spindly fingers seemed to wrap themselves around Tom's hand, touching him in all the wrong places.

'I hope you don't mind my being here,' the alien said, his diction perfect. 'Your brother said you wouldn't, but I'll leave if you'd rather...'

'No, no,' Tom said hurriedly, worried that his reticence might have caused offence. 'You've taken me by surprise, that's all. I wasn't expecting...'

'Someone like me to walk into your house?'

'Something like that,' he mumbled, not knowing what he was trying to say. Truth was, he could barely think straight. It had been one thing when he'd spoken to the alien in Drayton the other day, but this felt entirely different. There was an alien – a living, breathing creature from the other side of the universe – standing in the middle of his living room. It was an unexpected collision between the ordinary and the incredible, and it was hard to take it all in.

'This is my brother, Tom,' Rob said, dealing with the introductions which Tom was too tongue-tied to handle.

'Believe me, this is as awkward for me as it is for you,' the alien said.

'Oh, it's not awkward,' Tom said apologetically. 'I was talking to another one of your people in Drayton the other day.'

'One of your people,' Rob repeated. 'Bloody hell, Tom, we're not in the 1950's. You sound borderline racist.'

'Believe me, I've heard far worse,' the alien said.

'This is Siobhan,' Rob continued. 'Tom's girlfriend. She's far too good for him.'

When Siobhan didn't say anything, Tom looked around to see if she was still there. She was. She mouthed a couple of words, but no noise came out. Instead she just grinned, staring at the new arrival like a star-struck teenager.

'Close your mouth, sweetheart,' he whispered. 'You're catching flies.'

'What? Oh... sorry. I didn't mean to... I just...'

The alien took another few steps forward and reached out his hand again. She took it – slowly, hesitantly, respectfully – then shook it lightly. Tom almost expected her to curtsy.

'I'm pleased to meet you, Siobhan,' he said.

'And I can't believe I'm meeting you,' she replied.

'Well isn't this nice,' Rob said, bemused by the sudden awkwardness of the moment.

As the host – no matter how surprised he was – Tom forced himself to do something to try and break the ice. He gestured further into the room. 'Go on through,' he said. 'Can I get anyone a drink?'

'I'll have a beer,' Rob immediately replied.

'Beer,' Siobhan said also, still staring at the alien.

'And what about... Sorry, what was your name again?'

The alien looked at him. 'Call me Jall. You wouldn't be able to pronounce my full name.'

'I can try.'

'No, you misunderstand, you *wouldn't* be able to pronounce it. We have certain inflexions and subtleties in our speech that you can't detect, let alone recreate.'

'Fair enough,' Tom said, feeling strangely offended.

'Names have been a nightmare,' Rob said. 'Apparently they've tried all the movie clichés like giving them numbers or using typical names. Didn't work out.'

'Why not?'

'Twenty-three Johns, ten Stevens, and eight Michaels,' the alien explained. 'And when we tried numbers, everyone wanted to be number one.'

Tom laughed. The alien didn't.

'Some of them are using their position,' Rob said. 'The pilot, for example, calls himself Pilot. Others like Jall have chosen their own name.'

'Why Jall?' Siobhan asked.

'It's an approximation,' the alien replied.

'I like it,' she told him.

'So then, Jall, what can I get you to drink?' Tom asked again.

'Beer would be fine, thank you.'

'Are you able to drink beer? I mean, are you...?'

'I'm old enough, if that's what you mean. I know you don't allow your children to drink alcohol until they reach a certain age.'

'I wasn't thinking that. I just meant, are you okay with alcohol?'

'I've drank plenty with your brother. It's really not a problem.'

The supercilious tone of his voice was irritating. Tom couldn't tell whether the alien was deliberately trying to annoy him. *Give him the benefit of the doubt*, he decided. *He's probably as nervous as I am. And why the hell am I so nervous?*

'And have you got any chocolate?' Rob shouted after him as he went into the kitchen. 'Jall's a big fan of sweet stuff and we haven't eaten yet.'

Tom fetched four beers and a couple of Mars bars from the fridge, then returned to the others who were now sitting out on the patio together. It was dark outside and cool, though not unpleasant. Tom heard Rob explaining to Siobhan that the alien's metabolism was faster than that of a human, and that he often found being trapped indoors quite uncomfortable.

'So where did you two first meet?' he heard Siobhan ask.

*Christ*, he thought, *they're not a couple*. He fetched himself a chair (*nice of them to think of me*) and sat down next to her.

'Jall was brought in to do some work with Phil and the economics team,' Rob explained. 'We got talking after a meeting a couple of days back and we hit it off. We had a great day yesterday. I showed him the sights.'

'What sights?' Tom asked. 'There's bugger all to see in Willsham.'

'I had a good time,' Jall said. 'I've seen a lot.'

'So you're enjoying your time here?' Siobhan asked. 'Are you getting used to us yet?'

'I wouldn't say I'm enjoying it,' he answered as he struggled to open his beer with long, slender fingers. Siobhan took the can from him, opened it, then passed it back. 'Everyone has been very hospitable and accommodating,' he continued, sniffing his drink then cautiously sipping it. 'Everything's adequate for now.'

*Adequate? Just adequate?* Tom thought, fuming. He continued to watch the visitor with a degree of childish satisfaction. As well as being unable to cope with ring-pulls, he also couldn't get comfortable in his chair. His body was too long for his seat.

'You're looking forward to getting home, though, I'm sure,' Siobhan said.

'Of course I am,' he replied without hesitation.

'You must miss it.'

'More than you can imagine. I knew we were going to be away for a long time, and we were prepared for that, but this trip is going to take far longer than any of us imagined. At least twice as long, in fact.'

'So what exactly happened?' Tom asked.

'What do you mean?'

'To your ship? I can't get my head around how something as huge and powerful as your ship could become irreparably damaged like that.'

135

'Get your head around?'

'Sorry, local expression. I meant I can't understand it. You can see what I mean, can't you?'

'Of course. We were extracting ore in an asteroid field and were hit by debris from a collision.'

'Debris! Fuck me, must have been a bloody huge bit of debris to do so much damage.'

Jall fixed his baby-blue eyes on Tom's. 'It was.'

'But to cripple an entire ship like that?'

'It was a million-to-one chance. In fact, the odds were probably even higher. You can plan and prepare to the extreme but you can't allow for every eventuality. As Rob's friend Phil said to me earlier today, shit happens. We were hit by debris, one thing led to another...'

'You sound so dismissive. Aren't you angry?'

'Angry? Why would I be angry? It was no one's fault, and assigning blame after the event wouldn't make any difference. Getting angry, sad, frustrated, resentful... what good would it do? I am where I am and I have to deal with it.'

'That's where there's a big difference between us,' Rob said. 'If we could put aside some of our pointless emotions sometimes we'd get more done and get on with each other better.'

'You think?' Tom asked.

Siobhan wasn't interested in philosophising. She had more pressing questions to ask. 'Must have been a huge culture shock when you arrived here, though,' she said. 'I can't imagine what it must have felt like. What were your first impressions?'

'Relief was my overriding feeling,' Jall answered quickly. 'If we hadn't found you then our situation would have been far worse. Coming here has at least given us a chance of getting home.'

'Couldn't you have just stayed with the ship and waited to be picked up?'

'Not with the level of damage we'd sustained. We wouldn't

have lasted.'

'You didn't answer my question, though,' Siobhan said. 'Was it a culture shock when you arrived here? What did you think when you saw us?'

'I assume you want me to be honest?'

'Of course.'

'Then at risk of offending you, I'll admit that being here's like stepping back in time. But yours is an unfair question, because how can you compare anywhere else favourably to your own home?'

He finished his beer and set the empty can down on the table. Tom was surprised. He'd barely started his. He asked if he could have one of the Mars bars then demolished it in two large bites.

'So what's the biggest difference you've come across?' Siobhan asked, continuing her enthusiastic interrogation.

'Give him a break, Siobhan,' Tom said, but Jall dismissed his concern with a subtle hand gesture.

'It's fine. I don't mind. The biggest difference is the people, actually. Not so much physically, more in terms of attitudes. As I've said, everyone has been very helpful and welcoming, but I have to be honest, there's a huge gulf between our two species.'

'That's pretty bloody obvious,' Rob said. 'Just look at all the stuff you can do. We're still struggling to get people into space, you lot are all over the place.'

'Hardly, but you are right. There are some major differences between our planets and our people, but in general your technology and standards of living are similar to the position we were in a considerable time ago.'

'How long ago?' Tom asked.

Jall thought for a moment before replying. 'Two to three hundred years, I'd estimate.'

'Bloody hell, you're that far ahead of us?' Siobhan gasped.

'We're that far behind?' Tom said.

The alien nodded, the size and shape of his bulbous head seeming to exaggerate the gesture. 'Approximately. I'm not really qualified to talk about history in any great detail. I only had a basic education in the subject.'

'So what's your specialism?' Siobhan asked. 'What was your role on the ship?'

'I was involved in gradation and storage logistics,' he explained. 'Once everything we'd mined had been processed in the refinery, I was part of the team dealing with the cargo.'

'Bloody hell, you had a refinery on board?' Tom said, surprised. 'Christ, just what did that ship do? I imagined you just went around collecting whatever you needed then hauled it all back to your planet.'

'Yes, but think about it, that would be an incredibly inefficient way of working. We'd have ended up taking back huge amounts of unnecessary waste material. Also, because of the length of our mission, we had sufficient time to process the materials ourselves. Rather than return home with a hold filled with ores, therefore, we were instead due to return with everything extracted, refined, and processed for immediate use.'

'So I assume you'd probably reached the same position we're rapidly heading towards?' Tom asked. 'You've already used up your own planet's resources.'

'Far from it. From the little I know about your recent history, it seems that your race has done far less forward thinking that we were doing at a comparable stage in our development. We knew what we'd need to support our growing population. Rather than dig it all up from our own backyard – as I think you'd say – we went further afield. Nothing you have here is unique, and it was exactly the same for us. All the minerals we needed could be found or recombined elsewhere. There was no need to destroy our own planet.'

'Which is fine if you're able to leave your planet and look elsewhere,' Tom said.

'Granted. And we were fortunate in that we have several mineral-rich moons in low orbits which we could mine with relative ease. You'll have the technology too before long. You should just be careful not to plunder too much, too soon.'

'Tell that to the idiots who actually make the decisions,' Rob said.

'We are,' Jall replied.

The friends were quiet for a moment as they considered the alien's words. Tom thought it amusing that here was this visitor, dispensing wisdom and advice which would benefit the whole world, to just him, his girlfriend and his brother as they sat outside his little bungalow in the middle of nowhere. They couldn't have been much further removed from positions of influence and power if they'd tried.

'Anyway,' he said, smirking, 'isn't the real reason you're here to steal our resources from under our noses? To snatch our world away from us?'

'Absolutely not,' Jall replied, offended.

'Tom!' Siobhan protested. 'What the hell did you say that for?'

'Just kidding,' he said, back-pedalling furiously, cursing himself for having put his foot in it again. 'It's a staple of our old science-fiction movies, that's all. I was just joking. I didn't mean anything by it.'

Rob clearly wasn't impressed. 'You can't just go around saying stuff like that anymore, Tom, even if you are only having a laugh. This is too important to screw up with a stupid throw-away comment.'

Belittled, Tom wasn't sure how to react. 'Look, I'm sorry. Like I said, I didn't mean anything by it.'

To his surprise, the alien sprung to his defence. 'Actually, Tom's right,' he said. 'We are just here to steal your water.' He paused, long enough for Rob and Siobhan to exchange confused, slightly concerned glances. The slight upward curl of his top lip gave away the fact that he was toying with them. Tom relaxed slightly, happy to be mocked. 'Though I wouldn't blame anyone for wondering, we're not here for your water, your people or anything else. You have nothing we couldn't find elsewhere, and your planet doesn't have anything we don't already have in abundance.'

Keen to show that he really hadn't meant any offence, Tom tried to feign interest and prolong the conversation.

'So where exactly do you stand in the overall scheme of things, Jall?' he asked. The alien didn't answer immediately, and Tom qualified his question further. 'There are over three hundred of you, so how far up the chain of command are you? Do you sit at the captain's table, or are you...?'

'Am I what?'

He took a deep breath, knowing he was about to re-offend. 'Bottom of the heap? Ship's grunt?'

Jall was unperturbed. 'We don't have formal ranking structures, as such,' he explained. 'There's no real need. There are a finite number of jobs which need to be carried out, and all those individual jobs need to be completed correctly for the overall task to be successful. Success or failure can have the same repercussions whatever level one works at. Whether you're the pilot of the ship or you were involved in building it, the ultimate responsibilities are broadly similar. I was trained to carry out a role and I did that to the best of my ability, as did the pilots and the navigators, the technicians and the maintenance staff. Everyone. It's a collaborative effort.'

'So whose fault was it the ship got damaged?'

'No one's fault. As I said, it was a freak accident.'

'But shouldn't you have been prepared for freak accidents if you're all so highly trained and effective? Shouldn't all risk have been eradicated?'

'Tom, what's got into you?' Siobhan asked. 'Jall's a guest, not a prisoner. What's with the interrogation?'

'I'm just interested, that's all.'

'I don't mind,' Jall said, and Tom believed him.

'You can see where I'm coming from though, can't you? It doesn't matter how advanced and intelligent you are, you can still get caught out.'

'We had complete control over everything we *could* control, but there are always things which will be beyond even the most meticulous planners. We're largely scientists, Tom, not fortune tellers.'

'But shouldn't you have had some kind of contingency plans? Lifeboats or something like that? A get-out clause?'

'You're it, I think,' he replied.

'So do you enjoy your job?' Siobhan asked, again doing what she could to steer the conversation into more banal, safer waters. Rob returned from the kitchen with more beer. Tom hadn't even noticed him get up.

'There's no point liking or disliking it, is there?' Jall said. 'It's what I was trained to do. It's what I always knew I'd be doing, and I do it well. I know everything there is to know about the role.'

'But don't you ever yearn to do something different?'

'No.'

'Don't you ever look at the person who lives next door to you and think, *I want what he's got?*' Tom asked. 'Haven't you ever wanted to escape from your routine?'

'No.'

'So where's the passion? Where's the spontaneity and excitement?'

'There's no need,' Jall said, his tone beginning to sound frustratingly matter-of-fact, as if he was simply reciting learned responses.

'No need?' Tom protested. 'I'd argue there's every need. If everything's planned out for you and you know the end result, why bother? Where's the reward? Aren't you just going through the motions?'

'You're starting to become deliberately antagonistic now,' the alien said, still sounding maddeningly unflappable.

'Okay, okay. Look, I'm sorry. I'm just struggling to understand, that's all.'

'You don't have to. It's not your life.'

'And I'm pretty pleased about that. For crying out loud, you even know when you're going to die, don't you?'

'Approximately. But you make that sound like a bad thing. It's not. It allows us to prepare and be ready as the time draws near. We can say our goodbyes and get our affairs in order.'

There was a moment of quiet as the others paused to consider what he'd said, each of them individually thinking about how they might spend their own time differently if they knew how long they'd got. Tom imagined them all being stamped with 'Best Before' dates like the food on supermarket shelves.

'We're going to head back to Willsham in a while. Jall's staying in a place just off campus.' Rob said.

'How did you get here?' Siobhan asked.

'Pool car,' he replied. 'I've got to get it back by morning.'

'Which way did you come?'

'Straight into Drayton then out again.'

Tom looked at them both in disbelief. There was an alien in the house and yet all they wanted to talk about were travel arrangements. He wasn't going to let this opportunity go. He wasn't quite finished with their visitor yet.

'So what happens when two of you have a disagreement,' he asked. Siobhan groaned. 'Last question, then I'll shut up.'

'What do you mean?' Jall said. 'Be more specific.'

'Well we've all seen this utopian society of yours on TV. In spite of what you've said, I'm still having trouble believing that it all runs as smoothly as you say it does, particularly as you being here is living proof that things don't always go to plan. So what happens when two of you have a difference of opinion?'

'Even the most complicated decisions can be broken down to the most basic of choices. Everything boils down to yes or no, on or off, if you analyse it enough.'

'You think?'

'Absolutely. You just have to think logically.'

Tom barely managed to suppress a grin. The alien was getting dangerously close to the realms of parody now. He was starting to sound like Mr Spock.

'So what happens when you don't have time? What about when you need to make a snap decision? Life or death?'

'There's a process. A way of thinking.'

'So you all think the same way? How come you're not all just clones?'

'Because free thought and expression is still encouraged. We live and work within a specific framework, but what we do within that framework is still open to individual interpretation.'

'Do you believe in gods?' Rob asked

'No.'

'And you all get on?' Tom said.

'To an extent. There's plenty of tolerance and very little conflict, if that's what you mean.'

'What about when you meet someone you don't like. There must have been someone...'

'My race or alien?'

'Your race,' Tom immediately replied. 'Alien.'

He shook his head.

'No one's ever pissed you off?'

'Pissed me off?'

'Got on your nerves? Annoyed you?'

'You're the first for a while.'

'Any of your own kind?'

'No.'

'So let me see if I've got this right... you live in a perfect world where there's no resentment or discrimination, where everyone gets on with everyone else and...'

'Tom,' Siobhan snapped at him angrily, 'for fuck's sake, will you give it a rest?'

He ignored her and continued. '...and you all do everything for the greater good and...'

'What's your point?' Rob butted in, sounding equally annoyed.

'My point is I find it hard to believe any of this. I keep coming back to the same point, if everything's so perfect, why did you end up here with your bloody spaceship fucked?'

'Because, as I've already explained, although we're well-ordered and controlled, the rest of the universe isn't.' Jall sounded remarkably calm. 'Believe what you like, Tom, the fact is it's all true. We work together because it's the collective effort of each one of us that keeps the integrity of our society strong. We are all equal.'

'And do you feel superior?'

'Superior to what?'

'Us.'

The alien thought carefully for a moment, maintaining eye contact with Tom. 'Yes,' he finally answered. 'How could I not?'


The conversation continued long into the night without Tom who took himself away to cool off. He was disappointed with himself, but stood by the questions he'd asked and concerns he'd raised. He came to the conclusion that it was the alien's placid, Vulcan-like calm and holier-than-thou demeanour which had annoyed him more than anything.

He calmed himself down with more beer and loud music. He lay on his bed, headphones in, a half empty can in his hand, and tried to clear his mind of everything for a while. But the alien was in his thoughts constantly.

The music – an album he'd played hundreds of times over the years but which still mattered to him as much as when he'd first fallen in love with it – helped him to focus. Each song meant something different, every new track reminding him of a moment in time. The lyrics resonated. Every last note mattered. And he found himself thinking: how could something as unique as this music have been created without character, personality and spontaneity? Riffs were the results of happy accidents. Drum beats and loops were discovered through improvisation and chance. The lyrics were written by the vocalist in response to situations and people from his life... Christ, even the dire, manufactured pop music which was being mass-consumed these days sometimes still had a spark of originality. Maybe that would change? He wondered if, perhaps, in the not-too-distant future, music would be written and performed entirely by computers which had been programmed to create tunes which would tick all the right boxes and illicit the required emotional response from the listener? Was that what really scared him about the alien's words? Was this the shape of things to come?

The things he'd heard reminded him of *Brave New World*, *1984*, and other books he'd been forced to study at school. Bland, anodyne futures. Repellent and ugly. Everything he despised. A dystopia in a utopian disguise.

*How dare that fucker think himself above us. Where's their passion? Where's their motivation. There's got to be more to life than just living.*

# 17

'I'm worried about you,' Siobhan said, sitting down on the bed next to him. She'd come inside for more drinks. Tom had lost track of time. It was dark now but the conversation outside on the patio was still in full flow.

'I'm okay,' he said. 'Sorry about earlier.'

'It's not me you need to apologise to.'

'I know.'

'Look, Rob's taking him back in a little while. Come back outside, will you.'

She took Tom's hand and led him out to the others, pausing only to pick up a tray of hot drinks she'd made. Tom sheepishly followed her. Rob and Jall's conversation briefly stopped.

'I was out of order earlier,' Tom said to the alien. 'Sorry I gave you such a hard time.'

'It's understandable,' Jall replied. 'You weren't expecting me to come here. Maybe your brother should have checked first.'

'No, it's me. I'm sorry.'

'Tom's had a tough year,' Siobhan explained.

'I heard about your parents,' the alien said. 'That must have been difficult for you.'

'You can say that again,' Rob mumbled.

'You see,' Jall continued, 'there's not such an impossible gulf between us after all. My family back home must be feeling bereaved. In fact, I feel it myself. When we were drifting, before we found life on your planet, it looked for a while as if we'd have very little chance of surviving, never mind getting back home. Now we've more hope, but things are still uncertain. The thought of never seeing my wife, my children and the rest of my family again is too much to bear. What I'm saying, Tom, is that I think I understand your pain.'

*

146

Hours later, when the others were long gone and Tom and Siobhan lay together in bed, Siobhan leant across and stroked Tom's hair.

'I meant what I said earlier. I am worried about you.'

'There's no need to be. I'm fine.'

'No you're not.'

'Yes I am.'

'So what was all that about tonight then? You were downright rude to Jall. Honest, Tom, the poor guy's stranded millions of miles from home, separated from everything and everyone he cares about, and you were laying into him. It was completely unjustified. It was embarrassing.'

Tom struggled to answer. He was thankful of the dark so he could avoid eye contact.

'I just have a hard time swallowing some of the things I hear about the aliens, that's all.'

'Is that all? You're starting to sound like a bigot. I think there's more to it.'

'Like what?'

'There's all that stuff with your parents for starters, and—'

'Mum and Dad have got nothing to do with it. They're gone and I've accepted that and—'

'—and I don't think you have. I think you've just run away from it all.'

'How can you say that? What else am I supposed to do? The inquests have been completed, their estates have been settled... there's nothing left to run away from.'

'Yes there is. Bloody hell, Tom, you can be so blinkered at times. Don't get me wrong, I'm glad you came to Thatcham because you're the best thing that's happened to me in a long time, but I think you've left a lot of unfinished business behind.'

'You're wrong.'

'I think you should go back. You should take me. Show me

the place where you used to live and where you worked. Introduce me to some of the friends you left behind.'

'You wouldn't like them...'

'Let me make that decision, sweetheart. I think there's a lot you're not dealing with here, and it's starting to show itself as anger.'

'I'm not angry.'

'You were tonight.'

'I wasn't, I was frustrated. There's a difference between being angry and being frustrated...'

'Not from where I was sitting. Listen, I'm not saying you *shouldn't* be angry, I just think you need to try and deal with it better. More constructively. Stop aiming it at the aliens.'

Another silence. Tom didn't know what to say. Was she right? He wished she'd go to sleep. He didn't want to think about it tonight.

'You okay?' she asked after waiting too long for him to say something.

'I'm okay.'

'Are you going to talk to me?'

'I don't know what to say.'

'Will you take me to Birmingham? Let me have a look at who you used to be.'

Tom thought he didn't have any option. He couldn't think of a good enough reason not to. 'I suppose. Can't promise it'll be very exciting.'

'Let me decide that. I'm not looking for excitement, I just want you to be okay. Anyway, you might be surprised. You might want to go back there permanently.'

'I doubt it.'

'You might. The world's changing, Tom. You never know what's around the corner these days.'

'The world's always changing. It changes every day. Always has been, always will be.'

'Yes but the pace of change is different now and if anything it's going to get even faster.'

'Bloody hell, stop patronising me.'

'Then stop being so touchy. I just think you need to open up some more. Give these people a chance. You're a bloody pessimist, and it's doing my head in. You're right, all the things we're hearing do sound incredible and yes, a lot of it *is* hard to believe, but we *have to try*. You've said yourself, the human race is on a downward spiral and people are pre-programmed to fuck up and fight with each other, but there's no reason why we can't change the programming, is there? Not now they've shown us how.'

'Why does everyone think they're bloody philosophers these days,' he grumbled unhelpfully, turning onto his side. She pulled him over onto his back again.

'Maybe it's because we've all been given an incredible opportunity,' she said. 'This is our chance to turn everything around and make something of ourselves. They said on the news we've reached a pivotal moment in history, and we're right at the centre of it all, Tom, you and me. I don't want you to miss out and get left behind. You've got to get over this anti-alien mind-set because it's not doing anyone any good. Accept them for who and what they are.'

# Part iii
# ACCEPTANCE

## 18

Almost three weeks passed before Tom finally reneged and agreed to take Siobhan to where he'd lived before breaking away and settling down in Thatcham. She'd taken a day off mid-week, her first day's holiday since the end of summer. It was autumn now. All the greens had turned to reds and browns.

Siobhan seemed genuinely excited. 'I've never been to Birmingham before.'

'Hope you're not disappointed.'

'Oh, I won't be. I'm easily pleased.'

The journey took the best part of two hours. They talked intermittently, but neither felt the need to chatter constantly. Tom thought that was a good thing. He remembered his mum telling him it was a sign of being relaxed in someone's company not to have to fill every moment of silence with unnecessary noise. Being close to someone didn't just mean talking to them, she used to say. He thought that was ironic, because Dad used to complain that she never shut up.

The traffic on the motorway increased in volume and decreased in speed as they approached the city. Tom felt a strange fluttering in his stomach, an unexpected attack of nerves. He didn't know what he had to be scared about; they were only going to be here for a few hours, if that, and these were all places he'd been to countless times before. It had been more than six months since he'd last been here. He'd rather have left it a little longer before coming back.

They drove right into the city centre. The amount of traffic took Tom by surprise initially. It seemed busier than he remembered, but he accepted that was probably because he'd had half a year living in a village where, until the aliens had arrived, it had been unusual to see more than a handful of cars at any one time.

They parked at the Bullring, a large, distinctive-looking shopping mall. At one end of the development, the bulbous, futuristic-looking building nestled up alongside St Martin's Church, a place with roots traceable back hundreds of years. Even now it was a startling contrast of old meets new. Siobhan's small-town upbringing was immediately apparent.

'Wow,' she said, mouth hanging open. 'Fancy, isn't it?'

'Didn't think you'd be that impressed. You've seen aliens now. Your imagination knows no earthly bounds.'

'Don't take the piss,' she grumbled as they disappeared down into the underground car park.

'I wasn't.'


'Funny how it's just like all the other malls inside, isn't it?' Siobhan said as they wandered through the crowded shopping centre. She was right, of course. No matter how visually striking the building appeared from the outside, once you were in it looked much the same as every other shopping centre built in the last fifteen years. The same shops, the same décor, the same layout to an extent, all of it carefully designed either to maximise the experience for the shopper or generate the most profit, depending on your perspective.

'Any shops you want to go to?'

'Nothing in particular,' she replied, 'but you know me and shops.'

Tom wasn't one for stereotyping, but as far as shopping was concerned, he thought it amusing how men and women all too easily slipped into their expected roles. When he needed something, he'd go to a shop he knew sold the item, and then buy it. Even better, he'd get it online. Siobhan, on the other hand, liked to browse and compare endlessly before spending a single penny.

She started down the familiar route, spending an age looking at shoes she didn't really need, before checking herself and remembering why they'd come here.

'Sorry, Tom,' she said unexpectedly. 'This is your day. We're not here to go shopping.'

'It's okay,' he replied. 'We've got plenty of time.'

She smiled. 'You'll regret saying that! Mind if I just have a look here?' She gestured towards another boutique. 'Last one, I promise.'

'You carry on,' he said. 'Mind if I don't come in? I'll meet you out here somewhere.'

She tenderly squeezed his hand, then disappeared into the shop. He looked around for inspiration, wondering if there was something nearby which might distract him for a while and stop him thinking about where he was and why he was here. There were a few stores he used, but nothing which really grabbed him. He didn't want any clothes, wasn't in the mood for watching films, hadn't read any books for a while, had all but given up on games... He ambled a short distance further into the mall, cutting through the early lunchtime crowds, thinking about finding somewhere to eat once Siobhan had finished shopping. It was then that he noticed the crowd up ahead, in a space near the middle of the mall usually reserved for promotional displays. Semi-interested, Tom walked towards it. He'd seen all kinds of crap here in the years he'd worked in the city, from Barbie to Mario and everything in between – underpaid students in fancy dress costumes, doing all they could to attract the attention of passing kids, demonstrating the latest game, console, or whatever the current trend was.

But this was different.

As he approached, he saw an alien standing on a plinth. It was such a damn good likeness, that it was only when he'd got to within a couple of metres that he realised it was a dummy. It looked like Jall, perfectly proportioned and uncannily life-like.

'Anything I can help you with,' a smartly-dressed woman said, taking him by surprise.

'No. No, thanks, I'm fine.'

She smiled and offered him a brochure which he took without thinking. He walked further into the crowded area, and followed the general flow of the people around him. There was a number of large display units, some of them with screens built in, all of them providing information on certain aspects of the aliens. More specifically, he realised, it was information about getting along with aliens and the finer points of alien-human etiquette. It was strangely fascinating and, he had to admit, very well put together. The details were genuinely useful, if a little unnecessary in his opinion. He glanced at the brochure he'd been given which was similarly comprehensive.

'Here you are,' Siobhan said, grabbing his arm. 'Couldn't find you. What's all this?'

He gave her the brochure. 'I forget, most people here probably haven't seen an alien close-up.'

'I was thinking that earlier. Goes to show how lucky we are in comparison, living in Thatcham. Bloody hell, Tom, your brother's best friend is one of them!'

'Bit over the top though, isn't it?'

'Do you think? Personally, I think it's fantastic. The more information that's available, the better. It's when we stop educating people about all of this that we'll start hitting problems.'

'I still think it's a bit much.'

Siobhan frowned at him. 'We've talked about this, Tom. You've got to ease up on the anti-alien sentiment.'

'And I keep telling you, I'm not anti-alien, I just—'

'I know what you keep telling me, but you're saying one thing and doing another. People will get the wrong impression.'

They left the Bullring after another hour. Tom saw an old work colleague in the crowds, and decided that enough was enough. He wanted out before he was recognised.

They walked the streets for a while. A comic book shop,

where Tom and Rob had spent far too many hours in their younger days, hiding from their parents and the rest of the world by escaping into magnificently drawn fantasies, looked very different today. Siobhan didn't pick up on it – she wouldn't have – but to Tom it was obvious. The window of the store was filled with posters and pictures of the aliens. A scale model of their ship dominated the main display. There were action figures, magazines, play sets, mugs and T-shirts...

'Do you want any of this stuff?' Siobhan asked. 'Can't see the appeal myself.'

'No thanks,' he replied. 'I preferred it when it was all make believe.'

Harborne.

Like many parts of Birmingham, this green and leafy suburb was a mix of the old and the new, the affluent and the not so. Tower blocks rubbed shoulders with large, detached homes. A new hospital (which looked like something the aliens might have built) dominated the skyline.

Siobhan watched Tom intently as they drove down quiet streets. It was much of a muchness to her, really, nothing special. A nice place to live, but nothing to write home about. But for Tom this *was* home. At least it had been. From age six until the end of last year, this place had been where he'd spent much of his time.

The narrow roads were filled with cars. There was barely any space, residents and office workers jostling for limited positions. Tom gave up trying to get parked. He drove around and around, then stopped in the middle of one street which Siobhan was sure they'd been down several times already.

He was looking out of his window, face turned away from her, hiding the tears.

'This it?'

'Yep.'

'We could go in.'

'Someone else lives there now.'

'They wouldn't mind.'

'I would if I was them.'

'It's a nice place.'

'It was.'

'Things change, Tom.'

'Feels like everything's changed.'

'You should go in. Seriously. Leave the car with me.'

'I'm not going in. What would that achieve?' he snapped at her angrily. He glanced across and saw that he'd hurt her, then looked away again. 'Sorry.'

'It's okay.'

'I just want...' he started to say then stopped.

'I just want you to be happy,' Siobhan said, finishing the sentence for him. 'I love you, Tom. I hate seeing you like this.'

'Like what?'

'So full of hurt. So angry with the rest of the world. You've got to let it go. You've got to deal with it. It's eating you up.'

Tom wanted to tell her she was right, but he didn't think he could. The words felt trapped at the back of his throat. He put the car into gear and pulled away.

# 19

The following Tuesday evening, Tom arranged to pick Siobhan up from work. He arrived at the office in plenty of time, but she was seeing a client. He waited for her at her desk.

'Want a coffee, Tom?' Mona, Siobhan's manager, asked.

'If you don't mind. Don't you want to get going though? It's gone five.'

'Nah, it's fine. I'm going to be stuck here a while yet. Got a stack of paperwork to do, but I could do with a break.'

She locked the door, switched the sign to 'closed', then went out to the small kitchen out back. Tom waited for her to return, trying not to look at Siobhan's paperwork, but finding his eyes wandering. Her diary was open and was full of appointments. There were post-it notes stuck around the edge of her computer screen reminding her to email one client and phone another, to set up a meeting and chase up a file. Her wire in-tray was full to overflowing with papers. It reminded him of the desks he used to sit behind, and he felt a strange sense of nostalgia. Christ, was he actually beginning to miss work?

He felt uncomfortable sitting in her chair, and so got up and walked across the room and looked through the window onto the damp streets of Thatcham outside. This was Siobhan's world, and he didn't want to intrude. It wasn't that he didn't have any interest, more that he was keen to respect boundaries. His life, by comparison, was completely open to her. Problem was, he decided, right now there was very little in his life worth seeing.

'You okay?' Mona asked. He spun around, startled. He hadn't heard her return.

'Fine,' he replied. 'Miles away, that's all.'

Siobhan's appointment finished half an hour later. Tom had

wondered whether she'd want to go out for dinner then go on and see a film, but she wasn't keen.

'I'm knackered,' she'd said as they walked back to the car through the rain. 'I'd rather just spend the night at home if you don't mind.'

They agreed to go back to her flat and spend the night there, calling into one of the large, hangar-like supermarkets on the outskirts of Drayton to pick up supplies first.

'This is good, isn't it,' she said, pointing at a huge display rack full of confectionary and puddings.

'Is it?' He couldn't understand what was so special about it. In fact, the more he looked at it, the less sense it made. Since when did supermarkets display this kind of unhealthy, artificial crap alongside the fruit and vegetables? They were usually at opposite ends of the store.

'Yes,' she said. 'It's good that they're thinking of everyone.'

'Are they?'

'Bloody hell, keep up, Tom!' She picked up a tub of sickly sweet honeycomb. 'Jall was saying he can get through a couple of tubs of this stuff in a day. And he stays so thin! It's not fair. You know me, I only have to look at this kind of stuff and I put weight on.'

Tom walked on, keen to fill their trolley with stuff they needed, not waste time looking at what they didn't. Thankfully the store was relatively quiet. Siobhan's late finish meant they'd missed the bulk of people who shopped on the way home from work, and the school-related traffic was long gone too. Once done, Tom loaded their shopping onto the conveyor and watched as the glassy-eyed checkout operator scanned it all through. He handed her his bank card.

'Can't use that,' she said.

'What?'

'Can't use that at this till. There's a sign.' She pointed to a large sign hanging above her station, blowing slightly in the breeze from the air conditioning. Tom looked up.

'Biometric payments only. What's all that about? I've been coming here and using the same card for months. What's the problem?'

'It's a trial. We're a trial store. This is a trial till.'

'Well no one told me.'

'Like I said, there's a sign,' she repeated, pointing up.

'This is a joke. What the hell's a biometric payment anyway?'

'If you want to use that card you'll have to go to another till.'

'But I've unpacked all our stuff now.'

'You could re-pack it.'

'Or you could just take my payment. This is ridiculous. Is there a manager here I can talk to?'

Siobhan swapped places with him, conscious there were people waiting. 'Leave it, Tom. I'll get it,' she said, and she put her thumb on a finger pad where the card reader used to be. Tom continued bagging up their food. 'Did you not get a letter from the bank?' she asked.

'I get loads of letters from the bank. Most of them are crap and I bin them. Just marketing junk.'

'Don't you think it'd be a good idea to read them from time to time?'

'I don't know,' he grumbled, picking up their bags. 'They're only ever trying to sell me something or get me to invest money I haven't got with them.'

'Or they might be telling you about the new payment system they're trialling.'

'I haven't heard anything about it.'

She put the last bag in the trolley and started back towards the car. 'Well you should have. It's been all over the TV. They're trialling it here first because we've got a relatively high proportion of visitors. Honestly, Tom, that was embarrassing.'

'What have aliens got to do with it?'

'Jesus, you really haven't been paying attention. It's based on their tech. I mean, we've had this kind of stuff for years, but they've helped the banks take it to another level. It makes payment processing more efficient, cuts down the risk of fraud.'

'So what are you saying? That your thumb is now linked to your current account?'

'Something like that. Yours would be too if you'd read the letter like everyone else.'


Tom cooked their meal in the small kitchen of Siobhan's one-bedroom flat. It was a decent enough place – she had half the ground floor of a large, Victorian house which had been converted into four apartments. The rent was reasonable, and the surrounding area was pleasant enough. Siobhan kept the place pristine and had been there long enough to make her mark, tastefully decorating the limited space and making it her own. But Tom had been wondering for a while now if it was time for them to reconsider their living arrangements.

'Are you coping with the rent on this place?' he asked clumsily as they ate in front of the TV.

'Of course I am,' she said, surprised by his question. 'Why do you ask? I've been here almost three years.'

'I was just thinking, it's a lot to be paying out each month.'

'Are you offering to pay my rent for me?'

'No, I was just wondering if it was time to get rid of the flat, that's all. We've been together more than six months and...'

'I like my space,' she said quickly. The speed of her answer took him by surprise. Hurt him.

'Oh, okay. It's just that you spend a lot of time at mine, and I was thinking about all that cash you're paying out each month.'

'Tom, are you trying to help me save money or are you asking me to move in with you?'

'Both,' he said, sounding unsure. 'Actually, I'm asking you to move in with me. Or at least think about it.'

Siobhan put down her knife and fork. She looked across at

him and smiled. 'That's really sweet.'

'Sweet? Is it?'

'Yes.'

'So what do you think?'

'I'm not sure.'

Tom's heart sank. Frantic thoughts rushed through his mind. *Have I read too much into this relationship? Does she mean more to me than I mean to her? Thank God I didn't ask her to marry me...*

'Why?'

'Two reasons,' she explained, 'one is a practical reason, both are equally valid. First, I'm halfway through a twelve month tenancy. I signed an extension just after we started seeing each other, remember?'

'I remember,' he said. He'd forgotten.

'Second,' she began, pausing to choose her words carefully, 'I want this to be something we're both completely sure about.'

'I'm sure.'

'Are you?'

'Yes,' he answered, beginning to doubt himself. 'I wouldn't have mentioned it if I wasn't.'

'It's just that you've not been yourself these last few weeks. I think you've got a lot going on in that head of yours, and until you sort it all out, I don't think you'll be able to know what it is you really want.'

'I already know that. I want you.'

'I'm not talking about sex.'

'Neither am I.'

'I'm talking about commitment and long term plans. I feel like you're on the rebound from your past, and I don't want to make any decisions about what I'm going to do with my life until I'm completely sure you want me to be a part of yours.'

'But...'

'Tommy, sweetheart, I'm not saying no. I already know that I want to be with you for the rest of my life. I just want *you* to be sure that this is the life you want before we both take that leap.'

# 20

Friday night. The Badger's Sett. Punter levels in the pub had reduced to almost normal. Tom was relieved. Drinking sessions were becoming much more pleasurable again.

'Business good, John?' he asked.

'Mustn't grumble,' the landlord replied as he pulled Tom's pint. 'To be honest, I made so much over these last couple of months, it wouldn't matter if no one else came in here for the rest of the year. I'd still be quids in.'

'I'll be here,' Tom smirked, 'don't you worry.'

'I knew you wouldn't let me down,' John laughed.

Tom returned to the others. Siobhan and James were waiting for him, Rob was due shortly.

'Work okay, James?' Tom asked, regretting his words the moment he'd spoken them.

'No.'

'Ah right,' he said, supping his pint and hoping that would be the end of it.

'Got me on a bloody disciplinary now, haven't they.'

'Disciplinary,' Siobhan said, 'what for?'

'Insubordination.'

'Thought that was just if you were in the army,' Tom said. 'What did you do?'

'You see, that's what really pisses me off. You've already assumed I'm guilty. What chance have I got if my own mates turn on me like that?'

'I haven't turned on you,' Tom said. 'I just asked what happened. All right, I'll rephrase it. What have they *alleged* you've done?'

'Oh, I did it all right,' he replied, barely concealing a self-satisfied smirk. 'I told Sachs he was out of his fucking tree.'

'You didn't,' Siobhan gasped. 'Your boss?'

'I did. Right in the middle of a bloody staff meeting. Well, it was his own fault. He pushed me too far.'

'You idiot,' she said.

'Couldn't help myself. There's only so much I can take. I'd had enough.'

'But your boss! And with all those witnesses. You divot. What did Steph say?'

'Haven't told her and I don't intend to. I'll probably just get my wrist slapped.'

'I hope so for your sakes.'

'Well, the hearing's on Tuesday morning, so if I come knocking on your door looking for a job on Tuesday afternoon, Siobhan, you'll know things didn't go well.'

She looked over at Tom and shook her head in disbelief. James was about to speak again when, to the others' relief, the pub door opened and distracted him. Rob came inside, followed by Jall.

'Here they come,' James said. 'Glad I'm not getting the next round in. He drinks like a fish, that boy.'

'Who, Rob?'

'No, Jall. They all do. They can certainly take their beer.'

Rob and Jall got their drinks at the bar then joined the others. James was right; the alien had two pints to everyone else's one. And two bars of chocolate.

'Evening,' Rob said, pulling up a chair next to Tom.

'Everyone all right?' Jall asked, sitting down across the table. Tom watched him, and he couldn't help but think how much the alien had already changed in the short time he'd known him. It was a given that the Earth and its indigenous population would have been affected by the arrival of the extra-terrestrials, and that had certainly proved to be the case. He'd seen footage of fields of crops being grown in the desert, for example, and a test spaceship which had been launched last week that looked like one of the old, decommissioned space shuttles, redesigned by alien eyes. But Tom hadn't counted on how the aliens too would have been altered by the experience of being here. He remembered the night he'd first met Jall, when they'd sat out on the patio and Tom had given him hell about various aspects of the visitors' lifestyles. He'd seemed cold and distant that night, understandably guarded. Now that guard had most definitely been dropped. He leaned back in his chair, overlong legs crossed casually, wearing a bizarre amalgam of alien and human-style clothes. Maybe they were selling them in the shops now, next to the displays of alien preferred food. For a moment he was gone, daydreaming about seeing new signs in department stores: menswear, womenswear, childrenswear, alienswear...

'Did you hear that?' Siobhan asked, nudging him.

'No, sorry. Did I hear what?'

Rob answered. 'The stuff Jall's been doing at the uni today. It's incredible.'

'Go on.'

Rob looked at Jall, then continued. 'The staff there have been using some of Jall's lot's medical tech, and the results have been remarkable. You tell him, Jall.'

'A while back,' the alien began, 'we made a series of breakthroughs which allowed us to work on the individual components of any molecule at any level. I won't bore you with the detail...'

'But it means you can cure cancer and turn coal into gold,' Rob interrupted.

Jall nodded and finished his first pint. 'Pretty much.'

'So what are you saying, that you can turn anything into anything?' Tom asked.

'Not quite,' the alien replied, 'but the potential's there.'

'And that's what they were doing in the medical centre today,' Rob added. 'Changing cancer cells back to healthy cells again. Oh, and they've already been fixing broken bones and damaged nerves.'

'We have to be cautious,' Jall said. 'It might be that there are complications when adapting our processes to humans. That's why we're only working on people with terminal illnesses, and physical injuries that aren't otherwise going to get any better.'

'But that's not the best bit,' Rob continued. 'You'll never believe this. He took me into the lab this afternoon. They're only growing someone a new fucking arm! It's amazing. There's this kid who lost his arm in a bomb blast in Afghan or somewhere, and they're growing him a new arm!'

Even Tom had to admit that was impressive.

'The implications are vast,' Siobhan said. 'People might never get sick again.'

Tom thought about what she'd just said, but resisted the temptation to respond, worried that she'd see any questioning as a thinly veiled attack on the aliens. That was never his intention, but he knew that was how he'd probably come across. Tom used to bullshit for a living, but since leaving the corporate world he'd definitely lost his touch. Since coming to Thatcham he'd found it increasingly difficult to be anything but completely honest, and that wasn't always for the best.

'Good technology gets smaller and smaller, and once you can manipulate things at the most minute level,' Jall continued to explain to his enthralled audience, 'you start to look at the universe in a whole new way. Anything becomes possible.'

'It's a whole sea-change,' Rob said. 'You wouldn't believe the guys in the labs, they're going crazy for this stuff. It's a fundamental shift.'

'We were talking earlier,' Jall continued. 'One of our colleagues said it felt like the invention of the silicon chip and the development of the microprocessor.'

'How so?' Tom asked.

'Think about it... you start by using those discoveries to create computers. Fast forward twenty or thirty years, and you have the descendants of those computers everywhere, affecting every aspect of your lives. Transport, communication, entertainment, healthcare...'

Rob felt obliged to state the obvious, more for James' benefit than anyone else. 'So one major discovery, or set of discoveries, has almost infinite repercussions.'

'Like changing cancer cells back into healthy cells again?' Siobhan asked.

'Exactly,' Jall said. 'Back home we've long since stopped thinking about medicinal care purely in terms of the individual parts of the body. We're more concerned with the individual parts which make the individual parts, which make the individual parts. Does that make sense? I remember saying to you a while back, Tom, every problem can be reduced to a yes or no decision if you drill down far enough.'

'So what are you really saying?' Tom asked. 'Are you saying you can change *everything*?'

'Theoretically, yes. But being *able* to do something doesn't necessarily mean you *have* to do it.'

'This is getting too heavy for a Friday night booze-up,' James said, putting down an empty glass and getting up to go to the bar. 'I can't keep up with it all.'

The others were distracted by his interruption. Tom wasn't. 'How many people would have that kind of power and not use it?'

'You're thinking in human terms again.'

'They're the only terms I know.'

'We're different. Very different.'

'So why do you die?'

'Oh, don't start this again,' Siobhan groaned.

Tom squeezed her hand. 'I'm not. Honestly, I don't want to pick a fight. I just want to understand.'

'We die because it's all part of the plan. There has to be progression. We can't keep bringing new life into the world and

169

not let the old lives go. It wouldn't be right. We still age.'

'But you could sort that little problem out if you wanted to.'

'Theoretically we could, but there are incredibly strict ethics codes which control such things.'

James was back with more beer. 'Drink, chill out, stop talking bollocks,' he ordered.

# 21

More than two months had passed since the aliens had arrived. The days were shorter and the nights much colder and longer now. The sun seemed to rarely show its face, hidden almost permanently behind a layer of heavy grey cloud. Dense fogs frequently blew in off the sea, often so impenetrable that Tom could barely see anything from the windows of his home. Sometimes it was easy to believe that the village and everything else had completely disappeared, leaving just the bungalow on the hill.

But it wasn't just the physical appearance of the world which had continued to change. The influence of the aliens was far reaching, so much so that it was difficult now to remember what life had been like before they'd arrived. The visitors seemed to have skewed all perspectives. On one hand, the Earth now felt like just one small speck of dust amongst billions: fragile and insignificant. On the other, the aliens appeared to be giving the human race a 'bunk up', their influence having substantially increased mankind's reach and ambition. Tom thought it felt as if the physical size of the human race had been diminished, but at the same time the volume of its collective voice had been cranked up to previously unheard levels.

Tom found it easier to accept the aliens now that he could see tangible benefits starting to appear. Last week, the first manned expedition to Mars had been announced. It was due to launch mid-April. Gone were the days when years of planning, selection, research and training were necessary. The farmers in the former deserts were preparing to harvest their crops, grown in previously lifeless dustbowls. Just last week a massive earthquake in the Pacific Ocean had, with alien help, been predicted, then prevented. Had they not been here, thousands of people, maybe even tens or hundreds of thousands, would have lost their lives or at the very least their homes as a result of the quake and subsequent tsunami and aftershocks.

In the short time they'd been here, the aliens had changed the face of the planet at a faster rate than humans had ever managed. They never gave the impression of taking over or preaching, rather they were careful to offer their help when appropriate and point out things which could be done better, or things which were being done wrong.

But Tom still didn't feel entirely comfortable.

He lay in bed next to Siobhan, unable to sleep. The numbers on the alarm clock glowed in the dark. Half-four. He'd been watching the clock since just after two when he'd first woken up. Siobhan rolled over, turning her back on him, and he put his arm around her and edged closer, hoping she'd wake up. Back in those first frantic days and weeks of their relationship, it wouldn't have taken much to start something at moments like this, no matter how tired they were. The first rush of passion which accompanied their love affair was definitely beginning to fade. She grumbled something, half-asleep, but otherwise didn't respond. *Maybe she's just cold*, he thought. *It could just be the time of year, or the time of the month. Or the fact she's got to go to work in the morning. Then again, it might just be me.*

He held her tightly, not wanting to let go.

# 22

The following day was uneventful. Tom took Siobhan to work then returned home. With Rob at university, the small house felt deceptively huge. His footsteps seemed to echo off the walls. Even the constant soundtrack of brain-atrophying daytime TV didn't do anything to make him feel less alone. He felt disconnected from the stream of news reports, soaps, alien documentaries, dramas and re-runs. He tried reading, gaming, drawing... nothing helped. Even wasting an hour surfing the Internet for soft-core porn felt like a chore.

Just before four, when the last light of the afternoon had begun to fade away, he drove to Clare's house. It was Penny's birthday, and he'd planned to drop a card and present around. He thought it was a sad indictment of what his life had become lately, that delivering a card to a nine year old on her birthday was the highlight of his week. He'd planned virtually his whole bloody day around this one non-event.

When he arrived at Clare's, there was no one there. He was on the verge of writing a note on the back of the envelope saying he was sorry he'd missed them and pushing it through the letter box, when Clare's heap of a car pulled up. He recognised the distinctive rattle of its struggling engine. He was parked on the other side of the road and they didn't notice him at first. He watched Penny race towards the house. She was her typical self – a bundle of effervescence and energy, cranked up to extreme levels because it was her birthday. Clare, by contrast, seemed subdued. She smiled at her daughter and said all the right things, but something clearly wasn't right.

'Clare?' Tom said. She spun around.

'Jesus, Tom. You scared the hell out of me.'

'Sorry.'

'Not your fault. I was miles away. Bad day.'

'Another one? Bloody hell, every time I see you you're having a bad day.'

'Yeah, well, that's just how it is at the moment.'

'What's happened?'

'Oh, the usual. Typical day at work, that's all. I'm sure you remember how it is.'

'I remember.'

He helped her unload a couple of bags of shopping from the back of the car and carried them over to the house.

'We had a meeting at the end of my shift,' Clare said as she unlocked the door and fumbled for the light switch. 'There was all the usual bullshit – typical staff arguments and the like – and I lost my patience. They're all going on and on about nothing and I'm just looking at the clock, trying to get out because I've got to get Penny from after-school club and it's her birthday and so on and so on.'

'You made it though.'

'Walked out in the end. I left them talking about the aliens.'

'What about them?'

'Whether we should offer them a dental service in the time they're here.'

'Are they here long enough?'

'Exactly. And if they can fly around the universe, I'm pretty bloody sure they can look after their teeth without our help.'

It wasn't as ridiculous as it sounded – Tom had heard the issue of alien healthcare being discussed on more than one occasion on TV recently – but it sounded like Clare was right to be annoyed. Debating the issue in the staff room of a two-bit dental surgery in the backstreets of Drayton was never going to be a constructive use of anyone's time, particularly not when Clare had far more important things to attend to at home.

Penny flew into the kitchen, arms loaded up with the presents she'd opened before leaving for school this morning. The house had been empty all day and it was uncomfortably cold, but she didn't seem bothered.

'I won't stop long,' Tom said. 'I'll be out of the way before everybody else turns up.'

Clare looked at him, then looked around. 'Everybody else? This is it, Tom.'

He was surprised, and for a moment a little uncomfortable. Was he missing something? Should he have been there? Clare was in a strange mood, and he thought he might be intruding on their routine, impinging on their mother-daughter time together. And yet he didn't sense she was trying to get rid of him. Did she need to talk? Did he want to listen?

'So what's really up?' he asked, deciding to take the bull by the horns.

'Nothing. I told you.'

'Come on, Clare, you do this to me every time. It's obvious there's more going on. Do you want to talk, or should I just piss off home?'

'Don't have a go at me,' she sniffed, unexpectedly close to tears. 'Why does everybody always have a go at me all the time? It feels like it's me against everyone else.'

'I'm not having a go. I want to help.'

'There's nothing you can do.'

'Try me.'

'Unless you're a hit-man on the quiet and you fancy taking someone out on the cheap.'

Aiden. No surprise. 'So what's he done this time?'

'It's what he hasn't done that hurts,' Clare explained, her voice cracking with emotion. Tom had never met her ex, knew nothing really about their relationship and why it had fallen apart other than what she'd told him, but he despised Aiden for the pain he'd caused and was clearly continuing to cause Clare. The fact it was Penny's birthday was no doubt compounding the problem, whatever the problem was.

'What do you mean? Tell me.'

175

'Well you've made the effort to come and see Penny on her birthday, haven't you.'

'You've not seen him yet today?'

'You've managed to get her a present and a card. That's more than that fucker has.'

'You can't be serious,' Tom said, genuinely appalled. 'On his daughter's birthday?'

'There was a note scribbled on a bit of paper and a twenty pound note shoved through the letter box before we got up this morning.' Clare wiped away a tear, making sure Penny hadn't noticed. 'That's all she means to him, Tom. Christ, that bastard was outside the house and he couldn't even be bothered to come in and see her.'

'Fucker.'

'And that's why I lost my rag at work just now. They're all fawning over these bloody aliens when I can't even get Penny's dad to spend five minutes with her on her birthday. It's like they're all living in cloud-cuckoo land. I phoned Aiden a couple of days ago, you know. I swallowed my pride and kept down all the hate and anger for Penny's sake, and I asked him if he was coming over on Monday. You know what he said?'

'No.'

'He asked me what for! Can you bloody believe it? The fucker hadn't even remembered it was her birthday. I mean, he remembered as soon as I reminded him of the date, but he's too busy sleeping around with slags to give a damn about anyone but himself.'

'So how's Penny taken it?'

Clare wiped her eyes and helped herself to an early glass of wine from a half-empty bottle in the fridge. 'To be honest, she's starting to get used to not having him around, and that's probably a good thing. She doesn't miss him like she used to, doesn't expect anything from him. Call me stupid, though, but I *want* her to have a decent relationship with her dad. I want her to be able to make her own mind up about what kind of a father he's been when she's older. No nine year-old child should have to discover their dad's a cunt like this.'

Clare's use of the word *cunt* caught Tom off-guard. He'd never heard her use it before. *Change the subject*, he thought, *get her talking about something else before things get* really *heavy here.*

'So you've not got anyone else coming around tonight?' he asked. Clare shook her head and sniffed back more tears. 'Penny's not having a party?'

'We're doing something on Saturday. You can't get anybody to do anything on a Monday.'

'So this is it? This is her birthday?'

'Christ, Tom, don't make me feel any worse than I already do. I asked some of the family around, tried to build a few bridges, but no one was interested. Even her grandparents on his side didn't want to know. They've all got far more important things to be getting on with. But I tell you something, if that bloody alien friend of your brother's was going to be here, they'd be queuing at the door to get in.'

'So shall we do something?' Tom asked, regretting the words the moment he'd said them. 'Come on, this isn't right. Regardless of everyone else, Penny can't spend her birthday at home on her own. Let's take her out or something. My treat. Just a quick burger in town or something like that?'

'We can't, honest. Thanks anyway, Tom.'

'Why not? You've just been telling me you're not doing anything else. Penny won't care that it's just you and me.'

'I know, but you've probably got your own plans. I wouldn't want to impose.'

'It's not imposing, and I don't have any plans,' he said and, right on cue, Penny walked into the room. 'Hey, Pen, fancy going out for a burger?'

He'd barely finished speaking before she was gone. He

heard her thumping up the stairs. 'Got to get changed... down in a minute.'

'That's that then,' Clare mumbled, clearly unimpressed. She wasn't in the mood to go anywhere. Her daughter, on the other hand, obviously was.


Two long, loud hours later and it was done. Tom felt as out of place in the burger bar as the two aliens sitting diagonally opposite. At least they had the excuse of being tourists of sorts. He joked with Clare, wondering what they would have thought of the food. Regardless of his, Clare's, or the aliens' opinion, Penny clearly loved every second of being out. From the carbonated drinks filled with so much ice they diluted the taste to half-strength, to the quickly prepared but otherwise wholly unsatisfying burgers, to the cheap plastic toy which came free with her meal, she enjoyed every second of it. Tom and Clare sat opposite each other, bored stiff but doing everything in their power to hide it. Clare regularly thanked Tom for forcing her out, and seeing Penny happy made the bittersweet day a little more enjoyable, but there was no disguising the fact that she'd rather have been anywhere else. If she'd had the choice, being at home in front of the TV, wearing her pyjamas, watching a crappy movie and slowly getting pissed on cheap wine would have been the ideal way to spend the evening.

Tom again found himself staring at the aliens in the corner and wondering what they made of this place. All uncomfortable, plastic furniture and Day-Glo decoration, it was as artificial as the food on its menu. These people, he thought, had travelled millions of miles to be here, and must have seen such unimaginable sights along the way... and yet the two of them seemed perfectly content to while away their time in this bland, corporate shit-hole of a place.

*Maybe they're not so different, after all.*

# 23

Tom dropped Clare and Penny home, then drove on to the bungalow. It was only just after seven but it was already dark, the long days of summer now a memory. His heart sank when he saw that there were lights on in the house. Siobhan had told him she was spending the night at her own place, so it could only mean that Rob was home. And that inevitably meant his friend Jall would be there too. The two of them were inseparable. Tom wondered why it annoyed him so much. Was he jealous?

He let himself in and shut the door behind him. He found them both in the living room – *his* living room – relaxing on *his* sofa, drinking *his* beer.

'All right?' he asked, sticking his head around the door. Jall acknowledged him but Rob didn't even look up. They were watching TV like an old married couple.

'You've been out a long time,' Jall said. 'We thought you'd have been back ages ago.'

'Didn't know I had to check in with you,' Tom said, less than impressed. He continued through to the kitchen and made himself a drink. No need to offer anything to the other two, he could tell from the detritus littering the worktop that they'd already helped themselves.

He wanted food. It had only been an hour or so since he'd eaten, but his burger had been less than filling. He'd always harboured a suspicion that fast food was deliberately engineered to give a brief false impression of satisfaction, then trigger something in your gut to make you hungry again. It was a conspiracy, he'd long ago decided, to get you to keep buying food.

He needed a sandwich, but there was only one crust of bread left and the cupboards were as empty as his stomach felt. The fridge had been raided and stripped clean. His bloody brother again.

'Have you seen the state of the kitchen?' he asked, standing in the doorway, seething.

'Of course we have,' Jall replied.

'I think he knows that,' Rob mumbled.

'Of course I know that, you fucking idiot. I know you've been in the kitchen. I can tell because you've eaten all my bloody food and not replaced it.'

'We'll sort it out tomorrow,' Rob said. 'Want me to go out and get you a burger or—'

'No I don't want you to get me a burger. I just had a fucking burger!'

'Then you shouldn't be that hungry,' Jall said, again managing to miss the finer nuances of human conversation by about a mile.

'Well I am hungry!' Tom yelled at him. He slammed the door in anger, then returned to the kitchen where he managed to scrape something together from the few scraps which remained: a few crackers, some low-fat spread, and a jar of sandwich pickle.

He'd barely taken a mouthful when he remembered to check his phone. He'd had a message from Siobhan while he was out with Clare and Penny, but he'd forgotten to reply. He saw that there were a couple of missed calls now too. He quickly phoned her back. It rang out several times before she answered.

'Hello you,' he said. 'You okay?'

'Where've you been?'

'What?'

'Where've you been? You didn't answer.'

Siobhan sounded unexpectedly angry. Her abruptness caught him by surprise and for a moment he didn't know how to respond.

'I went to see Penny and Clare, remember? I told you yesterday. It's Penny's birthday.'

'Right.'

Another pause before he hesitantly spoke again. 'Is there a problem?'

'You tell me.'

'What?'

'You didn't answer my message. Didn't pick up my calls.'

'Yeah, sorry about that. I didn't hear the phone. We were in McDonald's in Drayton. Like I said, it's Penny's birthday and—'

'I know where you were.'

'Pardon?'

'I know where you were. I saw you.'

'Then why didn't you come in.'

'Didn't want to interrupt anything.'

'Interrupt anything? Bloody hell, Siobhan, what's the matter with you?'

'It was humiliating. Mona said she'd seen you there. I went to look for myself.'

'And is that a problem? Like I said, it's Penny's birthday. I called around and they were on their own, not doing anything. I didn't think it was right for the poor kid to be stuck in on her birthday, so I took them both out. This is stupid, Siobhan. I don't know what the problem is. You've known Clare longer than I have. Are you accusing me of something here?'

She didn't answer for a few seconds which felt like forever. She eventually spoke again. 'I wanted to talk to you, but you didn't answer. You ignored me.'

'I didn't ignore you. You know what it's like in that place. Remember that time we went there and left because of the noise? Ended up driving back to the village and eating chips on the beach in the pouring rain. Remember? Siobhan? Siobhan, are you still there?'

She'd gone.

# 24

Tom tried calling back several times but Siobhan wouldn't pick up. He was at a loss. He tried talking to his brother about it, genuinely concerned that he might have done something wrong or forgotten something important and not realised, but Rob couldn't say more than a couple of words before Jall interrupted again. With no other option, Tom got in the car to drive to Siobhan's and sort things out.

He'd barely been out of the house five minutes when a car drove into the back of his. He was at a junction, waiting for the lights to change so he could turn right, when the driver behind tried to turn left and clipped his rear wing. The accident sounded and felt far worse than it was. He pulled up and stopped the car on the far side of the road then ran back over to talk to the other driver. His car hadn't moved. Tom knocked on his window, then opened his door. His heart sank. He knew who it was straightaway. It was Ray Mercer, his neighbour. *Of all the bloody people*, Tom thought, readying himself for another confrontation.

'Evening,' Tom said politely. 'You all right, Mr Mercer?'

Mercer didn't immediately react. He slowly looked up. 'Sorry...' he mumbled.

'You went into the back of me and I was stationary, so there's no argument really.'

'I know. Sorry,' he said, sounding unexpectedly docile.

'I'll take some pictures with my phone, okay? Doesn't look like there's a lot of damage to either car. We can swap insurance details in the morning if it's easier. It's not like we don't know where the other driver lives.'

Tom stared at Mercer who just nodded his head. His apparent lack of concern was infuriating. *You cantankerous old bastard*, Tom thought, *that was completely your fault. I'd be well within my rights to go absolutely fucking mental if I wanted to.*

'Sorry... don't know what happened.'

'Have you been drinking, Mr Mercer?'

'No. Haven't touched a drop.'

'You sure?' he asked.

Mercer mumbled something unintelligible.

Tom sniffed at the air. He couldn't smell booze. 'Maybe you'd better go home. I'll call around and see you tomorrow and we can sort everything out. Okay?'

'Okay,' the older man said, and with that Tom stepped back out of his way.

He watched as Mercer tried to turn the car around in the mouth of the junction. He stalled, then restarted the engine, bumped up the kerb, then drove back up the hill towards home.

*Wish you'd been as agreeable as that when I pruned your bloody tree,* Tom thought, remembering the battles they'd had. The two of them had almost come to blows over his Laburnum. Mercer had been like a Rottweiler, going for the jugular before Tom had even had chance to explain.

Tom finally reached Siobhan's flat. The street was quiet. *The calm before the storm?* He had a key, but he didn't want to presume. He rang the buzzer and waited. And waited. Was she ignoring him? He was on the verge of trying to phone her again when she answered. Her tinny voice crackled through the loudspeaker. 'Hello.'

'Siobhan, it's me. Can I come in? I need to talk to you.'

Nothing. He was about to ring again when the door clicked open.

The door to Siobhan's flat was slightly ajar and he went inside. There were no lights on, and the only illumination came from the TV in the corner. Siobhan sat opposite the flickering screen, still dressed in her work suit. Tom waited at the door, not sure if he should go any further until she'd acknowledged him. He looked into her face, her perfect features picked out by the constantly changing light.

He cleared his throat. 'There's nothing going on between me and Clare, you know,' he said before adding, 'if that's what you were thinking.' He continued to watch her anxiously, desperate for a reaction. He thought she nodded slightly – or was it just the light? The movement was so slight he thought he might have imagined it.

Then she spoke. 'I know.'

He walked further into the room and crouched down in front of her, kicking away food wrappers and moving an empty mug. Almost afraid of what her reaction might be, he took hold of her hand. It remained limp at first, but then her fingers slowly moved, her grip tightening around his own.

'I love you, you know,' he said. 'I'm sorry if I've done something to upset you, I didn't mean to. You're the only one for me, do you know that?'

This time her movement was more definite. She turned away from the TV and looked straight at him. 'I know. I'm sorry.'

'So what was that all about on the phone?'

'I don't feel too good.'

'What's wrong? Something you've eaten? Have you had any dinner today?'

'Not yet.'

'So what's up?' He felt her head for a temperature. 'Do you have a headache?'

She nodded. 'Had it all day.'

'Want me to make you something?'

'Yes please.'

'Do you want to go out?'

'Want to stay here.'

'Shall I run you a bath?'

'That'd be good. Thanks.'

'Are you going to be okay?'

'I'll be fine.'

'If you're still like this in the morning, maybe you should see the doctor.'

'I think I will.'

Tom stood up and went through to the bathroom where he closed the blind and started her bath running. He returned to the living room and switched on the light. Siobhan flinched at the sudden brightness. He watched her closely, concerned by her apparent lethargy.

'That too bright?'

'It's okay,' she replied, squinting.

Tom looked around. 'Bloody hell, this place is a tip,' he said, instinctively picking more stuff up off the floor.

'Sorry.'

'Don't apologise to me, sweetheart, it's your flat.'

She smiled briefly, and sat up in her seat. Tom closed the curtains then fetched her a drink. She took it from him and managed a couple of sips before putting it down again. She took off her jacket and unbuttoned the front of her blouse, then moved towards Tom. She wrapped her arms around him and pulled him close.

'Sorry,' she said again.

'Want to talk about it?'

'Talk about what?' she asked, her face still buried in his chest.

'Whatever it is that's going on. Whatever it was you thought I'd done. I just don't want there to be any problems between us. You're all that matters to me.'

'I shouldn't have taken it out on you,' she said, kicking off the rest of her clothes as she disappeared into the bathroom.

'But to accuse me of—'

'I'm sorry,' she said again, and Tom sensed he should end the conversation. He watched her as she turned off the tap, checked the temperature of the water, then slid slowly into the bath, stark naked and completely uninhibited. He watched for

185

a moment longer, catching glimpses of her under the water, intermittently hidden by patches of bubbles.

'You sure you're okay?'

She nodded and smiled. 'Hungry.'

He went through to the small kitchen, pausing only to pick up her clothes and lay them on the end of the bed.

'Tom,' she shouted to him, 'could you turn the TV up please?'

# 25

Tom spent the night with Siobhan. She was quiet all evening, and was asleep virtually the moment her head hit the pillow, but Tom lay awake for hours, staring at her in the darkness. What had happened between the two of them earlier concerned him. If he'd given her the wrong impression or made her doubt his feelings towards her, then he needed to know. He couldn't afford to let it happen again. He couldn't risk losing Siobhan. He blamed himself. *I'm spending too much time alone. I'm on the outside of everything else. Have to start making more of an effort.*

He woke briefly when she got up and left for work. He lay in bed and watched her dress and get ready in the half-light of morning. She stood opposite him and brushed her hair in the mirror on the wall, then put on a little make-up, not as much as usual. She left without eating breakfast or even drinking anything.

'You all right?' he asked as she pulled on her coat, about to leave.

'I'm fine,' she replied.

'Will I see you tonight?'

'Okay.'

She opened the door. He called her back. 'Wait, is that it? Don't I even get a kiss?' She smiled, walked back to the bed, then leant down and kissed him.

'See you later,' she said.

Siobhan had been gone for some time when Tom finally got up, got dressed, and left the flat. The light outside had the cold blue-white sheen of early morning and the air was cool and still. It was unexpectedly quiet as he drove home, and the house too was empty. Rob and Jall had gone. Remembering that his cupboards were bare, before taking off his coat and boots and settling down he walked into the village to re-stock.

The normality of the day-to-day unfolded all around Tom. People went about their daily routines, literally side-stepping him as he ambled down the footpath, everyone else keen to get past and get on with their lives. He didn't miss work at all but he couldn't help feeling a real disconnection this morning. It felt almost as if everyone else had a reason – a right, almost – to be there but him. Even the school kids, who crowded into the supermarket to fill up on chocolate and junk food for the day, looked at him as if he shouldn't have been getting in their way. He stood in front of a chiller cabinet, taking his time to choose something decent to cook for Siobhan later. Someone reached past him to take something from the display, then Mrs Grayson asked him to move the other way so she could replenish the stock. He could almost feel their eyes burning into the back of him. *Look at that lazy bastard*, they were all saying. *He does nothing all day, every day.* Self-conscious, he picked up some steak – Siobhan's favourite – and moved on.

*Is it me? Am I pushing everyone that matters away?*

Mrs Grayson was back at the kiosk when he was ready to pay. He tried to make small-talk, not wanting to say anything but doing his best to be pleasant all the same.

Tom walked up the hill towards home, the handles of the plastic carrier bags digging into his hands. He stopped when he drew level with Ray Mercer's house, his heart sinking when he remembered he'd have to speak to the odious old bastard about the crash last night. Maybe he could put it off until tomorrow...

It was only when he walked a little further that he noticed Mercer's garage door was wide open. His car was parked inside. And was that Mercer sitting in the front seat? He was probably off out somewhere, Tom decided, but to all intents and purposes the strange old bugger looked like he hadn't moved since last night.

# 26

Siobhan left work early, feeling unwell. Tom forced himself out for a short run and didn't find out until he found a message on his phone when he got back. Siobhan's flat was closer to the office than Tom's house, so Mona had dropped her home. Tom showered and changed, then grabbed a few things and drove straight over. He found Siobhan in bed, already asleep. She woke up a while later, the smell of cooking and the noise of Tom in the kitchen disturbing her. She sat up in bed, bleary-eyed.

'How long have you been here?'

'Not long. I got your message. Let myself in and made you some dinner. Is that okay?'

'Not that hungry.'

'You feeling sick again?'

'Not sick, just tired. Been overdoing it, that's all.'

'I'm cooking steak,' he said, returning to the kitchen. 'It's your favourite. Will you at least try and eat something?'

She nodded and waited for him to bring her food over. She poked and prodded at it and managed to swallow a few mouthfuls. He sat in a chair and ate, his appetite slightly reduced by gnawing nervousness and concern for Siobhan.

'I'm really worried about you,' he said.

'Don't be. I'm fine.'

'You don't seem fine. This isn't like you.'

'Seriously, I just need some sleep. Stop fussing.'

'I'm not fussing. I care about you. I get worried when—'

'I'm fine,' she said again, her voice louder, bordering on angry. 'Stop it.'

'Okay. If that's what you want.'

Tom's phone rang. He glanced at it and then put it back in his pocket.

'Not going to answer it?'

'No.'

'Who was it.'

'No one.'

'So no one phoned. That's weird. Tell me, who was it?'

'Does it matter?'

'Yes.'

'Okay, it was Clare.'

'I might have known. What did she want?'

'How am I supposed to know? I didn't bloody answer it, did I? Don't start accusing me of—'

'I'm not accusing you of anything.'

'Not directly. Look, Siobhan, for the last time, there's nothing going on between me and Clare. I don't know why she called.'

'You should go and phone her.'

'To give you another reason to have a go at me?'

'Maybe you should just go.'

*What the hell is going on?*

'Siobhan, I can't keep up here. I don't know what I'm supposed to have done or why you're acting like this. It makes no sense. I haven't done anything to—'

'I'm tired. I want to go to sleep. I'll see you tomorrow, okay?'

She shoved her tray further down the bed then lay down and turned her back on him. Tom remained sitting in his chair, stunned. What had he done now? She'd made it clear she wanted him to leave. He didn't seem to have any choice. Staying was only going to antagonise her further. He took his plate to the kitchen and scraped the remains of his half-eaten meal into the bin, then picked up his coat, close to tears.

'I'll come back in the morning, okay?'

'Okay.'

'I love you, Siobhan.'

Nothing.

# 27

Rob was back at the house, fast asleep in his room. Tom was relieved to find no sign of Jall. The last thing he needed tonight was to have to listen to that sanctimonious prick droning on.

There was nothing on TV other than the usual mix of reality TV, third-rate dramas and documentaries, and Tom wasn't in the mood for any of it. He tried watching a film but turned it off before he'd got even half an hour in. He couldn't even derive any satisfaction from hunting down and killing aliens in video games tonight. Instead he sat in the dark in front of the gas fire and stared into the flames, trying to make sense of what had happened tonight, toying between either going back to try and talk to Siobhan again or drinking himself stupid. He'd just gone to get his first beer when the phone rang. He picked it up quickly, hoping it would be her. It wasn't. It was Clare. Tom struggled to hide his disappointment. She immediately picked up on his tone and he explained what had happened.

'So where is she now?' she asked.

'At home asleep, I think. She pretty much threw me out.'

'Doesn't sound like Siobhan. Time of the month?'

'I don't think so.'

'Whatever it is, I don't think it's you,' she said.

'And how'd you come to that conclusion? What do you know that I don't?'

'It's the reason I was phoning. I wanted to check you were feeling okay.'

'Me? Why?'

'I think there might be something going around. Some kind of bug.'

'What makes you say that?'

'Penny's not right.'

'Is she ill?'

'Not as such...'

'Could it be something to do with her birthday? Her dad, maybe? I've heard about kids who don't outwardly react to something, but then—'

Clare interrupted. 'It's nothing like that.'

'What then?'

'It's hard to explain... she was a little off-colour this morning when I took her into school, but I couldn't afford to miss work so I made her go in thinking she'd pick up once she was there. Since I collected her this afternoon, though, it's like she's...'

'She's what?'

'Oh, I don't know. I feel stupid even saying this, but it's like she hates me, Tom.'

'What are you talking about?'

'I swear, I've never known her like this before. It's like I've brought someone else's daughter home by mistake.'

'Why? What's she doing?'

'Last night she was fine. In fact, we had a lovely evening after you'd dropped us back. We sat and watched telly for hours, a proper girly night in.'

'So maybe she's just tired after that. Is she—'

'Please don't patronise me, Tom. I know when my daughter's tired. This is different.'

'Sorry,' he said quickly, feeling embarrassed. 'Maybe it does have something to do with yesterday? You're her mum, Clare. You're the closest person to her, the one who's always there for her. So maybe it's just that she's angry about something, and you're the easiest one to take it out on. She's only young. Christ, I find it hard enough trying to work out how I'm feeling half the time, a kid's got no chance.'

'You think she picked up on my vibes yesterday and now she's paying me back?'

'I don't know. I don't think so. Maybe me being there didn't help. Probably made her realise how different this birthday was to the last. I should have stayed away.'

'It's nothing to do with you, you're just paranoid.'

'You might be right about that.'

'No, there's more to this, Tom, I'm sure there is. Maybe she is coming down with something. You should have seen her, though. She kept hanging back at school like she didn't want to get into the car. Can you imagine what that felt like? She went straight up to her room when we got in and I've hardly seen her since. She came down for her dinner but barely touched it. Christ, she could hardly bring herself to look at me. I tried to talk to her but she wouldn't say a frigging word. She all but blanked me. She's been up in her room ever since.'

'Do you think her dad's been in touch through the school?'

'I doubt it. Like I told you, Aiden doesn't give a shit. If he can't be bothered to come around and see her on her birthday, he's hardly going to be trying to get to sneak in and see her at school, is he?'

'Maybe someone saw us out last night and said something to her?'

'You're not listening to me, Tom. This has got nothing to do with you or the three of us being out together yesterday. It's more than that.'

'One of the other kids then? Trouble with a teacher?'

'They'd have told me. Look, I appreciate what you're trying to do, but this is *different*. I've never seen her like this before.'

'So what are you going to do?'

'I don't know. I guess I'll have to see what she's like in the morning, and if she's the same then I'll...'

'Clare?'

For a few seconds all Tom could hear was the static hum of the phone line. He was about to hang-up, thinking he'd lost signal strength, when he heard more. Clare's breathing. Heavy footsteps. The creak of a floorboard. Then a loud crashing noise which clearly startled Clare as much as it did him.

'Jesus!' she cursed.

'What the hell was that?' Tom heard another noise, then another. 'Clare...? Are you still there...?'

'I'm here,' she said quietly, muffled noises continuing in the background.

'What the hell's going on there?'

'It's Penny. She's trashing her room. I'm going to have to go.'

'Do you want me to come over?'

'No offence, but what good's that going to do?' she said, sounding breathless.

'Is there anyone else who can help? Anyone I can call for you?'

'Like who? I've tried the family but no one's answering. Look, I'm going to have to go. I'll talk to you later, Tom.'

And with that the line disconnected.

# Part iv
# CHANGE

# 28

Tom slept in next morning, doing all he could to avoid facing the day for as long as possible. The temperature had dropped significantly and he lay with his head sandwiched between two pillows, trying to keep warm and at the same time block everything else out until he had no choice but to get up. He wanted to go and see Siobhan again, but the thought of how she might be when he got there was enough to make him find excuses to stay home. He decided she'd probably have gone to work anyway. It felt better to try and fool himself like that than to have to face up to a reality he couldn't bare to imagine. He didn't know what he'd do if he lost her. He didn't know what he'd done.

He forced himself out of bed and traipsed through the dark house, scaring himself shitless when he literally stumbled over his brother who was lying on the sofa in the living room, one leg on the floor. Tom decided to leave him sleeping. It was easier than having to explain what he was doing and why. There was only one person Tom wanted to talk to.

He dressed and drank a mug of strong coffee before putting on his coat and getting ready to head out. He needed to fill up with petrol, then get straight over and sort things out with Siobhan. He grabbed his keys, marched up to the front door, then stopped. He didn't want to go. *Pull yourself together, you fucking jerk*, he ordered himself. *Get a grip*. Was he going to add agoraphobia to his list of self-inflicted problems now? Maybe if he tried hard enough he could convince himself he was OCD too? That'd give him something to stop himself getting bored, he thought, washing his hands a hundred times a day or religiously checking, double-checking, then triple-checking light switches and power sockets.

He made himself leave.

*

From outside his house, Tom thought Thatcham looked quieter than usual today. That was a relief, as he'd decided he wanted to avoid speaking to people as much as he could this morning. He zipped up his coat and breathed in the cold, fresh air. Everything looked suitably grey and miserable, a light mist obscuring the view and leaving the outskirts of the village hidden as if they'd been rubbed out. The trees on the hillside were uniformly spindly and brittle-branched, their trunks twisting and climbing up into the fog like they were trying to escape.

Tom got into his car and drove away from the house. He stopped when he'd only travelled a short distance. There was someone leaning up the low stone wall at the side of the road as if they were catching their breath or being sick. It was Will Preston. Tom had been introduced to him in the pub by John Tipper a couple of months ago. He was one of the local lifeboat crew – a group of volunteers who lived and worked around Thatcham. Tom had considered volunteering himself. He liked the idea of running through the streets like a hero. He'd seen it happen regularly since he'd been here: a sudden siren would wail and a single flare would be fired up over the small lifeboat station, then the crew would come running from different directions and they'd be launched in minutes. Tom had already decided he'd wait until next spring to put himself forward though. The winter didn't seem the most sensible time to learn how to sail and rescue people from the sea.

Tom wound down the window, concerned. 'Morning,' he shouted over at Will. 'Everything all right?' Will didn't react. He remained looking ahead, staring out towards the ocean which, because of the mist, could barely be seen. The lack of any visible response briefly wrong-footed Tom. Perhaps he hadn't heard him? He cleared his throat and tried again. 'Morning.' Still no response. Ignorant bastard.

More concerned with getting to Siobhan, Tom continued

down into the village and pulled up on the petrol station forecourt. He killed his engine and everything became quiet, save for a constant, high-pitched yapping noise. He walked back towards the road and found a small dog tied to a lamppost, spinning circles and barking continually. He recognised it immediately. He'd heard the damn thing too many times before. He knew its owner too. It belonged to Ken Trentham, the old drunk who spent his days either in the Badger's Sett or wandering through the village causing trouble. Tom found Ken sitting on a bench a few metres further along the road. His scruffy head was hanging forward and he looked like he'd passed out. He was probably off his face on something as usual, Tom decided. For all the negative social stigma attached to being the town drunk, Tom found himself thinking that Ken might not have been as hard done by as he'd always presumed. He spent most of his time in an alcoholic daze, his uncomplicated life completely free of any responsibility or pressure, all booze and lodgings paid for by the state. On the face of it, it looked like a pretty good deal. Tom checked himself. *Are you serious? Listen to what you're saying.* And then an even more frightening thought materialised: *Did Ken start off like me? If I don't sort myself out, is this what I'm going to become?*

Tom noticed that Ken's eyes were open and unblinking. Shit, was he dead? He stepped over the growling dog, whose frayed rope lead was at full stretch, then shook Ken's shoulder. He was relieved when the drunk looked up, mumbled something, then looked back down again.

'Pissed, as usual,' an unexpected but immediately recognisable voice said, startling Tom. It was John Tipper. 'This happy little bunny spent his giro in the pub last night. Drinking like a fish, he was.'

'Might have guessed,' Tom said. 'How are you this morning, John?'

'Top of the world,' he said quickly, putting down the bags he was carrying. The tone of his voice was far from convincing.

'What's up?'

'It's probably nothing,' he replied, his face dropping. 'Just put my foot in it with the missus, and I can't work out why.' Despite the fact that the normally unfailingly positive pub landlord was clearly out of sorts, Tom took satisfaction from his demeanour. It was nice to know he wasn't the only one having a miserable time of things. 'Ever get the feeling you're pulling in a different direction to everyone else?' John said.

'Most of the time,' Tom replied without hesitation.

'I'm bound to have done something wrong, but I'll be damned if I know what it is. Honestly, Tom, thirty-five years we've been married and there's hardly been a cross word between us in all that time. This morning she can barely bring herself to look at me. She's still in bed, as far I know. At this time of day! I'm supposed to be opening up in half an hour and we've got a big booking for lunch today. I had to come out and get a few things from the supermarket because my delivery from the caterers hasn't turned up. I tell you, Tom, it's enough to turn a man to drink.'

'Well you're in the right place for it,' Tom joked.

John ignored him. 'I just wish she'd tell me what it is I'm supposed to have done, you know? Give me a clue, at least.'

'You can't think of anything?'

'We were quiet last night and I was moaning about there not being enough punters in. I was talking about changing the food menu, you know, re-launching it, spicing things up a bit. You know what she's like about her kitchen. I probably said something that upset her. She didn't say anything at the time, mind. She was still talking ten to the dozen in bed when I was trying to get to sleep.'

'Maybe that's it then?' Tom suggested. 'She's got the hump because you went to sleep while she was still talking to you.'

'Truth be told, that happens most nights. She's usually had

a few halves of Special Brew and she doesn't even notice. No, Tom, this is different.'

The two men stood together for a few seconds longer, the only noise coming from Ken Trentham's dog.

'Best get back with all this,' John said, lifting his bags. 'I'll see you later, Tom. You'll be in on Friday night?'

'We'll be there,' Tom said. John nodded, managed half a smile, then walked away, hunched forward and with his shoulders rounded as if just being alive this morning was too much of an effort. Tom watched him disappear into the mist then returned to the car and started filling it up.

Christ, he thought as he entered the kiosk shop to pay, even this place looked like it couldn't be bothered today. There were holes in the displays which hadn't yet been re-stocked. Darren Braithwaite, the part-time cashier, was working at a speed which was slow even by his miserable standards. He was filling a display of chocolate bars, moving one or two at a time as if it was all too much effort. His lank hair covered much of his face but Tom could see his mouth hanging open gormlessly. His eyes were glassy, probably still stoned from last night. *At least he's acting normally*, Tom laughed to himself.

He picked up a few things as he walked around the small store. He noticed there was another car on the forecourt now, and as he made his way to the check-out, the owner of the car, a short, white-haired man, burst through the kiosk door and crashed into him.

'Bloody hell, take it easy.'

The man apologised immediately. 'Sorry,' he said breathlessly. He began to regain his composure. He was in his late fifties, Tom thought, and he didn't recognise him as being from the village. His face was flushed red and he constantly looked back at his car.

'Everything okay?'

'Don't know what's the matter with them,' he said.

'With who?'

'All of them.'

With that he threw a twenty pound note at the cashier and rushed back outside.

*What is this?* Tom thought, *Invasion of the bloody Body Snatchers?* As dumb as it sounded, there was no denying the man's behaviour left him feeling uneasy.

Tom waited as the cashier lethargically processed the payment, then rang through Tom's purchases. While he was waiting, his phone rang. He answered it immediately, hoping it would be Siobhan. For a few seconds he wasn't sure who was calling. It was a little girl. It sounded like Bethany, one of James and Stephanie's kids, but he didn't know why she'd be phoning him.

'Beth? Bethany, is that you?'

'Yes.'

'Did you mean to phone me?'

No answer. Tom finished paying and went back out to the car.

'Daddy's not very well.'

'Beth, this is Tom, your dad's friend. Did you know you'd phoned me?'

'I just kept trying numbers.'

'What do you mean?'

'I kept trying the numbers in Daddy's phone.'

'Right...'

'You're the only one who answered.'

'How many people did you try, Beth?'

'Nearly all of them.'

'Where are your mum and dad?'

'They're here.'

'Can I talk to one of them?'

'They won't talk.'

'What's wrong with them?'

'I don't know.'

'Are you okay?'

'Just a bit worried.'

'I bet you are,' Tom said. He could hear the nervousness in her voice. 'Wait there, Beth. I'm just at the petrol station, not far from your house. I'll be there in a couple of minutes.'

Tom pulled up outside James and Stephanie's house and rang the bell. There was an uncomfortably long delay before the door opened inwards. Beth was standing in front of him, still wearing her pyjamas.

'You okay?'

She nodded. 'I'm okay.'

'Shouldn't you be at school today?'

'Mummy didn't take me.'

'Where is she?'

'In there with Daddy.'

She opened the door fully and stood to one side, giving Tom a clear view into the heart of the narrow little house. Stephanie was lying on the sofa, barely dressed. James sat bolt upright in an armchair opposite, staring into space, his mouth hanging open. Tom shut the door behind him, stepping over Mark, Beth's younger brother, who was lying curled up in a ball in the middle of the floor. He crouched down and checked the young lad. He was awake and alert, sucking on his thumb. 'You okay?'

'He's just tired,' Beth answered for her brother. 'He keeps falling asleep.'

Tom turned his attention to the children's parents. 'James? Steph?'

Neither of them reacted. After a few seconds, James turned his head slightly and looked at Tom. He had a puzzled expression on his face, as if he was waiting for things to come into focus.

'What's up, mate? No work today.'

'No work today,' he replied, his voice quiet and slightly slurred.

'Are you sick? Has something happened?'

No answer this time. Tom turned his attention to Stephanie who was gazing up at the ceiling. He discreetly leant down, picked up the flap of her open dressing gown, and covered her legs. She was showing herself, and it made him feel uncomfortable.

'Stephanie?'

He crouched down beside her and shook her shoulder but she didn't respond. Aware of movement behind him, he turned around and saw Beth trying to watch over his shoulder.

'What's the matter with them?' she asked, her wavering voice quiet, almost like she didn't want to be heard.

'I'm not sure,' Tom replied, wishing he could give her a better answer – any answer, even. 'How long have they been like this?'

'Just today,' Beth told him. 'I don't like it.'

'Me neither.'

A sudden, high-pitched cry from elsewhere in the house made Tom catch his breath. The baby. He cursed himself for not thinking about little Felicity sooner. When neither of her parents reacted, he stood up.

'Where's your sister?'

'Still in her cot,' Beth replied. 'She keeps crying. I tried to get her to stop, but she won't.'

'Does she have any milk or anything like that?'

'Mummy feeds her.'

Now what did he do? Things were happening at such a rate in this house that he didn't know which way to turn. He ran upstairs and checked from room to room until he found the baby in her cot. Although he knew she'd probably be able to do very little to help, he was relieved when he heard Beth follow him upstairs.

'I don't know very much about babies,' he admitted as he peered into Felicity's cot. The smell was worse than the noise. He was no expert, but it was clear both from the stench and the bulge around the baby's middle that it had been a long time since her nappy had been changed.

'Stephanie,' he shouted downstairs, hoping she'd hear him and snap back into life. 'The baby needs changing. Will you come up and do it?'

He waited for an answer he knew wasn't coming.

'She won't,' Beth said. 'I've asked her loads of times.'

'Do you know what to do?'

'I've seen Mummy do it, but I can't. Can you?'

'Looks like I'll have to. You'll have to tell me if I'm doing it right. Where's all the stuff?'

Beth dived over to a corner of the room then returned clutching a fresh nappy, a bag of cotton wool, a tub of cream and a packet of wipes. Not at all sure what he was doing – and feeling distinctly uncomfortable about touching the baby – Tom slowly removed her pyjamas. He braced himself and undid her bulging nappy, gagging both at the smell and what he saw and doing what he could to hide his disgust from Beth.

'I don't like that,' she said, backing away.

'You and me both,' he admitted, eyes watering, swallowing down bile. 'Now be a good girl and try and find me some clean clothes for your sister.'

Ten minutes of struggling – both with the distressed baby and his delicate stomach – and the job was done to a decent enough standard. He carried Felicity downstairs to her mother and, between him and Beth, managed to get Stephanie sitting upright. He propped her up in a comfortable position so she could feed her child. Tom cringed at every moment, drowning in the awkwardness of the situation, trying to pull the top of Stephanie's nightdress down low enough so the baby could get to her breast without inappropriately touching her flesh himself. She didn't react when he inadvertently touched her breast. Thankfully instinct at last seemed to take over. Stephanie finally held onto her daughter, and the little girl latched onto her mother's nipple and began to feed.

Tom turned his attention to James and Mark. He picked the young lad up and laid him down on another chair, covering him with a blanket, then focussed on his father.

'James!' Tom shouted in his face, pulling him forward and shaking his shoulders. 'James, mate, what's going on?'

No response. His eyes barely flickered. Tom shook him again and then dropped him back into the chair.

'Shall we get the doctor?' Beth asked.

Tom couldn't bring himself to look at her. He didn't want her to pick up on the fear he was beginning to feel in the pit of his stomach. 'I don't know.'

He put on his coat and moved towards the front door.

'You going?' Bethany asked. 'Please don't go.'

Tom didn't want to leave the children, but he knew he had to go. They weren't his responsibility, Siobhan was. 'Is there anyone else who can look after you?'

'Mrs Price,' Bethany said.

'Who's Mrs Price?'

'Don't know. Just this old lady who comes around when Mummy and Daddy go out sometimes.'

'Do you know where she lives?'

'No.'

'Does she come in a car?'

'No, I think she lives near here. Mummy makes Dad walk her home. I've stayed up and heard them talking before now.'

'Which way's her house?'

'Don't know.'

'I'll go and find her.'

With that he opened the door and took a step out onto the

street. He turned back. Bethany was standing in the doorway, eyes wide. Behind her he could see Stephanie, head drooping, just about managing to hold onto her baby.

'Will you come back?' Beth asked.

Tom steadied himself. He had to do this. 'I'll go find Mrs Price. Either she'll come and look after you or I will. I won't leave you on your own, okay?'

She nodded and he forced himself to go.

Tom tried five houses before he got any answer. It wasn't Mrs Price, but he did find a Mrs Simpson, a reassuringly lucid woman in her late-sixties. When he explained what was happening she immediately agreed to look after the kids. She knew them – rather, she'd *heard* them – and, more importantly, she too had realised something was seriously wrong this morning. She tried to ask Tom about it, pleaded with him to explain the inexplicable, but he couldn't. Despite her protests, he left her.

He felt like a callous, uncaring shit as he drove away, but the truth was James, Stephanie and their family were not his main concern. He needed to get to Siobhan.

# 29

Tom continued out through the village and on towards Siobhan's flat. He fought to keep his attention fixed on the road, struggling despite there being hardly any other traffic or pedestrians around.

What he'd seen at James and Stephanie's house had terrified him. Until then he'd been trying to convince himself that this morning had just been a series of bizarre, unconnected events, but the further he travelled, the more he began to realise that was bullshit. He'd been lying to himself, trying to keep calm and not blow things out of proportion, convincing himself that the reason everything felt so quiet today was just because he'd got used to everywhere being busy these last few bizarre months. The truth was, whatever it was that was happening to the people of Thatcham, it was no bizarre coincidence or isolated issue. It was fucking huge. Fucking terrifying.

He passed only one other car and just a handful of people in all the time he was driving. One young lad was sitting on the step of a driverless bus going nowhere. A woman was walking along the side of the road like a drunk. If only drink had been the reason for her freakish behaviour, he thought. Once he'd passed he looked back in his rear view mirror and saw that underneath her long brown coat she was completely naked. Elsewhere he saw several other folks who looked like they'd just given up and stopped. Some were lying on the pavement. One man was face-down on the white line in the middle of the road. Everyone was grinding to a halt. The more of them he saw, the more frightened he became.

Tom's heart thumped in his chest as he pulled up outside Siobhan's flat. He looked in through the window, his breath clouding the glass, but couldn't make out anything in the gloom. He rang the buzzer but there was no reply. He unlocked the door and went inside.

He found Siobhan sitting on the end of the bed, naked but for a bra which wasn't even done up. She didn't move, didn't react to his presence at all. Her hair was a mess. The remains of yesterday's makeup smudged around her eyes.

'Siobhan?'

She didn't flinch.

'What's the matter with you?' he asked. Still nothing. 'Are you sick?' He reached across and touched her arm. She felt ice-cold. 'Siobhan,' he said again, his voice louder, 'what's wrong?'

Very slowly, almost undetectably at first, she moved her eyes slightly. He couldn't tell if she was looking at him or trying to look away. He picked the duvet up off the floor and draped it over her shoulders. Not knowing what else to do, he filled up the kettle and put her last two slices of bread in the toaster. The sink was full of dirty plates, the bin overflowing.

*Is this the best you can do, you useless fucker?* He screamed at himself. *Your girlfriend's catatonic and you're making toast?*

He didn't know what else to do. Was there anything else he *could* do? If he called for a doctor or an ambulance, would anyone come, or were they all in the same state as this? His mind filled with images of silent hospitals, all the people there completely unmoving, lying in the corridors, slumped at the bottom of staircases. He imagined Drayton in the same state as Thatcham was this morning, then cities like Birmingham and London, then the rest of the world...

The toast popped up, the sudden noise making him catch his breath. He took the plate through to Siobhan and put it down next to her, then tried tearing a strip of toast off and offering it to her like she was a pet. He even pushed it up against her mouth but she didn't react at all, didn't even lick away the crumbs on her lips. Should he force feed her? Try and make her eat? Did it even matter anymore?

His mobile rang. He fumbled for it in his pocket and answered quickly, hands shaking, heart thumping.

'Tom? Tom, is that you?'

'Clare?'

'Where are you?'

'I'm at Siobhan's house.'

'Can you come over?'

'Not really... Siobhan's sick. I don't know what to do.'

'Penny too.'

'No better than last night?'

'Worse. She's barely moving. I'm scared.'

Tom looked down at Siobhan, still comatose. Should he bother telling Clare everything he'd seen this morning? He struggled with his next question, knowing it would sound bad, no matter how carefully he phrased it.

'Clare, is there anyone else who could—'

'There's no one else,' she answered immediately, cutting across him. 'You're the only person still answering.'

Tom paced the room. The plate of toast slid off Siobhan's bed and hit the floor. Holding the phone to his ear with one hand, he struggled to clean up the food with the other. Siobhan still didn't move.

'Tom... you there?'

'I'm here.'

'I need help. Can you come? Please, Tom.'

'I can't leave Siobhan. She's hardly moving, Clare. Barely even knows I'm here. I think Rob might be the same. He's still at home...'

'Sorry... I'll keep trying, see if I can get anyone else to answer. Sorry, Tom.'

She was about to disconnect the call when he realised he didn't want her to go. Didn't want to lose her voice.

'Wait, Clare. Just give me a little time. I'll come over.'

'But what about Siobhan and your brother?'

'Don't do anything,' he said, not entirely sure what he was

agreeing to anymore, just glad to have found someone else still able to communicate. 'Stay there and I'll be over.'

Tom's head was spinning as he ended the call, trying to balance Clare and Penny's relative importance against Siobhan and Rob's. And then there was the mess he'd left back at James and Stephanie's house... Where the hell did he start? Could he do anything for any of them?

He made a half-hearted attempt to move Siobhan, pulling her arms and trying to get her up onto her feet, but she didn't respond. She remained a dead weight.

'Help me!' he yelled at her, but her face didn't flicker. He yanked her arm again and pulled too hard, almost dragging her over. She fell onto her side and remained where she'd fallen. She looked at him – *through him* – with vacant eyes, and he gave up. Admitting defeat, he draped the duvet over her again. 'I'll be back. I'll go and get the others and I'll be right back.'

# 30

Clare was out of the door before Tom had even stopped the engine. She ran across the road and grabbed hold of him. He revelled in the sudden close contact of another lucid person.

'You okay?' was all he could think to say. Stupid bloody question.

'No,' she answered. 'I don't know what the hell's going on. I can't get anything out of Penny. I tried calling the doctor, but no one answered. I tried 999, Tom. I couldn't get an answer on bloody 999!'

He followed her inside. The last few times he'd been here, the place had been full of Penny's noise and bluster. Now the building felt cold and unwelcoming, as unnaturally quiet as everywhere else. Clare stopped at the bottom of the stairs.

'Where is she?'

'Her room. She hasn't moved all morning, Tom.'

'Can I see her?'

She nodded and took him up to her little girl's bedroom. She seemed to slow down as she approached the door. She reached out for the handle but didn't open it, turning back and looking to him for reassurance. He braced himself, not sure what to expect. Clare pushed the door open, peered inside, then stood out of the way to let Tom through.

The small room was just as he remembered; bright, colourful, innocent. There were toys scattered all about the floor, but no sign of Penny. The bed was unmade and empty. Clare gestured over to the other side of the bed. Tom walked a little further, cringing as the floorboards creaked loudly under his weight, and then he found her. She was slumped on the floor in the corner of the room, her head lolling over to one side as if she'd cricked her neck. Her eyes were open. She was staring right at him, and yet at the same time it was as if she wasn't looking anywhere at all.

Penny's unnatural appearance increased his unease. Tom wanted to get out but he made himself move closer. He crouched down in front of the little girl, feeling sure that at any second she'd snap out of this trance and start laughing like a kid again, as if it had all been one big joke. But she didn't. She remained completely still. She didn't even react when, out of sight of her mother, he gently picked up one of her hands and pinched her skin so hard it must have hurt.

'Well?'

Tom looked over his shoulder. Clare was standing just behind him, waiting at the foot of the bed.

'Have you seen anyone else today?' he asked.

'No, why?'

'Because they're all like this, Clare.'

'All of them?' The disbelief in her voice was evident.

'Pretty much.'

'That doesn't make any sense...'

'I never said it did. I know, Clare, it's fucked up. I don't have a clue what's going on. Penny's exactly the same as Siobhan. And James and Stephanie too.'

'James and Stephanie? Christ, Tom.'

'One of the kids phoned me and I went around. Same reason you managed to get me – I'm the only idiot still answering. It's like they've all just stopped...'

'But why? What's caused this?'

'Come on, Clare, how the hell am I supposed to know?'

'You should try and find your brother's alien friend. He'll know. It's got to be something to do with them. Where is he?'

'For Christ's sake, how am I supposed to know?' he snapped at her. He hadn't realised he was yelling, but he could see it in Clare's frightened reaction. He tried to apologise but he couldn't find the words. He was scared, unable to think straight. He turned back to Penny, hoping she might have reacted to the noise too, but she hadn't. She was stuck in the same uncomfortable-looking position.

Tom got up and left the room, thumping back downstairs.

'Where are you going?' Clare shouted, chasing after him.

'Siobhan and Rob,' he replied, sounding as unsure as he felt.

'Please don't leave us here, Tom.'

Confused, he walked back out to the car. He paused before getting in. He walked up to the front of the house next to Clare's and rang the bell. When there was no immediate answer he began hammering on the door with his fist. 'Who lives here?'

Clare was right behind him. 'His name's Graham,' she replied. 'I've never had a lot to do with him.'

'Is he likely to be in?'

'Rarely goes out. Doesn't have a job, as far as I'm aware.'

There was still no answer. Tom rang the bell again, this time leaving his finger on the buzzer. Although muffled, they could clearly hear the shrill, continuous ringing from outside. He moved to the nearest window and peered in. He beckoned Clare over. She looked over his shoulder and saw her neighbour sitting on a sofa on the far side of the room, staring into space. He was just like the rest of them. Frozen. Unresponsive.

'This is fucking crazy,' Tom said, climbing over a low picket fence to get to the next house along. He used the brass knocker but had barely waited for the noise to fade before he tried the door and found it unlocked. He went inside. Clare was hesitant to follow. They could hear running water. The kitchen was flooded, the ceiling bowed, water dripping down.

'Let's go, Tom. Please.'

'Wait here.'

Tom ran upstairs. In the bathroom an overweight, middle-aged man was sitting in the base of the shower cubicle in several inches of water, his legs hanging out over the edge, water pouring over the top of the tray and flooding the carpet.

214

The man – head bowed, skin pruned, water running into his open eyes and dripping off his forehead, nose and chin, didn't react. Tom didn't say anything, he just rattled the shower cubicle door. The man did nothing. Tom pulled the power cord and the water flow immediately stopped, but even that failed to illicit any response.

Back to the car.

'What are we going to do, Tom?'

He looked at Clare but didn't answer. Couldn't answer. What did they do? He went to open the car door.

'Don't go,' she said.

'I have to.'

'You can't leave us here.'

'Come with me. We'll get Penny, then go and get Rob, then go on to Siobhan's. Okay?'

'Okay.'

# 31

It was already afternoon, the gloom of the day making it feel like the light was fading ahead of time, almost as if it was being snatched away. It was bitterly cold. Clare went upstairs to try and dress Penny, leaving Tom pacing the ground floor rooms, trying to make contact with other people. He rang every number in his mobile, but no one answered. He did the same with Clare's, then tried her landline, working his way through her entire phone book as well as any other numbers he could remember. Still nothing. He checked the computer upstairs, but information was loading incredibly slowly, and when he did manage to read something, it had been hours since anything had been updated. The flow of information had stopped along with the people who consumed it. He looked up the number and tried to call John Tipper at the Badger's Sett, the last person he'd spoken to other than Clare, but the line just rang out unanswered.

The silence outside gave him too much time to think. Was this some kind of sickness? A contagion? Was it somehow connected to the aliens – and he couldn't imagine that it *wasn't* – or purely coincidental? Some kind of infection they'd brought to Earth, perhaps, which had laid dormant until now? His inability to find answers served only to intensify the fear. He hadn't seen any aliens since he'd last seen Jall, and with only a few hundred of them scattered across the surface of the entire planet, there didn't seem to be any prospect of that changing. They could have been anywhere. For all he knew, they could have gone.

Clare was taking forever. Tom waited impatiently, flicking through the channels on the TV now. Several channels just showed blank screens, others test cards or station identifiers. A couple were still broadcasting, but he guessed their programming must have been automated. Having some noise in the house – any noise – was welcome and he left it on as he stood at the window, scanning the street outside for any signs of movement. He looked around when Clare turned the TV off again, but she wasn't even in the room. He tried the nearest light switch, flicking it up and down several times more than was necessary, then did the same in the hall. Clare was at the top of the stairs.

'Power's gone. Where's your fuse box?' he asked her.

'Under the stairs.'

'You got a torch?'

'Should be one in there.'

He found the torch and switched it on, but it wasn't working.

'Got any spare batteries?'

'Shouldn't need any,' she shouted down. 'I only changed them a few days ago. I've told you before, the wiring's dodgy here. The lights are always tripping.'

Tom checked the torch a couple more times and even unscrewed the base and removed and replaced the batteries before giving up on it. He felt for the fuse board in the darkness under the stairs and located and flicked the trip switch. Nothing happened. He pulled out the fuses and examined each of them in turn as best he could but couldn't see anything immediately wrong.

'Don't bother, Tom,' Clare said from upstairs. 'It's not just us.'

He reversed back out of the cupboard, banging his head and cursing with pain, then went to find her. She was in her bedroom, looking outside. And he saw that she was right. Although it was too early for every light to be on, he would have expected to see a few lights out there by now. There were none, not a single damn bulb lit up for as far as he could see. Instinctively – though he already knew it was pointless – he tried a few more electrical items. A table lamp and small TV in Clare's room were both dead, as was the phone.

'Not even a fucking dialling tone now,' he said, slamming the handset back down. He took his mobile from his pocket. His battery hadn't been fully charged, but he knew he'd still had some power remaining. The screen was blank. He panicked. 'I've got to go. Sorry, Clare, I've got to go.'

She followed him down and out onto the street. He pressed the key fob to unlock his car as he ran towards it, but nothing happened. Clare grabbed his arm and tried to pull him back.

'This is pointless. Don't, Tom. It's too late...'

He unlocked the car door with the key and shrugged her off. 'I've got to go. Got to get back to Siobhan and Rob.'

He slammed the door shut, shoved the key in the ignition and turned it. Nothing. The engine didn't turn over. Every light and indicator on the dashboard remained unlit. Clare banged on the window then opened the door.

'Come back inside, Tom. Please.'

'I can't just leave them.'

'Come in and wait with me. Maybe the power will come back on. Please, Tom...'

He kept trying, forcing the key around, pumping the pedals... anything. He popped open the bonnet and checked the battery connections, then checked the fuses, refusing to accept the futility of his actions. He remained in the car alone, not wanting to move. Several minutes later, knowing he had little option, he reluctantly followed Clare back into the house. She shut and locked the door behind him.

'What are we going to do?'

He looked at her. 'What the hell can we do? It's like everything's running down.'

Tom crept upstairs to check on Penny again a while later. Clare was sleeping. The house was cold. Much of the earlier cloud cover had disappeared, and the intermittent light from a three-quarter moon occasionally provided him with a little welcome illumination.

He found Penny just where Clare had left her, half-dressed now but still on the floor, leaning over with her face pressed up against the wall. The moonlight played tricks, and several times Tom had to check himself because he thought the little girl's expression had changed.

He crept nearer, stopping when he was less than a metre away, reluctant to get any closer. He leant forward and listened for her breathing. There it was – shallow, but definitely there and reassuringly steady. He took hold of her wrist to try and take her pulse. Her skin was cold, her body limp. He pulled another sheet off the bed and covered her before going back downstairs to Clare.

'Any change?' she asked, startling him.

'Nothing,' he replied, feeling for a seat in the dark.

'What's happening, Tom?'

He didn't even bother trying to answer. How could he? And even if he knew, what difference would it make? What could he do about any of it? He got up and went into the kitchen. Clare continued talking, but he'd stopped listening. He sat at the table and screwed his eyes shut and covered his ears. He despised himself for being stuck in this damn house. He knew he should be anywhere but here but he was too scared to leave.

# 32

Tom woke with a start, sprawled across Clare's settee with her lying on top of him. He'd been drifting in and out of sleep for the last few hours. He couldn't remember her coming and lying with him but he was glad that she had. For a long time he did nothing more than lie perfectly still and listen to the soft and reassuringly normal sounds of her gentle breathing. He took comfort from the closeness and warmth of her body. As long as they stayed like this together, he didn't have to face what was happening outside.

The first grey light of morning trickled into the room. Tom closed his eyes and went over the events of the previous day again and again, trying desperately to make some sense of the bizarre things he'd seen and the inexplicable behaviour of the people he'd known and loved. He'd heard nothing in the night, so he assumed Penny hadn't moved. Regardless, he'd have to try and get home this morning, that much was clear. He plotted his route in his mind: home first, then he'd continue out through the village to Siobhan, maybe calling in on James and Stephanie and those poor kids if time and circumstance allowed. He felt an obligation to try and get to them. Maybe he should have been doing all of this last night instead of hiding away in the darkness here like a fucking coward?

He slid out from underneath Clare, doing all he could not to wake her, but desperate to relieve himself and also to check on the little girl upstairs. She'd be his barometer, he decided. Whatever state Penny was in this morning, Siobhan, Rob and all the others would probably be the same.

Tom used the downstairs bathroom and looked out of the window behind the toilet as he stood over the bowl. Everything looked reassuringly normal through the small rectangular pane of frosted glass: the fence and bushes at the end of

Clare's garden and the fields beyond, the occasional bird darting through the dull grey sky.

He flushed when he'd finished. The cistern was taking its time to refill. Low pressure, he decided as he washed his face and hands in a trickle of ice-cold water.

When he returned to the living room, Clare wasn't there. He heard her footsteps in the room directly above and went up to find her, hoping there'd been a change in Penny's condition. He knew the moment he entered the room that wasn't the case. Penny was where he'd left her last night. She hadn't moved a muscle.

'Any better?' he asked hopefully, although he already knew the answer.

'Same,' Clare quietly replied, gently stroking the side of her daughter's expressionless face. 'What are we going to do, Tom?'

He walked to the window, desperately trying to think of something constructive to say but failing miserably. As far as he could see, their position remained unchanged from last night. There was nothing they *could* do. He looked out over the back of the house and saw something which made his blood freeze.

Clare, still crouching on the floor with her daughter, immediately picked up on his sudden unease.

'Tom?'

He simply looked at her, unable to speak, then turned and ran. She sprinted after him as he raced downstairs, following him through the living room and kitchen, then out into the garden. He scrambled over the fence at the back of her property, then kept running until he was in the middle of the field immediately behind the house, sending a small flock of sheep scattering in all directions. He stopped and looked up.

'What is it?' Clare shouted. Tom pointed upwards.

Thousands of metres above them – maybe miles overhead – the hull of a huge alien ship was slicing through the cloud cover like a submarine.

'What the hell's going on, Tom? They got rid of that ship, didn't they? We saw them send it away. For fuck's sake, we watched it fly into the sun on live TV.'

Tom continued to watch the massive machine power down towards the surface of the planet. And, as more of the behemoth was revealed, he began to realise that this wasn't the same ship he'd seen previously. The alien vessel he'd seen arrive was long and narrow. This machine was more dart-shaped, almost like a flying wing.

'They must have faked the footage,' Clare said, craning her neck as the apparently endless metal monster continued to glide effortlessly above them.

'It's a different ship.'

'What?'

'This isn't the ship that was here before.'

'But they're not due to be rescued for another year or so, are they? Wasn't that what they said?'

There was another one of them. Tom rechecked, certain he'd just got confused. He looked around and saw there were definitely two ships now. No, wait, there were more. He ran over to the far side of the field and climbed up onto a low stone wall to get a better view. From there he could see another five alien ships in total. They were all different shapes and sizes. Some moved, others were stationary. Some were close to Thatcham, others miles away.

Feeling exposed, Tom jumped down and ran back to the house, following Clare who was already on her way inside.

# 33

Tom shut and locked the door behind him then leant against it, head spinning, numb with nerves and cold.

'Why so many of them?' Clare demanded, continuing with a torrent of obviously unanswerable questions. 'Why are they here?'

He ignored her and barged past to get to the hallway. He reached for his mobile – an instinctive reaction – then cursed his own stupidity when the screen remained as dead as it had been yesterday.

'Are they here to pick up the aliens or are they—?'

'How the fuck should I know?' Tom screamed at her. He threw his phone across the room and it hit the wall and exploded, sending shards of plastic and electronic components scattering over the laminate flooring. He looked up at Clare who backed away from him but continued to ask questions.

'But they must be here to take them home, mustn't they? There's no other reason, is there?'

'Just one.'

Tom sat down at the bottom of the staircase and held his head in his hands, unable to bring himself to spell out his worst fears. He covered his ears, trying to block out everything else so he could find another explanation for what was happening, something he might have missed before. But he couldn't. When he coupled the behaviour of the bulk of the indigenous population with what he and Clare had just witnessed outside, only one possible scenario remained: invasion.

He walked to the front door. The street outside was as quiet as it had been all of yesterday, deceptively peaceful. Nothing was moving out there, save for yet another huge ship which cruised silently across the grey cloud cover. It was smaller than the others he'd seen, but no less threatening.

Tom was numb. Terrified. And yet, bizarrely, he also felt sudden anger which stopped him being as scared as he knew he should be. It was more than just anger. He felt a genuine fury at the way the aliens had duped everyone, including himself. Sure, he'd not fallen in line to worship the visitors like just about everybody else had, but he was as guilty as the rest of them. Should he have made a stand... made more effort, asked more questions? Was there anything he could have done to prevent them taking a stranglehold on the human race then crapping on them from the greatest of heights like this? His mind wandered back to that night in Drayton, weeks ago now, when he'd first seen one of those extra-terrestrial fuckers in the flesh, and when one man had dared to stand up to them and question why they were here. And he thought about how everyone else had turned against the lone protester, and how he himself had done nothing to help. Things were immeasurably worse now. What chance did he have today?

*Am I going to keep being bloody useless,* he asked himself, *or do I make a stand?*

Tom knew he'd be pissing in the wind, and that this was no *Independence Day* moment. He wasn't going to help the human race pull off some miraculous, last minute escape, nor were the aliens going to be caught out by an earthbound germ or disease or anything like that. Fuck, he'd barely made a noticeable impact on the people of Thatcham recently, so what hope did he have of making a difference on a grander scale? But there were people out there who needed him. More to the point, there were people out there *he needed.*

'Where are you going?' Clare asked, panicking as he went to leave. 'Don't go, Tom, please. I have to stay here with Penny. You can't leave us now...'

'Stay here and keep out of sight.'

'You should stay here too. We should just wait until—'

'Until what? I've done all the waiting I'm going to,' he told her. 'Stay here and I'll come back for you later.'

'Where are you going?'

'To get Rob and Siobhan. I can't leave them out there. They're all I've got left.'

'What's the point? We can't fight back against this. We can't—'

'Don't, Clare. You'd do the same if you were in my position. Just keep the door locked and don't let anyone in.'

'There's no one else to let in.'

Deliberately moving quickly so he couldn't talk himself out of doing what he knew he had to, he left the house. 'See you later,' he said as he pulled the door shut behind him.

# 34

Tom ran to the car. He looked back and saw Clare watching from the window, then angrily gestured for her to get out of sight. The key fob was as useless as it had been yesterday, but he opened the door and tried the ignition in the vain hope that the engine might fire. There was no logical reason why it should, but he couldn't leave without trying. *Nothing.* The total lack of power was as unsettling as the sight of the alien ships soaring through the air overhead. It felt artificial, unnatural, as if the laws of physics themselves had somehow been altered.

He froze as another huge machine slipped silently across the sky above him. Back in the summer, the relative silence of the alien ships had been awe-inspiring, even to an alien sceptic like him. Today, however, their lack of noise just added to the cloying terror he now felt. The bastards could creep up on him and take him out in a heartbeat, the same way they'd managed to deceive the entire human race.

He studied this particular ship in detail as it flew by him with an arrogant lack of speed. It was lighter in colour than the others he'd seen, with an awkward shape which looked anything but aerodynamic. Five angled spokes stretched down from a central hub to an outer wheel, making the ship look strangely like a connective piece from a kid's construction set. It flew like a Frisbee which didn't spin, and the incredible illumination from several equally-spaced engines underneath its hull made everything brighter and warmer for a few brief seconds. But that warmth faded quickly, leaving the world below a colder, more inhospitable place than before.

With no means of transport, Tom had two options: he could either give up and stay where he was or he could try to get back into Thatcham on foot. The choice was a simple one.

*

Tom wasn't concerned about the distance – he'd run much further than this before now – but nerves and doubt conspired to make every footstep more of an effort than he'd imagined possible. He tucked himself in close to the sides of buildings wherever he could, but there were several stretches of open road between here and home which left him dangerously exposed. At one point he stopped and ducked behind a tree as another ship cruised overhead. This one looked like an undersized version of the first ship he'd seen last summer. The increasing variation in their designs distracted him momentarily. How many of them were here now? And if each ship could carry hundreds, possibly even thousands of aliens, then how the hell did he stand any chance out here alone? He'd keep moving as long as he could, he decided. If any of these ships were ordered to touch down and allow their crews to disembark, he'd have to think again. His mind filled with movie-inspired visions: garrisons of alien soldiers, hand-to-hand combat, forming a resistance...

The ship swerved through the eddying clouds, changing course directly above him, appearing to double-back on itself, almost as if it had missed something first time. He looked around, and when he realised he was the only thing moving down at ground level, he pressed himself flat against the tree. Were they tracking him? Was this huge fucker of a ship following him, ready to take him out? His questions were quickly answered when the vessel accelerated away. He felt cool relief wash over him. *I'm less important than I think I am*, he realised. *I'm one man alone. I'm nothing to them.* Feeling slightly safer, he started to run again. Within a short distance, however, his temporary optimism had again been replaced by pessimism. *What if I'm wrong? What if I'm the last man? Will they track me down in their thousands?*

Tom reached a more built-up section of road. The ship was still in view, hovering ominously over Thatcham now. It had slowed to a virtual stop. He couldn't help but still feel a sense of awe when he looked up at the incredible feat of engineering and technology hanging effortlessly in the sky, a triumphant culmination of unimaginable intellect and effort born on the other side of the universe. As he watched, a bright opening appeared in the craft's otherwise featureless underbelly, and from it a fleet of five smaller, dart-shaped ships swooped down. They seemed to plummet for several seconds before a single pulse of energy appeared from the rear of each of them and they levelled-out and raced away, all disappearing in different directions. Other than the light, he could see no other features on any of them: no windows or cockpit, no pilot. He thought they looked like military drones, the kind he'd seen used in desert wars which had blurred together. He wished that was what they were. He'd have felt safer under observation from an Earthly intelligence, no matter who it was or why they were following him.

Moving only his eyes, Tom traced the path of a couple of the smaller machines, transfixed. He was concentrating so intently on what was going in the air that he failed completely to notice things happening much nearer to him at ground level. A figure rushed him from the right, virtually rugby tackling him. He tried to fight back, but the force of the attack took him by surprise. He was slammed into the side of a large white Transit van. He wrenched himself free and spun around, ready to fight back. He expected to find himself face-to-face with an alien, but it was a young Asian girl. Early twenties, long black hair, a good twelve inches shorter and several stone lighter than him, her face bore a curious mix of panic and concern.

'What the fuck are you doing?' he demanded.

'Get into the van,' she ordered, pushing past him and opening the back of the Transit. He did as she said and followed her in.

'Who the hell are you?' he asked as he climbed into the van

and pulled the door shut.

'My name's Bhindi, Bhindi Shah,' she replied.

'You on your own?'

She nodded. 'You're the first person I've seen since yesterday who's not...'

'In a coma?'

'Pretty much.'

'Likewise. I've got a friend who's okay, though. I'm Tom.'

Bhindi crawled deeper into the van and crouched behind the driver's seat, looking up through the windscreen and watching the sky. Tom glanced around in the low light and saw a sleeping bag, some clothes, and the remains of a little food.

'How long do you think we've got, Tom? How long before...'

'Before what?'

'Before they do whatever they're planning to do. Before they wipe us all out.'

'No idea,' he replied, pressing his face against another window and looking up. 'How long have you been here, Bhindi?'

'Since last night. I've been staying with my uncle,' she explained, gesturing in the general direction of a couple of houses over the road. 'I couldn't stay there, though, not with him and Auntie like that, you know?'

'I know.'

'I put Uncle in his chair last night because he'd been lying on the floor all day. When I went back inside just now, he was in exactly the same position as I left him. He hadn't moved a bloody muscle.'

'They're all the same.'

'So what are you going to do?'

'I'm going home to get my brother, then I'm going to go on and get my girlfriend,' he answered without hesitation.

'Are they like us?' she asked. He shook his head. 'Then is there any point?'

'I have to try.'

229

She seemed about to argue, about to tell him he was wasting his time, but then thought better of it. 'What about your friend?'

'I'm going back to her when I've got them. She's with her daughter. She's like the others.'

'How?'

'What?'

'Your brother and your girlfriend... how are you going to move them?'

He didn't have an answer. 'I don't know.'

'I think you should just go back to your friend. Either that or stay here with me.'

'I can't. I can't just leave them.' Tom slouched down in the corner of the van. Was everything as futile as it was beginning to seem? 'I have to try.'

'What do they want?' Bhindi asked.

'Who knows? Us, water, clean air...'

'Well I wish they'd just fuck off. I wish they'd never come here. I never wanted them here in the first place.'

'You and me both.'

'All those fucking idiots talking as if they were some kind of gods. We've had them rammed down our throats constantly from the second they got here, and now look what's happened.' Her voice quickly turned from a whisper to a rant. 'People are so fucking stupid. So fucking gullible. Always so quick to believe the hype. It's the cult of celebrity, amplified a thousand times over.'

Tom sat and looked at her. He matched her anger, and also her frustration. No matter how much noise either of them made, he knew there was nothing they could do about their situation.

'I have to go,' he said.

'Don't go any further into the village,' Bhindi warned. 'You're a fool if you do. The place will probably be crawling with those things before long. It's only a matter of time.'

'Well they're not there yet,' he said, realising again that a part of him actually *wanted* the aliens to come down to the surface so he could go out fighting rather than just *watching*. 'You sure you're staying here?'

'It's where my family is. Anyway, I'm tired. Too tired to just keep running until they decide they've had enough of me.'

Keen to move on, Tom wished her well then climbed back out and shut the door behind him. He looked around anxiously but saw nothing and no one else moving. For a moment even the sky was relatively clear; the myriad alien ships all drifting away from the village for now. Why would they bother with Thatcham, anyway? It was as insignificant in the overall scheme of things as he was.

He began to jog then to run, his confidence returning. If the aliens had wanted to take him out, he thought, then wouldn't they have already done it? In any event, there was nothing he could do about it, no way he could defend himself against their technology and power, so why bother trying? His irrelevance was strangely reassuring; empowering, almost. *Why should they give a damn about me? I'm nothing to them.*

Before long Tom was sprinting towards home along eerily silent streets, his echoing footsteps the only noise.

# 35

The last half mile was the longest. From the moment the bungalow came into view, his pace dropped and the effort required to keep moving increased. The house looked as dead and uninviting as everywhere else, and actually being able to see the building made it somehow feel further away, not closer. His nervousness returned, amplified ten-fold at the thought of what he might find inside.

*What the hell am I doing? I can't take Rob with me, and I've got twice as far to go again before I even get to Siobhan.*

He stopped and almost turned around, but made himself keep going. He couldn't not go inside, not now.

This part of Thatcham was as deserted as everywhere else. Tom's heavy footsteps echoed off the walls of lifeless buildings, his laboured breathing amplified out of all proportion. He turned a corner and almost fell over a body lying sprawled face-down on the pavement, feet hanging out into the road. He recognised the man; he didn't know his name, but he'd regularly seen him around the village. He crouched down and shook his shoulder. No response. His eyes were wide open, unblinking, staring at nothing, just like the others.

In contrast with the malaise down at ground-level, the skies overhead were again teeming with activity. More ships were arriving by the minute. Some dropped down to perform unknown functions closer to the surface, then rose up and disappeared again. Others cruised imperiously through the cloud cover. One was so impossibly huge that Tom had assumed the sections of its hull he saw belonged to different ships until the entire vessel had cleared the clouds and revealed its full, terrifying magnificence. Another raced directly overhead, tipping over onto its side and zipping through the narrowing gap between two more, covering endless miles in a few scant seconds.

*If the skies are this busy here,* Tom wondered, *then what must it be like elsewhere?* How many thousands of ships were now crawling through the atmosphere above every country, swarming over every continent and every ocean? It was hard to believe that they'd taken over without a single shot being fired by either side; embarrassing, almost, that there'd been no final battle. Mankind had facilitated this and made it easy for the invaders. The aliens had almost been invited to browse the planet, then come and take what they wanted.

Tom stopped again at the bottom of the final climb up to the house, legs heavy with both effort and fear now. He looked up and saw Will Preston still sitting where he'd left him looking out to sea, in the exact same position almost twenty-four hours later.

The wind changed direction momentarily, carrying with it the instantly familiar noise and smell of the ocean, immediately taking him back to the summer just gone before the aliens had arrived, then further back still to distant holidays with Mum and Dad. His heart sank as he remembered when this place had still felt like home... when this place had, as far as he was concerned anyway, been the very centre of the universe.

*So what do I do now? Roll over and play dead like everyone else?*

Tom wiped tears from his eyes and looked up at his house again – little more than a black silhouette against the dark grey sky. That house had come to mean so much to him... it was the foundation of the new life he'd been building with Siobhan, a life which had been good and which had been getting even better until the aliens had arrived. That was when it had all started to unravel around him. That was when he'd begun to doubt and question himself. And as Tom stood and stared up at the house from the bottom of the climb, he realised *it wasn't me*. His increasing loneliness and self-doubt... the disconnection... wondering why he was alienating those people who mattered most... feeling a lack of worth, like he was the odd one out.

*There was never anything wrong with me, it was the rest of them. They were suckered in, I wasn't. I was right all along.*

With renewed energy, he dug deep and began the final climb home.

# 36

Almost an entire day since he'd left, Tom reached his house and let himself inside. He shut the door behind him and stood in the hallway, the noise of his entrance echoing throughout the small building. The house was cold, the air unnaturally still, and yet just being there made him feel immeasurably better. He peered around the living room door and saw his brother sitting on the sofa, eyes fixed straight ahead towards the lifeless TV, his body completely motionless. He ran to his side.

'Rob,' he said, his voice sounding too loud. Rob didn't flinch. He hadn't expected him to.

Tom felt a bizarre sense of vindication. Making it back here to this house against the odds was further proof that he'd retained more control than he'd allowed himself to believe. Almost everyone else had descended into catatonia, but not him. He looked around his home. There was the bedroom where he and Siobhan had slept and made love. The patio where they'd sat and talked. The computer he'd wasted half his life on. This was *his world*. No one else's. But he also knew that it was lost. He could feel his grip slipping away.

He crouched down in front of Rob. His brother was still breathing – just – and his eyes were open wide, but to all intents and purposes he was otherwise gone. A corpse with a pulse. What Tom would have given to see him smile again, or to hear his voice. And Siobhan... a wave of remorse washed over him when he thought about her being like this, alone in her flat. He cursed himself for having left her yesterday, pictured her sitting naked on the bed where he'd left her. Christ, even seeing a photograph of her would have helped make things a little easier. He could have pretended she was still with him. He wished he could hear her voice. He'd have played back a voice message on his phone or looked through his pictures, but the damn thing had been rendered useless long before he'd smashed it up against Clare's living room wall. All he had left now were memories.

'Tom?'

The voice took him by surprise. For a second he was too shocked to react. He remained completely still, almost too afraid to look. But then he did. He stood up and turned around. 'What the fuck are you doing here?'

Tom felt himself filling with rage. Standing in front of him – no, not standing, *cowering* – was Jall. Tom couldn't control himself. All of the fear and anger he'd been swallowing down immediately came bursting to the surface. He ran at the alien, who tried to scuttle back, and threw a single punch at him. His fist caught the side of Jall's head, the force of impact sending him spinning away. He lay on the carpet, sobbing, with crimson, almost black blood dribbling from a split above his right cheek. Tom took a step back then came at him again, booting him hard in the gut and hearing something crack.

Jall groaned.

Tom repeated his question. 'What the fuck are you doing in my house?'

'I didn't know... where else to go,' the alien said slowly, struggling to breathe.

'Bullshit,' Tom spat and he came at him again.

Jall tried to move but was still caught just above the pelvis by another brutal kick.

'Please, Tom,' he said, sobbing freely, 'don't...'

Tom paced the room. 'Give me one good reason why I shouldn't kill you now, you spineless cunt.'

'It's not what you think,' Jall said, clutching his ribs and trying to sit up. His right eye was badly swollen, almost completely closed. Tom felt good that he'd inflicted so much physical damage. He hadn't even started yet. 'We're both victims in this,' Jall continued. 'You, me... all of us.'

'What do you mean? What the fuck are you talking about?'

The light in the room decreased ominously, distracting Tom. He glanced out of the window and saw another immense black machine power silently through the increasingly turbulent air, almost covering the entire village with its shadow. A noticeable change in air pressure made the whole house shake. A pair of dirty beer glasses on the coffee table began to rattle against each other.

'I didn't know,' Jall whimpered. He was still on the floor, looking up through the window at the ship in the sky with eyes which seemed somehow to match Tom's fear. 'You have to believe me. I didn't know this was going to happen.'

'Bullshit. How could you not have known?'

'I didn't, I swear. None of us did.'

Tom was ready to kill Jall, keen to wring the life out of the fucker with his bare hands, but he paused. He thought for a moment that he could detect genuine, unexpected emotion in the alien's voice. He sounded nervous. No, it was more than that, he sounded *scared*. There was a definite trembling uncertainty in Jall's tone. Vulnerability, even.

'What are you talking about?' Tom demanded. 'Tell me everything or I'll kill you.'

'Those ships out there,' he said, lifting an overlong finger and pointing, 'they're nothing to do with me. They're nothing to do with any of us here.'

'What are you saying? You're not making any sense. If these ships aren't yours, whose are they?'

'They belong to my race, but not to those of us here. I'm not who I thought I was.'

Tom ran forward again and kicked out at the alien, catching him off-guard. He screamed out with pain.

'Stop this! Isn't what you've done already bad enough? Don't make things worse than they already are. Start talking sense.'

The alien rolled over on his side, clutching his left arm and howling like a wounded animal. Tom grabbed his collar and pulled him up onto his feet then shoved him towards the other end of the room, into the space between Rob and the TV on the wall, literally backed into a corner.

'Talk!' Tom screamed at him.

'Things aren't what they seem,' he said, watching Tom's every movement. 'Remember that first night we met and we talked about what I did and why we were here?'

'I remember. What about it?'

'Most of it wasn't true.'

'That doesn't surprise me.'

'But it's not what you think. I didn't know. I genuinely didn't know... none of us did. I remember you getting angry because you couldn't believe the utopian society I was describing.'

'Well that was clearly bullshit...'

'Not to me. I believed it.'

'*Believed* it? Past tense? Start from the beginning and tell me everything.'

Jall's breathing was laboured. His one remaining good eye locked onto Tom's face. 'You were told we were on a mining mission, and that our ship was damaged in an accident, remember?'

'I'd worked out that that wasn't true.'

'I hadn't.'

'What?'

'I had no idea. None of us did. Our ship was a probe, sent here to record information about your planet to see if it was habitable.'

'Bastards.'

Tom took another step forward, Jall took several more back until he hit the wall and could go no further. He held his hands up in submission, wincing when he moved his injured left arm. 'I swear, we didn't know,' he said.

'How could you not have known?'

'The exact same way the entire human race were fooled. We've been reprogrammed, Tom, we all have. The truth was hidden from us. Since long before we arrived here, constant signals have been broadcast alongside your transmissions. Remember back when we first talked, I told you how we've learned to alter everything at a microscopic, sub-atomic level? We can change anything physical into anything else, and Tom, *everything* is physical. Even a thought. At the end of the day, it's just a series of connections in the brain. Everything can be reduced down to a yes or no answer, remember? On or off. Plus or minus.'

'But how...?'

'For you it was a long, on-going process,' Jall explained, re-gaining a little confidence. 'A process which has been running for the last seventeen months or so. Television, radio, the Internet, films... everything has been augmented.'

'Subliminal messages?'

'If you like, but far more complicated than you make it sound. The more advanced a society, the more susceptible it often is. You rely on so many different means of communication – you're lost without them. Everything you've consumed over the last year and a half has been interrupted and modified prior to it reaching you. Think about it, Tom, how else could we have been allowed to arrive here like we did? We were dropped right into the middle of your civilization – a civilization which has been steadily tearing itself apart for years – and most people accepted us without question. You've never trusted each other, never mind anyone else, and you were manipulated into letting us in. You had to believe the story, and so did we. Didn't you think it was strange?'

'Right from the moment I first saw your ship. But everyone just accepted it.'

'So did we. The illusion was complete. We were manipulated too.'

'What do you mean?'

The alien's voice wavered again. 'I'm as much a victim as you are, Tom.'

'Bullshit.'

'It's not. My colleagues and I fully believed the stories we were telling you. We didn't know what we were really here for. I truly believed I was stranded.'

'But you're not, are you? You'll be able to hitch a lift home on any one of those ships out there.'

He shook his bulbous head and wiped his eyes. 'There's no way out of here for me.'

'Why not? That doesn't make sense.'

Jall hesitated before answering. 'We're political prisoners,' he said, 'and this is our sentence. You were right, Tom, there is no utopia. Our world is ruled by a brutal regime far worse than any you've had here. Libya, Syria, Iraq... they pale in comparison to those who rule my people. I foolishly tried to make a stand, and this is my punishment. Exiled from home, and sentenced to death.'

'So how do you know? Have they suddenly switched off your programme?'

'Pretty much. I realised as soon as I saw things start to change yesterday. I recognised the pattern, and the arrival of the fleet today just confirmed what I'd thought. I know what those ships are for. As soon as I saw them, things started to unravel and I remembered. They planned it this way. They want us to know what's happening. It's the final part of the punishment, to be fully aware at the end. It would be better to be like Rob and all the rest of them. They won't know anything. They're already gone...'

Tom was punch-drunk, unable to take it all in. These new revelations were almost impossible to process. 'Why...?'

'Why do you think?' Jall said, his confidence beginning to increase as Tom's ebbed away. 'We were being used as biological probes. They needed to see how we adapted to living here, so they sent us here and monitored the effect of the atmospherics on us for several months. Now they know exactly what they need to do to make the planet fully habitable, and the fleet has been mobilised. They're here to colonize, to expand the empire.'

'You fuckers. You think you're just going to stroll in here and—'

'Look out of your window,' Jall interrupted. 'It's already begun, and there's nothing either of us can do to stop it.'

Tom's rage returned, a thousand times stronger than before. He threw himself at Jall, taking the spindly-limbed figure by surprise again. Tom charged into him with his shoulder dropped, knocking him back, slamming him against the wall-mounted TV and cracking the screen. Jall fell forward and dropped to his knees, then hit the ground, face first, out cold.

Tom looked up into the dead TV and could see the rest of the room behind him, reflected back in the shattered monochrome mirror. He sat beside Rob, turning his brother's head to face him, trying to shake him back to life. His eyes remained unblinking. Pupils wide. Vacant stare. At his feet, Jall was beginning to stir.

'So what happens now?' Tom asked, his heart breaking.

'The planet will be recalibrated. Re-engineered,' Jall replied, dribbling dark blood.

'How?'

'I don't know. I'm not a scientist, Tom, even though I thought I was. I'm a politician. A failed revolutionary.'

'Has this happened before?'

'This is the fifth time, as far as I'm aware. I don't expect you to believe me, but this was one of the reasons I stood up against the regime. I couldn't stand back and be a part of this.'

'But if you can re-engineer planets, why choose this one? Why not just choose some other place? Somewhere uninhabited?'

'The scientists can do a lot,' Jall explained, 'but they can't move planets yet. Unfortunately for you, yours is optimally placed.'

'But there are billions of people here...'

Jall cleared his throat. 'There's a process.'

'Go on,' Tom said, unsure if he wanted to hear more, but knowing he had to.

'The first stage is to disable the resident population.'

'Disable?'

'Switch them off,' he clarified, looking directly at Rob. 'If it's any consolation, I don't think any of them can feel anything. Only minimal brain activity is maintained, basic control functions. They are completely unaware.'

'And then what? Ship them off somewhere?'

Another hesitation.

'There will be a cull,' he said. Tom couldn't help himself and he laughed out loud. It sounded so clichéd and implausible. Jall remained stony-faced.

'A cull? You're fucking kidding me. But when? How?'

'I would think it's probably already started. They'll do it land mass by land mass, I expect. It won't be long before it begins here.'

'Did you not hear me? There are billions of people here.'

'Come on,' the alien said, forgetting himself momentarily and unwisely adopting a superior tone, 'I don't agree with what's happening, but is this really any different to what you've been doing here yourselves for hundreds of years? Just substitute a rainforest for the entire planet.'

'How can you say that? It's completely different. All those lives... We'd never treat another people like this.'

'You would,' he replied factually, without any malice or spite in his voice, but with a definite hint of anger now. 'You *have*. Think of all those indigenous populations you've driven out of their homes. Is this any different? At least this way most people won't even know it's happening. They won't feel anything.'

The enormity of what he was hearing totally floored Tom. He walked away from Rob and Jall, barely even aware of his own movements now. Everywhere he looked, all he could see were things which reminded him how much he'd lost. Rob, Siobhan... everything was gone. The life he'd made for himself here now felt as if it was a million miles away. Tears rolled down his face, and the alien's last words rattled around his head: *they won't feel anything*.

'So why am I different?' he asked. 'Why am I here talking to you when everyone else is...'

'Not everyone is as susceptible to the program, I guess. It's difficult to achieve one hundred per cent success in anything.'

'How many are left like me?'

'I don't know. It won't be many. I'm sorry, Tom. You know there's every chance it will still happen to you. If you feel yourself losing control, don't fight it. You should embrace it. It'll be a lot easier that way.'

Notwithstanding everything he'd seen and been a part of since the aliens had arrived last summer, Tom felt like he was trapped in a third-rate science-fiction film. His mouth was dry. He struggled to string enough words together to ask his next question.

'What if I don't conform?'

'Then all you can do is sit back and watch your world change around you. I'm in the exact same position. I don't have any option either. They don't give a damn about me. They sent me here to die.'

'My heart bleeds.'

'If I could change things, Tom, I would. But I can't. I'm scared... probably as scared as you. I don't want to die.'

'But there must be something you can do?'

'There's nothing. The process has already begun and it's

unstoppable. It's like a reboot of the planet, by all accounts. There's nothing either of us can do now. I don't know how long it'll take or what immediate effect it'll have. You might be able to survive for a few days, maybe even longer. You could try and find somewhere remote and watch it happen.'

Another ship drifted out over the village and moved over the ocean, the sudden change in light as it blocked the window refocusing Tom. *What the hell am I doing here?* He looked down at his brother – all but dead – and then thought about Siobhan alone in her flat and Clare and Penny... He needed to get out of here if he wanted to see them again. He tried to pick Rob up, but his useless bulk was too heavy. He knew he had no option but to leave him.

'Where are you going?' Jall asked as Tom moved towards the door. Tom didn't answer. The alien ran after him and pulled him back. 'Don't go. Stay here. I'm scared, Tom. I don't want to be on my own when—'

'*You* don't want to be on your own? I couldn't give a fuck about *you*! Look at what you've done to my brother. My girl-friend's out there like this. She's on her own...'

'And there's nothing you can do for her, I've already told you. Believe me, Tom, things will start to move quickly around here soon, and you won't want to be outdoors when it begins.'

Tom ignored his protests and shook him off. He reached for the front door handle and Jall put a hand on his shoulder. Tom glanced down, and the sight of those foul, elongated, pale alien fingers enraged him.

'Get off me, you bastard,' he hissed, turning around and pushing Jall away.

Jall winced and staggered back, holding onto his injured midsection. 'Please,' he begged. 'I'm as innocent in all of this as you are.'

'Innocent? As innocent as Rob and Siobhan?'

'Stop this, Tom,' Jall said. 'You're wasting your time. Do you want me to tell you exactly what's been done to them? Shall I tell you which parts of their brains have been disabled and which parts left operational? Nothing you can do will help them. It's over. The people you used to know are already dead.'

'As long as they're still breathing, they're alive—'

'Only physically. Emotionally they're—'

Tom moved towards Jall who continued to cower away. 'You can deny responsibility all you like, but the fact is none of this would have happened if you bastards hadn't come here. You've taken everything I had left. You've destroyed my life.'

'And they've destroyed mine too. This isn't my fault,' Jall whimpered. 'You're just making things harder for yourself, Tom. Admit defeat or keep fighting, that's the only choice we have left to make. And it doesn't matter what you decide, the end result will be the same.'

Tom stared deep into the alien's piercing eyes. He'd despised this particular fucker from the outset, and because he was here, an invader in his own home, he was going to make him pay for the crimes his entire people were now committing. He screwed up his fist and slammed it into Jall's face, catching him square on the jaw and completely off-guard. He tried to crawl away, but Tom wasn't finished with him. He grabbed him by the scruff of his neck and pulled him back upright, easily man-handling the alien's surprisingly insignificant weight.

'Fucking bastard,' he yelled at Jall as he spun him around and threw him into the kitchen. Jall fell and Tom picked him back up, pushing him up against the wall. He looked deep into the alien's face. There were tears rolling down his cheeks and blood was pouring from a split in his swollen bottom lip.

'Please,' he begged. 'It's not my fault...'

Tom punched him again, and felt his body slump. He almost believed Jall, but he was past caring now. He held him by his neck, pinned up against the wall, and he offered no resistance. Jall knew he was beaten and he shook and sobbed, his cries choked as Tom tightened his grip on his windpipe. Tom's pain was unbearable. He knew he'd never make love with Siobhan again and wake up next to her in the morning. He'd never go drinking with James, never watch bad movies and rip them to pieces with Rob, never listen to music or read another book... He hoped more than anything that the alien felt as much pain and loss as he did.

Tom covered Jall's face with his right hand. He squeezed hard, pulled his head forward, then smashed it back. Jall whimpered, but didn't cry out. He screwed up his eyes in pain, then opened them again and looked straight at Tom. Tom did it once more, thumping his head back harder this time, leaving a bloody smear on the wall. He let go of Jall, letting him slide down to the floor. He looked up at Tom and opened his mouth as if he was about to say something. Whatever it was, Tom didn't want to hear it. He kicked Jall in the face, then, when the alien slumped over, he brought his boot crashing down on the side of his head, feeling bones crack.

Before leaving the house, Tom collected food, water and clothes, then left much of it behind. If what the alien had said was true – and despite everything, Tom thought it probably was – then he didn't have long left.

He wanted to stay a while and say goodbye to Rob, but there wasn't any point. He lay him down on the sofa and covered him with a duvet to keep him warm. It was a pointless gesture, but it made him feel marginally better. Then he made himself leave. Standing outside, he looked down over the lifeless village of Thatcham below.

*Which way do I go? Siobhan or Clare?*

Despite everything, his mind was made up in an instant. He began running towards Siobhan, knowing it was futile but unable to stand the thought of not seeing her again.

# 37

The quickest way to Siobhan's by foot was to head into the centre of the village and out the other side. Tom ran down the uneven pathway which led away from his house, increasingly conscious that he was the only thing still moving. Even the birds seemed to have disappeared from the sky. He allowed himself one final look back over his shoulder before his home disappeared from view forever. The temptation to turn back was still there; to sit in familiar surroundings alongside his brother and watch the world he knew gradually disappear and become something alien and new.

He struggled to moderate his speed. He wanted to sprint to Siobhan, but he knew he'd never make it. He needed to conserve energy, knowing that after reaching her flat, he'd then need to try and get her to Clare's. How he was going to do that, he had no idea. A short time with Siobhan in an unresponsive state was infinitely preferable to never seeing her again, and this way, he thought, he might still have a chance, albeit a very slight one, of protecting her from the oncoming cull. That was what he kept telling himself, anyway. If he said it enough times, he thought he might start to believe it.

Another alien ship appeared overhead, overtaking him as he ran down the main street through the centre of the village. It was radically different to the others he'd seen. It flew much lower, and had an enlarged, rounded front-section with a stunted rear. With his mind filled with terrifying thoughts of the impending extermination of millions of lives, he panicked and ducked out of sight behind a metallic blue Ford Mondeo opposite the Badger's Sett pub, tripping over the outstretched legs of another lifeless victim of the aliens. He instinctively steadied the young woman's body.

On his knees, Tom looked through the car's windows

straight across to the pub, then got up and ran across the road, remembering that John Tipper had been as lucid as he himself when he'd last seen him yesterday morning. John was like him and Clare, somehow resistant to the alien's programming. The thought of seeing another familiar face gave him a faint flicker of hope.

Being inside the pub was a heart-breaking, almost surreal experience. Everything looked much the same as before, but it was all inherently different; unreal, almost like a film set. This was a dead place now, devoid of all atmosphere. The noise, the people... all gone. He walked around the end of the bar, helping himself to a lukewarm drink from a useless chiller cabinet, then went into the back of the pub.

Tom had been behind the bar several times before, always at John's invitation. He'd once helped him carry an awkward wardrobe upstairs, and had unloaded deliveries with him on a couple of occasions when he'd been short-staffed. Today, however, he felt like an intruder. He stood at the bottom of the long, straight staircase and called up.

'John? John... are you there? Betty?'

There was no answer. He knew he was wasting time, that he should leave now and keep going, but he couldn't go without checking. He crept upstairs, cringing at the disproportionate noise his heavy footsteps made on the creaking boards, then waited at the top of the landing and called out again. Still nothing. He walked further into John's home and found Betty sitting cross-legged on the living room floor, staring into space.

'Betty?'

She didn't move when he approached. He waved his hand in front of her face, but there was nothing. Betty's condition unnerved him more than most others he'd seen this morning. He'd never known this woman quiet before.

Tom found John in the bedroom next-door, slumped against the foot of his bed, as unresponsive as everyone else. He looked the same as always: a saggy, hand-knitted Aran sweater, and with his glasses still perched on the bridge of his nose. There was a cricket bat beside him, like he'd been ready for his last stand, but had then given up. He shook John's shoulder, virtually begged with him to wake up, but he knew he was wasting precious time. He was lost like all the others.

Tom paused in the doorway and looked back at his friend. As the initial disappointment faded, his sadness turned to terror. *If John eventually succumbed,* he thought, *will I go the same way? What about Clare?* The thought of losing control and being reduced to this was unbearable.

Tom was about to leave the building when the light in the upstairs rooms changed. He looked out of the nearest window and saw that the alien ship he'd come into the pub to escape had altered its position again. Ominously, it was directly over the centre of the village now. The size of the thing was impossible to gauge: he couldn't tell whether it was a mile above him or ten. As he watched, a single wide opening appeared in the base of the rounded front-end of the vessel and a long, stem-like object was lowered down. He dived for cover, terrified at what might be about to happen next. Like a frightened kid he scrambled under the bed, tripping over John Tipper's unresponsive legs as he did so. Tom buried his face in the carpet, covered his head, and waited.

Nothing happened.

He held his position for a while longer, still too scared to move, convinced that the second he looked up would be the moment the aliens unleashed whatever hell they had ready over Thatcham, wiping out its population, regardless of whether or not they had submitted to their programming.

Still nothing. The pub shook as the enormous craft held its position overhead. Ornaments and books fell off shelves. He heard glasses smashing downstairs. It felt like an endless earthquake.

*I'm dead anyway*, Tom thought, sick of hiding, and he crawled back out into the open and returned to the window. The glass rattled and shook in its frame. The alien ship was still there, but it was climbing vertically now, drifting up into the sky and rotating slightly as it did so. Tom remained there for a moment longer, pulse racing, holding onto the windowsill for support. *Pull yourself together*, he told himself. *Get out of here.*

He was about to move when he heard someone else moving in the building with him. An alien? He looked around for a weapon but could find only the bottled drink he'd brought up from the bar. He emptied the last dregs out onto the carpet then held the neck of the bottle and smashed the end of it against the wall. He crept around the edge of the room and was about to step out onto the landing when Betty Tipper strode past the doorway.

'Betty?'

He immediately regretted calling out, but she didn't react. She marched past him, her face emotionless. She'd have collided with him if he hadn't moved out of her way. He pressed himself up against the wall to avoid her touch, then leant over the banister and watched as she went downstairs. He spun around when he heard more footsteps behind him. He tripped over his own feet and ended up on his backside, looking up in disbelief as John Tipper marched towards him, his face vacant, terrifyingly expressionless. Tom scrambled back up and tried to grab hold of John but the older man was unnaturally strong and walked on regardless, following his wife down into the pub.

Tom crept down after the Tippers, maintaining a cautious distance. He watched them both walk through their pub, following the exact same route step for step, then heard them go out through the door. By the time he'd reached the exit, he could see through the glass that the street outside was rapidly filling with people. He stood on a bench and watched through a window as people emerged from virtually every building. The noise of hundreds of footsteps filled the air, the sound made all the more uncomfortable by the total absence of anything else. No speech. No coughs, splutters or sneezes. No cries, no one begging for mercy. Not a single damn word.

Hiding behind the edge of the curtain, Tom watched as the people formed themselves into a single line along the exact centre of the road. All facing the same way. All perfectly equidistant from the person in front and the person behind. Once they'd taken up position, they each became still again, and the lack of visible animation was as unsettling as anything else Tom had so far seen today. The people were like waxwork dummies, completely unaware of what was happening around them, and yet each of them was perfectly in tune with everyone else. It all seemed effortlessly choreographed, the movements of the people executed with military precision as if they'd practiced these manoeuvres all day, every day for months. He shifted his position slightly, standing on a chair now to get a better view without being seen, and saw that people were continuing to pour out of the side streets and join the queue which now stretched as far as he could see in either direction along the main road. There was little doubt in his mind that if this wasn't the entire population of Thatcham, it soon would be.

*What about Siobhan?*

Suddenly forgetting about his own safety, Tom left the pub and approached the nearest section of the queue. None of the people reacted to his presence in the slightest. He began to look at each of their faces in the vain hope he'd see Rob or Siobhan, but he couldn't immediately find either. Now completely exposed but no longer giving a damn, he walked further down the line.

He found James.

His friend was alone, the rest of his family nowhere to be seen at first. Then he found Stephanie a short distance back, and their son Mark a little further still. Where were the others? What had happened to Bethany and the baby? He hoped they were still together, but he knew there was nothing he could do to help them now.

And then Tom found his brother.

'Rob,' he whispered, pushing his way into the queue and standing directly in front of him. 'Rob, can you hear me?'

Rob remained motionless and impassive, eyes wide and unblinking, gazing into the distance at some undefined point. He tried to pull him away from the line but he wouldn't move. It was as if his feet had been nailed to the ground.

A new sound alerted Tom. The eerie silence was shattered by a loud noise coming from somewhere near the front end of this vast line of people. He took a few steps back to try and get a better view, but the beginning of the queue was too far ahead for him to be able to see anything. And then, without warning, the people began to move. Tom ducked out of sight into the driveway which ran down the side of the supermarket, his heart pounding. The ripple of movement quickly worked its way down to where he was, each person starting to walk as soon as the person immediately in front had shifted. The movement of the masses was bizarre, like production line robots. They were all still in perfect time, precisely synchronised in spite of their wildly differing size, age and physical condition. Every footstep matched. Each person lifted their feet at the exact same moment, then took a step of the exact same length as everyone else before putting their feet down in unison. The stomping noise which accompanied the march increased in volume with every additional person who moved. It was a wholly unnatural sound: *stomp – silence – stomp – silence – stomp – silence...*

Rob.

Tom's terrified malaise lasted a couple of seconds longer before he broke cover and sprinted further down the line until he found his brother again, then he grabbed his hand and tried to pull him out of formation. He managed to drag him a couple of metres away but couldn't match the force which was controlling Rob's movements, and their hands separated. All he could do was watch as his brother was re-absorbed into the vast column, those ahead and behind adjusting their speed and position enough to allow him back into the fold without missing a step.

Desperate now, Tom grabbed at the line again, this time catching hold of an elderly man so frail he looked barely able to support his own weight. Realising the futility of his actions almost immediately, Tom straightaway let the old man's hand drop and watched as he too melted back into the faultlessly formed line, matching the relentless pace of everyone else with ease, a pace he himself knew he'd struggle to match.

Tom staggered back, sobbing. He looked up again, hoping to catch one final glimpse of his brother, knowing with almost complete certainty that this would be the very last time. The pain was unbearable. Worse still, he knew now that there would be no point trying to reach Siobhan because she was inevitably lost too. She was probably already here... Was there any point doing anything now, or should he just stay and wait for the end to wash over him as the alien had suggested?

But he knew he couldn't just give up. What about Clare? He had to get back to her and hope she remained as lucid as when he'd foolishly left her earlier.

It was a safe assumption that this silent, snaking line of people were inevitably being marched to their deaths. He needed to find a different route to get back to Clare's, maybe avoid the roads altogether. Sensing that the next ship which appeared might be the one which carried some foul weapon of mass destruction to start the cull, he cut through the queue and then slipped down a side road towards Thatcham's small train station.

Like everywhere else, the quaint little building was completely silent and empty. His lonely footsteps echoed as he walked through the ticket office and waiting area. The platform was deserted, and he clambered down onto the tracks. The line ran close to the back of Clare's house and, as he hadn't seen any vehicles capable of movement since yesterday, following the track seemed a relatively safe and direct way of getting back to her.

He paused and looked in either direction. From down here the world appeared strangely uniform and simple – the repeating pattern of the sleepers and the rails stretching away into the distance for as far as he could see. He set off towards Clare's at a jog, deliberately pacing himself like before, not wanting to use all his remaining energy at once. He wanted to keep something in reserve, though he didn't know what for.

The track climbed a steady incline away from Thatcham for a short distance before dropping back down and levelling out again. At the highest point on the rise, Tom scrambled up the embankment to look down over the world below him. He could see for miles. The skies were teeming. Several vast lines of people were visible now, all moving in the same general direction. Others remained stationary as if waiting for orders. The ease with which thousands of people were being manipulated was terrifying.

All that mattered now was getting back to Clare. Tom didn't want to die alone.

# 38

The railway track was deceptive. Following the long, artificial scar through the frequently obscured landscape, Tom managed to convince himself on more than one occasion that he was either going the wrong way or following the wrong line altogether. It was just nerves. He needed to get a grip and stay calm. When the track crossed a tall stone bridge over a narrow road, he knew beyond doubt he was going the right way. Just a little further now...

The line carved a dark groove between fields on either side, and Tom knew he was close. He recognised this place. He left the track and jogged across the grass until he saw Clare's cottage in the near distance, nestled amongst a row of similar-looking homes. His nervousness increased again as he approached. Was this a mistake? Were the aliens following him and was he about to lead them straight back to Penny and Clare? He knew that was bullshit, but it was becoming increasingly difficult to stay focused and think straight. *Is this confusion how it begins?* The thought that he might be starting to lose control made him run even faster.

Soaked with dew and sweat and splattered with mud and sheep shit from the fields, he drew level with the fence which ran along the back of the houses. He climbed into Clare's small garden, allowing himself to slow down now he'd finally made it back.

'Clare!' he shouted. He tried to open the back door. It wasn't locked but it had been blocked with a table. A couple of rough shoulder barges and he'd managed to force enough of a gap to be able to squeeze through and get inside. Once in the middle of the kitchen he shouted again. 'Clare!'

The house was as desolate as everywhere else he'd been today. Tom checked the downstairs rooms, his mind filling with nightmare thoughts of John Tipper, and how he'd succumbed to the aliens. No sign of either Clare or Penny. He ran upstairs, pausing when he reached the landing. He continued through into Penny's brightly painted room and looked for the little girl in the corner, but there was no one there.

'She's gone.'

He spun around and saw Clare sitting in the diagonally opposite corner of the room, wedged into a narrow gap between Penny's desk and her wardrobe, wrapped in the duvet they'd used to try and keep Penny warm last night. She was staring into space, her face framed by the bedding. She looked beaten, empty.

'When?'

'About an hour ago,' she replied, still not moving. Her voice sounded detached and unemotional. 'I don't know where she went. I tried to stop her, but she was too strong. They've all gone, Tom. All the people in these houses... it was like someone flicked a switch.' She let the duvet fall away and she stood up. Tom reached out for her but she didn't want to be held and she pushed him away. 'I was shouting at her to stop, begging her not to go, but she was stronger than me. *She* was too strong for *me*. She unlocked the door. She's never been able to unlock the door before. She's nine years old. How could that be?'

'I saw it too. It's happening everywhere, Clare.'

'You should have seen them,' she continued, not listening. 'They were in perfect fucking formation.'

'Penny's gone,' Tom said, and for the first time Clare looked directly at him. 'Rob, Siobhan, James and his family... they're all the same. I watched my brother walk away like you watched Penny.'

'Did you find Siobhan?'

He shook his head and tried to answer but couldn't. The pain was unbearable. He managed to compose himself enough to speak. 'I only saw one other person like us in all the time I was out there.'

'Who?'

'A girl. She was hiding.'

'And you just left her?'

'She wouldn't leave.'

'She was the only one? You haven't seen anyone else?'

'Back at the house... Jall was there.'

'Who?'

'The alien that Rob knows... knew.'

'There to gloat, was he?'

'He told me he was hiding. Tried to make out it had nothing to do with him, said he'd been sent here as punishment for standing up against his people. He told me what they're here for, Clare. They're taking the planet.'

'I'd worked that much out for myself. Where is he now?'

'Dead. I killed him.'

She remained standing opposite Tom, and he could see her trying to make sense of the little he'd told her. It felt like minutes had passed when she next spoke, though it could only have been seconds.

'I'm going. I can't stay here with Penny out there on her own. I should have gone already but I stayed here for you.'

She left the room and ran downstairs. Tom chased after her. 'Don't go. There's no point.'

Clare wasn't listening. She was sitting on the bottom step, pulling on a pair of boots. 'There's every point. My little girl is out there. She might be surrounded by hundreds of other people but she's still on her own. She needs me...'

'There's nothing you can do for her. They're gone, Clare. They're all gone.'

'I have to try,' she said, grabbing her coat from a peg. 'I should have followed her. Shouldn't have waited for you. I'm the only one who looks out for her. It's only ever been me and I'm not going to stop now.'

'It's too late...'

Tom positioned himself between her and the door. She tried to push past him but he wouldn't move. She screamed at him with frustration as he stood his ground. 'Get out of the bloody way!' She shoved him again, and this time he caught hold of her arms and refused to let go. She fought for a few seconds longer, yelling and trying to beat him off, before giving up. Tom held her tight as she broke down.

# 39

Clare sat bolt upright. She and Tom were sitting in Penny's room together. Neither of them had moved for more than an hour. There hadn't seemed any point. They'd both been sitting against the wall, watching through the window opposite as countless alien ships silently criss-crossed the skies.

'What was that?'

'What?' Tom asked, immediately concerned.

'I heard something outside, I'm sure I did.'

She got up and ran through to her bedroom at the front of the house. Tom followed. They stood either side of the wide window, peering around the net curtains. There was someone out there, trying to get into the house next door. He looked like he was in his mid-twenties. Well built, like a rugby player.

'You know him?' Tom asked.

'Jim and Eileen's son-in-law. He's like us, Tom, he must be.'

Clare banged on the window and Tom cringed at the noise. 'Don't,' he snapped, still instinctively afraid of drawing attention to where they were hiding. 'I'll go. Wait here.'

He was gone before she could argue. He stumbled downstairs, legs stiff through inactivity, and unlocked the front door. He ran out onto the street but the man had already forced his way into his in-law's house. He was checking each room in turn, and Tom's sudden appearance startled him. He had a shotgun, and Tom found himself staring down its barrel.

'Don't shoot,' he said quickly, raising his hands.

'Who the fuck are you?' the man demanded, his desperate face streaked with tears.

'There are two of us next door. You should come and—'

'Have you seen Eileen and Jim?'

Tom shook his head. 'Everyone's gone, mate. It's the aliens.'

'No shit, fuckwit,' the man said, pushing past Tom and running upstairs. Tom followed and found him trashing an un-made bed, throwing the duvet and pillows off as if he thought his missing mother and father-in-law might be hiding under-neath.

'They've all gone,' Tom said again. 'Look, why not come back with me and—'

'I know they're gone,' the man yelled, marching threateningly towards Tom, who backed into a wall, unable to get away. Sud-denly the man's demeanour changed and his face crumbled. 'I tried to stop her,' he said, clearly heart-broken, his words punctuated by deep, painful sobs, 'but she wouldn't listen to me. Wouldn't speak to me. Wouldn't even look at me. Is that what happened to yours, mate? Did yours all go the same way?'

'That's what's happened to just about *everyone*,' Tom ex-plained, 'and there's nothing we can do about it.'

Tom looked on helplessly as the man dropped to his knees at the foot of the bed, his cries echoing around the empty house. 'Come on,' he said, wanting to give up and go back to Clare, but knowing he couldn't just walk out on this poor bastard.

'So what are you going to do?' the man asked, looking back over his shoulder at Tom with red-raw eyes.

'There's not a lot we can do. Just stick together, I guess, and stay safe for as long as we can. They're not interested in people like you and me. We're not part of the programme.'

'And what about those they've already got?'

'They're gone,' he said. 'There's nothing we can do for any of them.'

The man nodded and wiped his eyes. 'Thought as much.'

Tom, now standing in the doorway, looked back down the stairs. He could see the open door, and he wanted to get back to Clare. 'I'm going next door. You coming?'

'Give me a second, okay?'

'Okay.'

Tom had barely taken two steps down when a single gun-shot rang out, filling the house with noise. He kept walking.

# 40

The light was fading. Clare paced the downstairs rooms of the house. In the short time since Tom had returned from next door, they'd done little but argue. Clare wanted to go out and look for Penny, Tom knew there wasn't any point. He couldn't bring himself to spell out why, letting her cling onto the belief that Penny was still alive instead.

'I'm going,' she suddenly announced.

'Christ, Clare, we've been through this. You can't. It won't do any good.'

Her mind was made up. 'I've heard everything you've said, Tom, and I know you're right. It probably won't make any difference, but I have to try. My daughter's out there. I should be with her.'

'Even if you find Penny, you won't be able to help her. She won't know you. She won't respond to you.'

'I know that, but I can't just sit here any longer. Not while she's out there...'

Tom was on the verge of telling her about the cull but he stopped and checked himself. She'd probably already worked it out for herself.

'Thing is,' Clare continued, 'it's going to take time, isn't it?'

'What is?'

'For those bastards to do whatever they have to do to the planet to make it habitable for them. Our gravity is stronger, isn't it? And isn't the atmosphere supposed to be more acidic than theirs?'

'So?'

'So they're going to need to do something about it before they move in and occupy us, aren't they?'

'That's what Jall said. He called it re-engineering.'

'Chances are it's going to take a while, even with all their tech. I don't know about you, but I've been sitting here all day assuming the end could come at any minute. It might not. We might still have days left. Weeks... months, even. We should use the time. Get out and find the people who matter, maybe others like us.'

'But the end result's going to be the same, isn't it?'

'Probably, but what would you rather do? Are you prepared to give up on her like this? I'm not.'

Whether it was a clumsy attempt at emotional blackmail, or just something to say in these darkest of moments, Clare's words struck a chord: what kind of a man would he be if he just sat back and waited to die without even trying to find Siobhan? But then he remembered the condition Rob had been in when he'd left him, and he knew there was no point trying to save any of them. But Clare still believed there was hope, and who was he to tell her otherwise? She was right about one thing; time was all they had left. Maybe they should try to do something with it instead of sitting here like prisoners on Death Row. He tried to think more positively, logically.

'Maybe our best option is to get away from anything man-made,' he suggested. 'Jall said the few of us still conscious aren't a concern to them, so if we stay away from towns and villages and just head out into the middle of nowhere we might last a little longer.'

'Long enough to find Penny?'

He didn't think so – still didn't think there was any point even looking – but he didn't want to tell her otherwise.

'We should head for the sea,' he said suddenly. 'Just water there, no buildings. We might be safer if we can get off the mainland.'

'It's got to be worth a try. Can you sail?'

'No.'

'Do you know where we can find a boat?'

'Maybe.'

'Then that's what we should do. Get away from here, find out where they've taken everyone, get Penny and the others, then get the hell away from everything else.'

They were ready to leave within a few minutes. They worked quickly and quietly together to collect all the food and other useful supplies they could find from around Clare's little house. Clare cried as she worked, and Tom wondered if she was experiencing the same emotions he had when he'd left his own home for the final time. He thought it must have been even worse for Clare, the pain infinitely more intense. She'd lived here for years and had brought her daughter up in this house too. Her attachment to this place undoubtedly ran deep.

They managed to fill a rucksack each. As they readied themselves in the kitchen, rain began to clatter against the window. It sounded like someone was throwing stones against the glass. Tom looked out and saw that the clouds were whipping across the skies at different levels and different speeds, almost too fast. It reminded him of the storm he'd been caught out in when the aliens had first arrived. And overhead their ships continued to sail through the atmosphere untroubled. Impervious.

'We should go,' he said. 'We're not going to—'

His words were silenced by an intense flash of light outside. He thought it was lightening at first, maybe a double-strike, but the longer the light continued, the more obvious it became that this was something else entirely. It was too bright to keep watching, and Tom looked away until it faded again. He wondered if it was a signal that the invaders were readying themselves to make a long-overdue appearance on the surface of the planet they were claiming as their own. He hoped they were. In some bizarre way he thought that might even the odds slightly. He'd already killed one of them with unexpected ease. Maybe he'd have a chance to take out a few more yet, one for each of the people he'd lost.

264

'Ready?' he asked, sensing that Clare was standing right behind him.

'I'm ready,' she replied, though there was clearly much reluctance in her voice. Before she could dissuade herself, she opened the back door and stepped out onto the patio. Tom had already suggested they should stick to the train track he'd followed to get here – a relatively direct and well-sheltered route which would lead them to the coast. He followed her down the garden and clambered over the fence, stopping only when a number of smaller alien ships whipped through the air just above their heads, much lower than most others they'd so far seen. The wind they left in their wake was intense, and Tom held onto Clare tightly, struggling to stay upright through the sudden gale.

'Keep moving,' he said when the wind had faded again.

The ground beneath their feet was boggy, making progress frustratingly slow. The train track was just about visible as a dark black line stretching across the already dark landscape.

'Which way?' Clare asked. Left would take them towards the ocean, right would lead them straight back to Thatcham. There was a part of Tom that still wanted to go back there. There was still some familiarity in Thatcham – in the shapes of the buildings and the roads if nothing else – and that seemed preferable to just about anything else.

'Away from the village,' he replied, hoisting his rucksack into a more comfortable position, then scrambling over a low fence and down onto the track. Their pace quickened now that they were able to walk on the sleepers and shingle. Clare made an attempt to stay hidden, but Tom knew there wasn't any point. There remained some level of alien activity in the sky visible almost all of the time, but apart from the occasional smaller ship which hugged the ground, in the main they continued to operate at dizzying heights. Tom and Clare were of no interest to them.

# 41

Their initial burst of energy didn't last long. With only a vague, interminable aim, they both soon began to flag and the effort of the walk increased. At first Clare marched on and set the pace, thoughts of her missing daughter driving her forward. Within the space of a mile, however, the last light of day had all but completely gone and she'd dropped back, allowing Tom to take the lead.

There was another intense pulse of light in the far distance. Tom turned away and crouched down, waiting for it to disappear. He took his time getting up again, long enough for Clare to catch up. 'You all right?' he asked as she drew level.

'Dumb fucking question,' she replied. 'Of course I'm not all right. Fucking idiot. How can I be all right when I've just—'

The appearance of another alien ship overhead immediately silenced her. Its absolute lack of noise had taken both of them by surprise, allowing the huge machine to creep up and catch them both unawares. Although it remained hundreds of metres above them, its unannounced appearance chilled Tom to the bone.

Without needing to speak to one another, they both leant up against the steep embankment until the ship had disappeared. It was gone in less than a minute, but Tom remained on alert, determined not to be caught out like that again. He gently pushed Clare forward. She shook him off and grumbled at his unsubtle intervention.

'Leave me alone.'

'Can't be far now.'

'You've been saying that for as long as we've been walking. There's no sign of anyone around here, and there's no way we'll see anything from down here on this bloody train track. They're just words, Tom. If you haven't got anything constructive to say, don't bother saying anything anymore.'

'Another couple of minutes and we'll try and get onto the coast road,' he continued, ignoring her. 'We'll have more chance of finding them there.'

'Whatever.'

He watched her walk on, hoping that would be the end of the conversation. He wasn't interested in finding anyone, he just wanted to put as much distance as possible between him and the bulk of the aliens. But it was different for Clare. He'd already accepted that the others were lost, but she hadn't. She was very clearly still clinging onto the faint, fading hope of seeing her daughter again.

There were more flashes of light, miles behind them this time, lighting up the world like slow-motion artillery explosions. Tom kept walking, shuffling his pack into the centre of his back, then putting his head down and marching. It was still raining and the wind was gusting along the tracks, but the night now felt unexpectedly, almost artificially, warm. He undid the zip on the front of his jacket, struggling with the humidity. Was this something to do with the aliens too? He shook his head and trudged on, sodden boots squelching.

Clare had stopped again. He pretended he hadn't noticed at first and just kept moving. Beyond her the railway line seemed to stretch on forever. He overtook but didn't acknowledge her, just glancing back now and then to make sure she was still there. He didn't want to be alone. He didn't want to be out here anymore. He didn't want to be anywhere. But what was the alternative? Other than sitting down where he was and waiting for whatever was coming to take him and finish him off, he didn't have one. A nearby building, perhaps, to get out of the rain? That prospect was no more inviting. He imagined the two of them sitting in silence at opposite ends of a dark and unfamiliar room, nothing to do but wait... For a fraction of a second he thought about turning tail and heading back to Clare's house or even his own place, but those ideas were dismissed almost instantly. They were closer to the coast than they were to either house now. Pointless. It all felt so fucking pointless.

'What the hell are we doing out here?' Clare shouted at him, clearly thinking along the same lines. He stopped and looked up. For a few seconds he was distracted by the warmth and the rain and the movement of the clouds overhead. They looked like they were swirling, turning in on themselves and slowly sinking down towards the ground. When Clare repeated her question, virtually screaming at him this time, he forced himself to answer.

'Looking for Penny,' was the best he could manage.

'We can't even see where we're going,' she said, spitting into the rain. 'What chance have we got of finding her?'

'More chance than if we'd stayed back at your place, I guess.'

He looked into her face. She looked drowned, her hair plastered down, water dripping off the end of her nose and chin. He tried to walk on again, not knowing what else to say, but this time Clare stopped him. She grabbed the shoulder strap of his rucksack and pulled him back.

'I just want to see her again,' she sobbed, her tears mingling with the rain. 'You understand? Just once more.'

'And you will,' he lied. 'Keep yourself together. Keep moving.' He gently took her hands away and carried on walking. 'Let's get up,' he said, starting to climb the embankment, grabbing handfuls of long grass and weeds to help keep his balance and haul himself up. 'We'll see more from up there.'

Tom looked back from the top of the climb and saw that Clare had hardly moved. He shouted back for her to follow him but kept walking, trudging wearily across a ploughed field. He reached a hedgerow on the far side of the churned mud, but still hadn't seen her. Eventually she appeared, head peering up over the ridge.

He waited for her to catch up, using the time to find a way

through the tangle of hawthorn and undergrowth which bordered the field. When Clare finally reached him he held back a branch of spiteful, barbed-wire-like thorns and gestured through. She looked down and saw a steep bank on the other side. At the bottom of the bank she could see tarmac.

'Look, a road.'

'So?' she said, panting with effort. 'Which road?'

'Not sure. Doesn't matter. We'll find a way down to the sea from here. And there are hills up ahead too. We'll be able to see for miles from up there. We'll see the people.'

'You sure about this?'

'As much as I'm sure about anything anymore, yes.'

'I just want to stop now, Tom. I'm cold and I'm tired and...'

She stopped talking when he wrapped his arms around her. Her body remained stiff, her arms hanging at her sides.

'I'll go down first,' he told her. 'Give me a few seconds, then follow. Okay?'

He was gone before she could answer. He tried head-first, but the drop was further than it looked. He changed position, getting down on his hands and knees then turning around and reversing through the greasy mud. He held himself steady, his boots hanging in mid-air, not knowing how far a drop it was down to the tarmac. He looked up at Clare as the sky behind her was illuminated by another distant flash of alien light, then pushed himself down. Clare followed. He took hold of her feet and guided her down. The two of them stood together in the middle of the road.

'Recognise anything?' Clare asked.

'Think so,' Tom replied, adjusting the increasingly uncomfortable backpack on his shoulders again. He needed to be positive, to try and keep her moving. 'It's this way.'

Tom marched off, hoping he'd chosen the right direction but knowing that it mattered less and less if he hadn't.

# 42

Footsteps.

'What's that?' Clare asked. It sounded like footsteps, but it was too loud and too orderly... like the stomping of some advancing giant creature, increasing in volume as it came nearer. Tom instantly recognised the sound. This was the noise of hundreds of pairs of feet moving in perfect synchronisation, an unimaginable number of individual movements combining to create a single eerie sound. These were footsteps which were as unnatural and inhuman as the creatures which continued to crawl tirelessly through the skies overhead tonight.

'What is it?' she asked, frantically looking around but seeing only the road and the tall hedges on either side. Tom stopped, unable to tell from which direction the people were approaching. What he couldn't hear unnerved him more than what he could. There was still not a single voice of dissent. Not a solitary groan, moan or other voluntary or involuntary noise could be heard over the relentless marching noise.

He took a few more steps forward, and then stopped. He could see the first of them now, coming towards him. They walked in single file in the absolute centre of the road, their formation so perfect that it was only when they followed a slight curve to the left that he saw any of the others behind the man in front. He turned and ran in the other direction, grabbing hold of Clare's arm and dragging her along with him.

'Tom,' she hissed at him. 'Tell me!'

There was a gap in the hedge to his left; the entrance to a well-trampled public footpath. He pulled Clare down the dark path and off the road. She tried to pull back the other way to see what was happening but he restrained her, covering her mouth with his hand and keeping them both out of sight.

'This is what I saw in Thatcham,' he explained, whispering right into her ear, afraid of being overheard. 'Hundreds of people.'

Clare writhed and bit his hand. 'Let me go,' she spat at him. 'Penny...'

It took all his strength to restrain her. She slipped one arm from her rucksack strap and started to run but he pulled her back again. Still she fought as the thunderous marching noise continued, kicking out and trying to scratch at his face, anything to free herself. In desperation he kicked her legs out from under her, dropped her down and lay on top of her body, his weight too much for her to move.

'There's no point,' he said, still whispering, still terrified. 'There's nothing we can do. Even if we find Penny, we won't be able to help her.'

At the mention of her daughter's name, Clare struggled again. She tried to knee Tom in the groin but couldn't get enough leverage. Holding one of her wrists with either hand, he twisted his legs between hers and spread them, then pushed his weight down on her harder than before. She hissed and yelled in his ear, in real pain now, but he ignored her, even when she started spitting and biting again. He focused on the apparently endless queue of people still striding down the middle of the road, perfectly equidistant, unblinking and unseeing. He was hypnotised by their emotionless gaze. Whatever the aliens had done to them had stripped away their individuality and made them all the same. No longer people with personalities, capable of free thought, they were now just vacuous, easily manipulated shells. Soulless and dead.

'They're all lost, Clare,' he said. 'All gone.'

She finally stopped struggling. Tom lifted his head slightly and saw that she was looking up now. He looked over his shoulder and watched as an alien ship moved overhead. He'd seen one like this before. It had a distinctive engorged head and stunted body. This was the same kind of ship which had hovered over Thatcham when he'd been hiding in the pub, perhaps the exact same one. The ship, he assumed, which controlled the people.

'Are they looking for us?' Clare asked, slightly calmer now.

'They're not interested in us.'

Moments later – Tom wasn't sure how long – the end of the column of marching figures finally came into view. Tom watched as the last of them disappeared. The final person was a girl, older than Penny and darker-skinned, still wearing pyjamas. Her hair was tied into a ponytail which bobbed as she marched, its random movements completely at odds with everything else about her. He waited a minute longer, then relaxed his grip on Clare. He got up and brushed himself down, taking care to make sure he was still blocking the way through to the road.

'Where are they going?'

'Let's find out,' he said, taking her hand and starting to move. He could still hear the regimented footsteps. Rather than risk the road, he instead went further along the footpath they'd stumbled across. It curved left, running almost parallel with the road, then climbed a formidable-looking hill. 'Up,' he ordered.

The ground beneath their feet was increasingly steep, the narrow path little more than a greasy furrow. The climb was difficult and slow, both of them having to help each other to keep moving forward, the summit never seeming to get any closer. After several minutes Clare reached the top. She stood upright, hands on her hips, panting hard. Tom pulled her down.

The distinctive alien ship had stopped less than half a mile away, he estimated, and was now hovering over a large, open expanse of grass. Below it he could see the queue of people entering the field through a single gate. It took him a few seconds to realise, but there were far more people in the field than the number he'd seen on the road. He'd estimated that hundreds of people had just marched past them, but there were *thousands* here. What was this place?

'Look,' Clare said, pointing ahead. There were more of them filling adjacent fields. It looked like they were being grown here ready for harvest: some kind of bizarre crop. 'Penny must be here somewhere. And Siobhan and your brother too. Once that ship's gone we can go down there.'

'It controls them, I think,' Tom said. 'I saw it earlier.'

Tom sat up and fully unzipped his jacket, struggling with the inclement heat and the effort of the climb. He was transfixed by what he could see happening in the field up ahead now. The people were forming themselves into perfectly straight lines, their keenly paced, rhythmic movements strangely soothing and distracting to watch from this distance. They appeared to instinctively know the limits of their immediate surroundings, no matter how unexpected those surroundings were. The field was odd-shaped, and yet exactly the right number of people peeled off at a time to form each row. He doubted whether they still had any degree of control over themselves. Their movements were being orchestrated from the ship above.

As the field continued to fill, Tom was just about able to make out the faces of some of the people. Even now he caught himself still looking for the familiar, praying he'd catch a glimpse of Siobhan or Rob, wondering if, somehow, he really did have a chance of saving them. Despite their uniform movements and emotionless demeanour, the physical appearance of the people in the field still gave some clue as to who they used to be. Most were fully dressed. A few were naked. None of them reacted to the conditions or to any aspect of their surroundings in the slightest. Neither the wind nor the torrential rain affected them. He counted thirty-seven people in the furthest forward row, and each of those people stood at the front of columns more than fifty deep. He lost count after a while, but he'd already seen enough to know that there were tens of thousands of people out here tonight. Was there anyone else like him and Clare left, or were they the final two?

He was about to say something to Clare when she scrambled to her feet and started to run, catching him off-guard. She sprinted down the other side of the hill towards the fields full of people.

'Clare!' he yelled. 'Clare, don't...'

He got up and ran and almost immediately lost his footing in the wet grass. He rolled over and over, unable to stop or even to slow his uncontrolled descent until he reached the bottom. He landed in a deep puddle and swallowed a mouthful of filthy water, which he coughed out as he got up, and continued to run.

Clare had kept her balance and was racing towards a gap in the hedge.

Tom looked up and saw that the alien ship hovering over the fields was moving again. The hatch in the bottom of its rounded head began to slide open and the long, stem-like appendage he'd seen earlier was lowered down.

He ran faster, diving forward and managing to catch Clare by the waist, tackling her before she could step back out onto the road. He fell back and dragged her over with him. She pushed him away then scrambled to get up again.

'Clare, wait! Don't go out—'

His words were abruptly truncated as the world was filled with unbearably bright, incandescent white light. He was vaguely away of Clare staggering for cover as he buried his face in the mud, his eyes burning. He reached out for her but she pulled away when his outstretched fingers made contact with her leg.

Tom sat up, his back to the light, leaning into the hedge. He opened one eye slightly and saw that, bizarrely, the incredible illumination was limited to a specific area behind him, leaving the rest of the world shrouded in darkness. It was filling the field and nowhere else; a perfectly shaped beam.

And then, as quickly as it had appeared, the light was extinguished. Everything was immediately bathed in inky black, this time even deeper and darker than before.

'You all right?' Tom asked. His voice sounded weak. Frail, almost. Clare didn't answer. She picked herself up and continued through the gap out onto the road. He walked after her, no longer able to run, every footstep an effort now.

When they both reached the entrance to the field, they found it completely empty. The ground was littered with clothing, but every other physical trace of every last person had gone. The alien ship was already moving away, casually drifting further down the coast.

'You bastards,' Tom mouthed at the disappearing machine, his mouth too dry to properly form the words. 'You fucking bastards.'

He kicked his way through the rags covering the ground. Clare dropped to her knees and picked up a shoe, no trace of its owner. She stared at it in disbelief, even tipping it upside down and looking inside to see where the person who'd worn it might have gone. Everything was bone dry, covered in dust. The rain began to soak the arid ground again.

'It's a cull,' Tom told her. 'I didn't want to say anything, didn't think there was any point. They don't need us, Clare, they just want the planet. They're wiping us out.'

For a while they remained in the field, exhausted and beaten, the enormity of what they'd witnessed almost too much to bear. Thousands of people had been destroyed in seconds. Penny, Rob, Siobhan, James, John and Betty Tipper, everyone else they could think of... all gone.

# Part v
# CULL

# 43

The driving rain increased in intensity and although unnaturally warm, the swirling wind battered them from every direction. They kept walking, because they didn't know what else to do. They knew whatever they did was most probably pointless now, but carried on regardless. Better to be on the move when it happens, Tom had long since decided, than to just be sitting there waiting for the apparently inevitable. They were disorientated and lost, but it didn't matter anymore.

And then, just when he was on the verge of finally giving up, Tom saw something which both confirmed their location and gave him renewed impetus to keep moving. It was the dark, boarded-up shell of The Black Swan, the burnt out restaurant he tried to take Siobhan to early on in their relationship. The memories of that night both filled him with a crushing sadness while also reinvigorating him somewhat. He remembered how much of an idiot he'd felt as he pulled up outside the ruin of a building, and how Siobhan had laughed at him, unable to understand how he'd managed to avoid hearing it on the news all week: a cash-strapped celebrity chef setting light to the restaurant avoid bankruptcy. He remembered the evening they'd gone on to have together, and how they'd made love for the first time...

The memories of that night made him sob with pain, and yet that pain also made him more determined to keep moving forward. He wasn't prepared to give up, and getting off the mainland still seemed the only viable option.

'Down here,' he said to Clare. They'd reached the top of a muddy, uneven and well-worn footpath which wound down a steep slope towards the beach. He looked back and saw that she hadn't moved. She remained standing on the road outside the burned-out building. Behind her he thought he could see

Thatcham or, at least, the space where it used to be. The village itself – normally an obvious bright cluster of street lamps and houses – had melted into the landscape, wholly unlit. The only lights he could still see came from the myriad alien ships above and Christ, there seemed to be hundreds of them now, cross-hatching the skies at different altitudes and speeds, perfectly coordinated. He looked back along the coast line towards the cliffs from where he'd witnessed the arrival of the first aliens. A ship of a similar shape and size bore down towards the land from which they were now trying to escape. It was so black and so featureless that it seemed to be eating its way through the heavens, blocking out thousands of stars at a time.

Clare still hadn't moved.

'You coming?'

Before she could answer, another ship drifted overhead. It's vast belly slid open and a phalanx of seventeen smaller vessels dropped down into the squally skies. Tom crouched down, battered by the sudden warm wind and the change in air pressure, but Clare remained standing, looking directly up at the alien machines as they whipped through the air just metres above her. The physical closeness of the aliens unnerved Tom, but Clare seemed not to care. She'd seen enough. She'd *had* enough. Tom stood up again and tried to hold her close but the warmth and strength he'd felt in her previously had all but gone. She felt like a shop-window dummy: all life extinguished. But he refused to let go, and gripped her tighter still. Over her shoulder he watched as the aliens continued their work. In the distance, bright blocks of controlled light shone down intermittently, and he knew that each brilliant flash resulted in the eradication of untold numbers of innocent lives. He counted more than ten bursts of light as he scanned the horizon – hundreds of thousands of people reduced to nothing in seconds – and there wasn't a damn thing he could do to stop it.

The longer he looked into the clouds overhead, the more

alien activity he saw. The air was teeming with their smaller ships. Some were flying low, ground-hugging reconnaissance flights, others darted from one mother ship to another, the pulses of white from their engines illuminating their routes and drawing bright connective trails in the sky. It was like watching electricity flow around a circuit, like blood being pumped around a body. And it occurred to him that he was watching something new being created. The old being discarded. New life beginning. He thought about the words of the alien he'd killed, how he'd talked about mankind's plundering of the planet, filling the atmosphere with fumes, cutting down the rain forests, forcing natives out of their homes to build shopping malls and factories. Jall had been right. This wasn't any different. This wholesale reclamation of the planet was the same thing, but on a massively increased scale.

He dragged Clare down the narrow coastal path, forcing her to move. She was slow to react, almost falling over when her feet didn't move quickly enough. She didn't resist, but she didn't comply either. She was beaten. Empty.

The gradient of the path steepened, their footing becoming more treacherous with each step. The waterlogged, sandy loam made the ground impossible to read, particularly at speed. Tom almost fell, but he didn't dare stop or slow down, nor would he let go of Clare. He kept his eyes fixed downward, desperately trying to distinguish the zigzag route the path took through the darkness, but just for a moment he allowed himself to glance up. His stomach dropped and his heart leaped. The steep landmass seemed to have momentarily fallen away, and all he could see now was the ocean. It stretched out ahead of him for endless miles, a vast vista untouched. But the illusion was shattered seconds later when another alien ship swept out over the waves.

The slope worsened again, then gradually levelled out, the sandy mud eventually giving way to the shingle of the beach.

The noise of their footsteps as they crunched across the bay was reassuringly loud: a pathetic yet satisfying act of defiance. They stopped just short of the wet line where the waves hit the beach and Tom spat and cleared his throat, panting hard. He let go of Clare and stood with his hands on his knees, struggling to breathe. Was it his imagination, or was the temperature rising again? He looked over at Clare through another sudden shower of rain, and thought that he saw a flicker of emotion. She caught his eye.

'We did it,' he said. 'Told you we'd make it.'

She looked around. 'Now what?'

Tom shielded his face from the driving rain. He didn't immediately recognise the cove they'd found, but he knew roughly where they were. There were several of these small bays along this part of the coastline. He was certain he'd seen boats moored around here before now.

'This way,' he said, already marching back up the shingle shore. He checked back and when he was sure she was following, led her along the crescent shape of the beach. The land narrowed and he was soon ankle-deep in ice-cold sea water, its icy temperature a stark contrast with the unseasonably warm air. He ignored the discomfort, long past caring. They were both soaked through and exhausted, what difference would anything else make now? He steadied Clare as a wave caught her by surprise, and she almost lost her footing, then dragged her towards a shadowy headland which separated this bay from the next.

'I'm tired,' she said, shouting over the wind which had suddenly increased in ferocity. 'Want to stop now.'

'Keep going. Not much longer,' Tom yelled back. He began to climb, wondering if the aliens were somehow controlling the wind to spite them, using its speed to make life even tougher. He forced himself to focus, knowing that was as ridiculous as it sounded. The aliens weren't going to waste any time or effort on them. They didn't give a damn about the two of them. Whether they were standing in the middle of Thatcham or on a boat rowing out to sea, it didn't matter. They were of no consequence.

Tom waited for Clare to catch up then scrambled up the rocks behind her, pushing her forward and keeping her moving. The moss-covered rocks under his boots were slimy and his foot slipped as a large wave hit the headland and broke over him. He fell back, under the surface before he'd realised what was happening. Complete darkness. Muffled silence. An intense cold punch which sucked every last scrap of air from his lungs. He flailed in the water but couldn't find anything to hold onto until another wave seemed to cradle him and flip him back over onto his front. His feet and hands made contact with the ground and he stood up. Clare was standing right in front of him. He looked up and took her outstretched hand. She pulled him up, the lights from an endless procession of alien ships illuminating the sky behind her.

Tom vomited salty water and struggled to stay standing upright. He held onto Clare for support, urging her to start moving again and climb back down the other side of the rocks, so they could reach level ground once more. He followed her down to the next beach, tripping through pools of water. He was relieved when they were finally able to stop and rest, temporarily shielded from the wind and driving rain by the headland they'd just negotiated.

He looked around, the weather making it difficult to make out detail. And then, away from the beach, back towards the land, he saw a number of dark, rectangular outlines. Caravans. He started towards them, dragging Clare behind him as he struggled to remember if he'd been here before. It looked vaguely familiar, but the conditions combined with his state of mind and fatigue to leave him confused and disorientated. They walked further along the beach towards where Tom could see more caravans and then, in a flash of alien light, he caught sight of a concrete ramp and, next to it, a narrow wooden jetty stretching out into the water. The wild waves constantly battered the flimsy looking construction. And there, moored right at the very end of the dilapidated slatted walkway, bobbing up and down on the viciously swirling water, he saw several small boats.

'Clare,' he said, pulling her close and shouting into her ear to make himself heard over the storm. 'We've done it. Look!'

But she didn't look. He stared deep into her eyes and saw that they were gone, trance-like.

'One last push,' he said, and he began marching across the beach, head down into the wind, pulling her along behind him, almost having to drag her through the sand. He'd suspected she might be close to succumbing to the alien programming, but he wasn't going to give up on her now. Not here. Not after getting so far and coming so close. 'Not now, Clare,' he pleaded with her. 'Please stay with me.'

And then everything stopped.

It was as if someone had flicked a switch. One second, ferocious gales and driving rain. The next, nothing. Absolute calm.

Clare didn't even notice.

Tom kept moving, kept pulling her. Was it starting to get lighter now? He thought it was his mind playing tricks because, although it was late, he could definitely see more of his surroundings than he'd been able to just a few minutes earlier.

Tom continued along the beach, tired feet digging into the sand and fine shingle, then he climbed up onto the jetty and pulled Clare up after him. The three boats moored there looked reasonably seaworthy – not that he knew enough about boats to be able to tell for sure, and not that it mattered anyway because he didn't think they'd be out there long – and he threw his sodden rucksack onto the furthest of the three. It was little more than a small rowing boat, barely big enough for the two of them. He helped Clare on board, resorting to manhandling her when she wouldn't move, then scanned around for something to use as an oar. He ended up grabbing a piece of the jetty, struggling to free the sodden wooden slat, realising just how much energy he'd already used to get this far, and what little now remained. With a grunt of effort he finally wrenched the slat free and then, with numb fingers, untied the frayed knot which had so far kept the boat moored.

Tom half-climbed, half-fell into the boat. It rocked precariously. He used the wood to push them away from the jetty, and then began digging into the water on alternate sides, desperate to get away. The light levels seemed to have increased another notch, because now he could definitely see more than before – far more than he wanted to. He took one last look at the land they were leaving, then turned his full attention to the water which stretched out ahead of them. He looked out towards the horizon, and what he saw there made his already heavy heart sink further.

'Oh fuck.'

Coming towards them, as silent as every other alien machine he'd so far come across, was a bizarre looking craft. It was unimaginably long and narrow, gently curved, appearing to span several miles across. It looked like it was flying sideways, disobeying every known rule of aerodynamics in the process. And as it flew, a curtain of intense blue-white light shone down onto the water from beneath its entire length, sweeping across the surface of the waves.

Was this it? After getting so far, would this be the light that finally ended his life? Tom watched the ship steadily approaching, knowing there wasn't anything he could do now. Maybe he could get in the water and try and get under the boat? Maybe he could paddle back? Maybe not. What was the point? He could see even more of them now flying tip to tip: lines and lines of them steadily sterilizing everything. The ship and the light came nearer and nearer, seeming to increase in speed the closer it got. Tom dropped his makeshift paddle and reached across for Clare. He held her tightly and buried her face in his chest, then screwed his eyes shut and waited for the inevitable, for the light to cover them both and reduce them to nothing.

# 44

When Tom next opened his eyes, the sea was as flat and steady as a millpond. Artificially motionless. The waves had stopped. The only ripples came from the rocking of their boat. It was light now, and there were no signs of the peculiar ships which had been scouring the planet when he'd last looked up.

*Am I dead?*

'Clare?' he said, his voice sounding disproportionately loud in the suddenly overwhelming silence and calm. She was sitting at the other end of the boat to him, her feet entangled with his, her head hanging back over the side. 'Clare, are you okay?'

She shuffled, then raised her head and looked up at him, but he wasn't sure if she'd understood or if she'd even heard him. She lay back again.

The temperature was intense. Tom stripped off his sodden clothing, discarding his jacket, sweater and T-shirt, dumping them in the middle of the boat. Steam snaked away from his clothes, just visible in the unnatural light. He crawled over to Clare, struggling to keep his balance, then lifted her head up again. He held her face in his hands. Her eyes flickered then focused, her pupils dilating.

'What?'

'We did it, Clare. We got away.'

'So?'

'So we did it. We escaped.'

'What now?'

He struggled to answer. 'Now we make the most of what's left.'

'There's nothing left. All gone. They've taken it all.'

'We've got a little food, enough to get us through a few more days.'

'Then what?'

Another hesitation. He didn't know. 'We could head back to the shore. Get more stuff.'

'No point.'

'Come on, Clare. We'll survive.'

'We won't.'

'We *will*. They're not interested in us, can't you see? We could last for months out here.'

'Until they click their fingers and snuff us out.'

'Don't do this. Please, Clare... you have to stay with me and...'

He stopped talking. Her expression had changed. She was staring into the sky beyond him, watching something over his shoulder. Tom got up and spun around, steadying himself as the boat rocked, and saw that it was one of the smaller, dart-shaped alien machines. It was moving slowly, and there was no question that the little rowing boat was its intended target. Tom's heart raced, pounding in his chest so hard he thought he might pass out. There was nowhere left to run now, nowhere to hide. He picked up his wooden paddle, one last act of defiance.

The alien ship came to an abrupt halt less than a metre away, its pointed nose level with Tom's face. The backdraft from its powerful but silent engines was boiling the water. Tom stood his ground. When the alien ship did the same, refusing to move, he swung his wooden plank around and smashed it against the vessel's hull. It hit the metal with a sonorous clang and the shuttle seemed to waver slightly, the impact having an unexpectedly dramatic effect. Encouraged, Tom did it again, and this time the ship lifted itself several metres higher in response, just out of reach. He threw the paddle at it like a spear. It glanced off the side of the machine then splashed down into the water.

Tom was ready to fight, willing the alien piloting the craft to reveal itself and face him. But the vessel simply angled itself to port and went on its way, the force of its sudden acceleration knocking Tom off his feet. He lay on the deck of the boat and laughed out loud as the alien ship disappeared.

*Batter me and beat me and wear me down for a hundred years and I'll never give up*, he thought. *I am Tom Winter, and I will always be Tom Winter. You'll never take that from me.*

The light never faded. It was permanently like the middle of day. Tom lay back in the boat alongside Clare and watched hundreds of alien ships teeming through the light blue sky overhead like worker ants. They filled the sky like dark stars. More of the long ships appeared on the horizon and dragged their curtains of light across the land. They were cleansing the face of the planet, setting in play the changes which would remove the last traces of man, sterilising the land and making it hospitable for its new masters.

# EPILOGUE

Tom talked to Clare constantly, though she rarely replied.

'Look at the sky, Clare,' he said as the colours changed. Purple turned to pink. By the third day, stars were visible all the time. 'The sun's not yellow anymore. It looks grey now.'

Hour by hour, the level of the ocean dropped until the water had almost completely disappeared. Where once there had been nothing visible but the waves, there now lay a vast and silent tundra. Tom and Clare hid under the upturned boat which they propped up with the plank of wood.

'It's hot, Clare. Can you feel it? The air tastes different too. It's sweet.'

No answer.

'You still with me, Clare?'

'Tired,' she said, her first word in more than a day. Her last word.

They both slept. The heat was exhausting. When Tom next woke, another day had dawned. He shook Clare to wake her. 'Look,' he said, 'they're going.'

Every alien ship had risen up. They now held positions at unimaginable heights. Tom could barely see them.

'Are you hungry?' he asked her. She didn't reply. 'I'm going to go back and find some food. Will you be okay here? Stay with me, Clare, please. I don't want to be on my own.'


Once I was running I was fine. The nervousness, the trepidation, the apprehension, it all disappeared in seconds. I just kept putting one foot in front of the other. It was easier than I expected. I ran faster than I remembered and with less effort, as if gravity itself had been reduced.

The aliens and I regarded each other with a mutual lack of interest and respect. They ignored me, and I did what I could to ignore them. I felt strong enough to run all the way back to Thatcham, but when I got there I couldn't find it. The entire village had disappeared, as had every road, building and other landmark. In their place was an unending blanket of blue-green tinged moss.

There was no food or water anywhere. I stopped looking and walked to the place where my house used to be. Even though everything had changed, I knew I was in the right place. I could see the moss-covered stump on the cliffs which used to be the war memorial. I stood in the spot where my living room once was and looked down over the space where the village had been. It all looked so very different, and yet the undulating shapes of the land still bore an undeniable familiarity. I felt strangely proud to be back there again. Vindicated. I'd doubted myself as the people around me had succumbed, but I'd been right all along. My only regret was not having more faith in myself when it mattered most. Maybe I could have done more to help the others. Then again, maybe not.

The moss which had already covered the land was starting to spread out farther from the shore. I rested for a short while longer before returning to Clare. Above me I could see thousands of aliens sitting and waiting for whatever they were doing to my planet to be completed so they could come down and claim it as their own.

I walked back to the boat, too tired to run.

I held Clare close and talked to her for as long as I could, although it had been days since she'd last answered. It was like she was sleeping with her eyes open: still alive, but no longer aware, just like the rest of them. I wish she'd wake up. I wish she'd talk to me again. We'd talk about the fact that we'd survived, and we'd remember all the people we'd lost.

No matter what those bastards have done to everyone and everything else, they haven't beaten me. I know I don't have long left now, but when I die, I'll die remembering who I was. They can't take that from me now.

*For the next seventeen hours, Tom Winter was the last man alive.*

# ACKNOWLEDGEMENTS

With thanks to my family and friends for their continued love, support and patience. Particular thanks – as always – to Lisa, Emma, Katie, Megan, Becca and Zoe.

Thanks to all those people around the world who've picked up the AUTUMN and HATER books in bigger numbers than I ever dreamed possible, particularly those who were with me right at the start for the original incarnation of Infected Books.

Here's to Moody's Survivors – again, thank you for your support and best wishes to each of you in all your endeavours.

To Wayne Simmons and Rebecca Stranney, thank you for going above and beyond the call of duty.

Finally, thanks to Craig Paton (www.craigpaton.com) for the magnificent TRUST artwork and designs.

Lightning Source UK Ltd.
Milton Keynes UK
UKOW050756300612

195265UK00001B/8/P